Kan Pai Nichi

KAN PAI NICHI

A story of revenge

Ivan Scott

Copyright © 2014 by Ivan Scott.

Library of Congress Control Number: 2013918639
ISBN: Hardcover 978-1-4931-1474-0
Softcover 978-1-4931-1473-3
eBook 978-1-4931-1475-7

All rights reserved. No part of this book may be reproduced or transmitted in any form or by any means, electronic or mechanical, including photocopying, recording, or by any information storage and retrieval system, without permission in writing from the copyright owner.

This is a work of fiction. Names, characters, places and incidents either are the product of the author's imagination or are used fictitiously, and any resemblance to any actual persons, living or dead, events, or locales is entirely coincidental.

This book was printed in the United States of America.

Rev. date: 08/25/2014

To order additional copies of this book, contact:
Xlibris LLC
1-888-795-4274
www.Xlibris.com
Orders@Xlibris.com
539265

There is something exasperatingly simple-minded about the Americans who go off to Hiroshima each summer to ask to be forgiven, and about the Japanese who, with calm, long-suffering, tea-ceremony smiles, forgive them.

Edward Seidensticker

Chapter 1

He didn't care for Harry, Luke thought, as he stared out the plane's window; too coarse, too brutal; he hesitated to think, too American. He had to wonder. How old was the man? At least sixty years old, yet as vigorous as a man half his age.

Across the aisle, Luke could hear Harry talking to the other American businessmen. He shut it out of his mind, reluctant to listen to his colleagues.

Through the window he could see the Japanese coast coming into view. The leading edge of the jet's wing cut through patches of clouds. For a moment the city of Tokyo appeared below, a vast patterned mosaic, stretching in the late afternoon sun from the coast to the distant mountains. The perfect cone of Fuji appeared briefly, as though snapped by a photographer, and then the whole picture faded, caught in another mass of wooly clouds.

In this dimmer light he saw his reflection faintly in the windowpane, oriental features with a Caucasian caste. Son of a Nisei, he thought, son of the second generation. That's what it meant. He was half-Japanese, half American. He was coming home. But no, it was not his home; it was his grandmother's home.

Home for Luke had been Honolulu, where his Japanese grandmother and his American grandfather had settled after World War Two. Patrick Sullivan, a bluff loving man with the tangled traits and genes of the British Isles; part Irish, part Welsh, part English. He was a police officer, a devoted family man, an admirer of Japanese culture. He doted on his only son Patrick Jr. who like his father, became a police officer, killed while still young by a suspected drug addict when Luke was a small child. His Japanese mother died the next year; then his grandmother passed away a year after that.

It seems the Sullivan family was disappearing almost as fast as it was forming.

Luke was a third generation Sullivan, Patrick Lucas Sullivan the third. The nickname Luke was fixed on him, almost from infancy. Like father, like son, like grandfather; he chose a career in law enforcement. A degree at the University of Hawaii, five years on the Honolulu police force, then a security specialist for a Los Angeles security firm, full years, Lucas thought. Work had filled the long hours, giving him skills and experience, a black belt in karate, the mastery of two languages, and a position of importance with a multinational corporation before he was thirty-three.

A lifetime seemed to pass in a few minutes for him, fleeting memories as he watched the clouds flashing by the side of the plane. Half-Japanese, half-American, a racial mongrel, he knew the two languages as mother tongues. The Japanese heritage had been easy for him to absorb. In Hawaii the Japanese community never loses touch with the natal homeland.

A slight smile came to Luke's face. An only child, self-contained, brain and body disciplined, in perfect harmony. What had all the education and training come to? Industrial espionage. It was as though his life had been only a preparation for the deceptions and the perils a spy knows.

The flight attendants were coming down the aisle to collect cups and trays, checking seat belts as they went. They chattered and kidded the passengers in that friendly, provocative way of all flight attendants.

Walt, a heavyset, middle-aged man, one of the American businessmen, was sitting next to Luke. "The English of these girls is damn good," he said.

"When the Nips make up their minds to do something, they're almost unbeatable," said Harry. His big voice boomed, but the passengers, mostly Japanese, didn't seem to notice.

Luke glanced at the faces of the passengers around them. He wondered if they knew enough English to understand Harry's remarks. But the faces, he almost blushed to think, were inscrutable.

Walt filled the silence. "I doubt if the Japanese will ever forgive us for Hiroshima and Nagasaki."

Harry snorted a little. "They ought to. If they hadn't been forced to surrender that way, there would have been a slaughter on both sides. There would have been a million casualties on our side; they would have lost more than that."

He looked around, waiting for an argument. "They were fanatics. They would have lost half their people before it was over."

"They were fighting for their existence," said Walt mildly.

"Bull! They wanted to take over the world, that's all."

Luke intervened. "The leaders maybe, but not the people."

"Ah, the people. The people let their leaders take them down the road to hell, and they were glad to go along."

Luke felt surprised that such old issues could generate this much emotion. Suddenly subdued by these exchanges, they fell silent. Finally, Walt said meditatively, "So we killed and maimed the populations of their major cities, and they ought to thank us because we didn't destroy half their country."

"Listen," said Harry resentfully, "we can't really know what the war in the Pacific was like. In the end, neither side was taking prisoners. The Japs fought to the death, and they got what they wanted: a quick trip to Synada Heaven."

"They did surrender," Luke said quickly.

"No, they didn't," retorted Harry. "Their Emperor surrendered, and they obeyed him. There's a difference."

Mark, the other American, sitting alongside Harry, had said nothing up to now. Occasionally he gave Luke a glance, the kind of look that suggested that they shared something the others didn't know.

Mark had been chosen for this trip because of his background. Harry and Walt were company veterans, workhorses, with long years of office experience. They had learned the business, kept up with the successive revolutions taking place in cyber technology. Harry, for all his vulgarity, had the common touch that made him every man's man, and was a mathematician of international prominence. He had entered the computer field in its infancy, knew it from top to bottom. If he was not the father of the microchip, then the internet, he liked to brag that he was a member of the founding family.

Mark, like Luke, was of another generation. He had gone far in a few years. A public relations executive, he had spent the first ten years after college working in the Honolulu office. He learned thoroughly the banalities and the clichés, the ways of meeting and mastering the public. Cynicism is the eventual price of over simplification, the need to reduce the normally complex to a common denominator. Briefly, his and Luke's careers had touched. Then, Luke went to the L.A. office as a security manager. His police background and his family's police connections in Honolulu had given him the position.

"Security" meant preserving the company's secrets from other rivals. Security really was, and remains, a euphemism for industrial espionage.

In Honolulu, "public relations" meant for Mark, foreign contacts, techniques in industrial diplomacy so that his company might monitor the progress of its international competition. For both Mark and Luke the line between domestic law and order, on the one hand, and the international piracy of a rival's ideas on the other, became blurred over time. Eventually Luke accepted it for what it was: a world of willful conduct, beyond the normal reach of law, not quite criminal, not quite legal. It was rather like, and here he groped, reaching back for a college course he had taken . . . . it was sort of like old time European feudalism. Patrons, the lords of industry, held their minions in a state of moral bondage: loyalty to the company over all else. For what reason? To serve the cause of commerce and huge profits.

The problem of a double loyalty, to the corporation and to one's country, seemed appropriate he thought. It was a divided affection for two communities: Japan, his mother and grandmother's country; and America, his father and grandfather's country. The twilight zone between two national loyalties was not more obscure than the twilight zone between international corporate piracies on the one hand and the legal codes of the two societies he honored.

Mark was called to L.A. when the company officers at the highest level, decided that a crucial piece of their technology had fallen into a rival's hands. Looking across the aisle at Mark, Luke recalled that critical meeting vividly. The purloined technology was being called the "formula." Once stolen, it could not be recovered. "An idea, after it is generalized," said one of the vice presidents, "can never be taken back."

On the other hand, a primary idea, such as the "formula" represented, could serve as the basis for a breakthrough to a new idea: a new "formula." It was a new idea (apparently based on the old "formula") which seemed to have appeared in the hand of the rival, the Tushimi Corporation. The manifest result of the supremacy of this newest "formula" was a product almost revolutionary.

"It was," said another company officer to Luke, "a magnification of human intelligence, reduced to something small enough to put in your pocket, yet potentially powerful enough to devastate a large city. "A dirty bomb," said Luke, understanding at once; the ideal weapon terrorists long to possess.

"They couldn't have accomplished this without our formulas," said another officer.

"OK," said another. "They stole our information. We'll steal theirs."

Mark and Luke followed this esoteric conversation well enough, without comprehending the technical complexities of it all. When one of the Big Brass complained that the Tushimi Corporation had stolen a five year march on them, he was not employing an exaggerated metaphor. He meant Tushimi had established an insurmountable lead. Great statesmen and generals, in the crisis of a losing war, could not have appeared more alarmed or felt more imperiled than the company officers on that day.

There followed a year's preparation. The Tushimi Corporation was wooed, in the ways of business diplomacy, complicated and protracted, and not to be reduced to mere words. In the multinational environment one proceeds by stealth, indirection, and tentative moves. Good offers mask less than good intentions. In this case, they made Tushimi an offer to merge. That opened doors and a visit was arranged. Merging with Tushimi really meant being absorbed by the Japanese behemoth, but that they intended not to do.

Harry and Walt, the best experts available on the newest technology, were prepared for a tour of the Tushimi plants. Mark and Luke prepared to go underground in Japan, in effect to live a clandestine life in the host country. They were company executives, but in fact, they were spies, wise to the world of industrial espionage.

Mark's Honolulu connections paved the way. Harry and Walt, big genial men, more technically competent by far than their banal appearance might suggest, would offer an imposing front of American mediocrity, while the younger men would make the necessary contacts.

It was appropriate for this conspiracy that the two older men should go uninformed of the real purpose of the two younger men. Harry played his role naturally, Luke thought, with a certain ignorance and crudity. It was all to the purpose of the plot. Anyone on the Japanese airliner would have recognized the ugly Americans abroad.

"Hirohito may have surrendered," said Harry, determined to get back to his argument. "His people may have surrendered, but I doubt the military clique surrendered."

"What do you mean?" asked Mark.

"I mean, they probably went underground. You know. They were fanatics. They would never quit."

"That war ended more than half a century ago," said Mark. "They'd all be dead or in the old folk's home by now."

That irritated Harry. "I bet they're still around, some of them anyway. More than that, they've probably indoctrinated the next generation. That's the Jap way."

Walt agreed. "They never give up. I read somewhere that after the Japanese High Command signed the treaty of capitulation in 1945, no one of any importance in Japan, not even newspaper writers, ever used the word surrender. They used terms that meant cessation of hostilities, termination of war, all euphemisms. They called the American Occupation some involved expression like Advanced Base of the Foreign Army."

"In other words," said Mark, "they didn't surrender, and they weren't occupied."

"Right," argued Walt, "if you want to interpret their language that way."

"And if you interpret it that way," said Harry, "they didn't lose the war, and the past half century has been a truce to them, time gained; so they can recover, regroup, and get ready for the next round."

"You make it sound like a national conspiracy," said Luke skeptically.

"But it is strange," said Walt, "mystifying when you think about it. Their country was humiliated the way few nations have ever been. Yet, no hard feelings. I mean, they smile at you all the time."

Harry sneered slightly. "That's the way they are, polite. It's the root of their phony culture."

"It's a way to hide their real feelings," said Mark. "No one could be that self-effacing."

Harry had made Luke think about it. "I wonder if the old military party has really survived," he murmured, almost to himself.

Harry heard his soft words, "Maybe a remnant, but it's broken up for good. General MacArthur saw to that."

"I doubt it." said Walt.

They felt the wheels of the plane touch down, tires squeal, and then the jet shuddered and the engines roared briefly. They were at Haneda Airport. As soon as the plane stopped at the gate they started to get their things together.

"The Japs fight the great economic war today," said Walt, "in search of the mighty yen."

"You mean in search of the almighty dollar," said Mark.

"Right," agreed Harry. "It's our money they're out to get."

"They're winning this war," said Luke.

Walt thought that was ironic. "We beat them into the ground, rebuilt them afterward, and now they're rubbing our noses in it."

Harry's bitterness and jealously was apparent. "Damn right. We're coming over here to take lessons from the bastards in the things we used to do best."

The passengers were beginning to unfasten their seat belts and stand up in the aisle. So involved had the conversation become Luke had forgotten to wonder any longer if the silent Japanese around them heard and understood the drift of their talk.

"You sound as though you hate them," he said to Harry.

Harry stared into Luke's smooth young face. "We're from different generations, son. I carry the prejudices of the nineteen thirties and forties. I admit that and I'm damn proud of it."

Luke laughed good naturedly. "Let me finish your thought. I'm half Japanese, reared in an affluent era. I grew up on Japanese motor bikes, plasma TV's, karate lessons, cell phones, personal computers and the internet. I have to be neutral."

Harry grinned, reaching out to punch Luke's arm. "You said it, kid. I didn't."

Chapter 2

They came off the plane in that half-disoriented, somewhat hesitant manner of strangers in a strange place. They were looking for a welcoming host, a representative of the Tushimi Corporation. They didn't have to wait long. Harry and Walt, big portly men, towering over the other passengers, were something like a Caucasian nucleus in the moving tide of oriental travelers. The Japanese contingent sent to meet them quickly identified them.

Their representative was a small man, thin, erect, with silvery hair. The bright eyes behind the steel-rimmed glasses seemed hard and metallic like the gold fillings that gleamed when he smiled.

The flurry of introductions, a confusion of handshakes and the low bows by the Japanese, made an immediate recollection of names impossible for Luke. The representative's name was a long one, unintelligible, the last syllables sounding like Taki. The Americans seized upon it as though an acronym.

Getting through customs didn't take very long. "Where can we pick up our luggage?" asked Luke.

"It will be delivered to the hotel," said Taki.

They were escorted to a company limousine. Luke sat in one of the back seats, Harry and Taki more toward the front. They were an arresting pair, Luke thought, the hulking American next to the window, sitting alongside the diminutive Japanese man.

The contrast was not less striking than the similarities. Luke judged that they were about the same age, silvery haired, and the eyes hard and sharp in their expressions. Each took measure of the other, as though old rivals. Even their perfunctory remarks were something like an unspoken contest.

Harry was looking out the window when he said, "I was here at the end of the Korean War, spring of 1953." His head came around and he and Taki looked into each other's eyes.

"What do you remember," Taki said finally.

"Not much, actually. I was here about three months and then they started shipping us back to the states."

Taki seemed interested. "Did you see any action?"

"No. I had just turned eighteen, drafted, sent to boot camp, then on to Korea. We never got into it. President Eisenhower had his people arrange a sort of truce that ended the fighting."

Some more silence, then Harry said, "Wait a minute. I remember the Ginza."

"It hasn't changed," said Taki.

Harry betrayed a little enthusiasm. "It was lined with shops and sidewalk vendors."

"Still the same," said Taki.

There was a brief silence between them after that. Then Harry winked. "How about the whore houses?"

Taki seemed hesitant. "Disestablished now, by law."

Harry turned around to face those behind him. "Now, that was a sight you wouldn't forget. Every night was like a carnival. When it got dark, they turned on the lights, making several blocks as bright as day. Then some guys would take down wooden barricades. And you know what was behind there, don't you?"

"No, what?" asked Mark.

"There were cages, like wood lattice work; and inside whores, maybe a hundred; all young, all good looking. I never saw anything like it."

"Fantastic," said Mark.

"It's a fact, in downtown Tokyo. It was called something like *Yushi*, *Yushiwakara*, I think."

Taki had been listening intently. "*Yoshiwara*," he said quietly.

"That's right. Now I remember. There would be a pimp standing beside each cage, and he would try to sell the woman. If he didn't get an offer in a few minutes, she would go out of the cage, and another would take her place."

"Sounds like a slave market," said Luke.

Taki's voice was cold, formal, and hard as ice. "*Yoshiwara* was closed in 1958."

A silence followed. It seemed strained. Even the ebullient Harry lost his words. Walt, sensing Harry had gone too far, said to Taki, "There's a lot of building going on here." He paused. "A lot of cars, not so many bicycles."

"Much change," said Taki. "And no change."

"You take pride in that, don't you?" asked Luke. "You progress, yet you keep your traditions."

Taki turned around enough in his seat to look back. It was apparent that Luke's Asian features piqued his curiosity. "We want to keep up in the world, to compete with the West."

Another silence followed. Walt tried to break it. "You speak good English," he said to Taki.

Luke realized by now that the other Japanese businessmen in the limousine had said nothing, listening intently, smiling, yet silent. He had heard that the Japanese business class learns to read English, rather than to speak it. Their system of education is one of intensive memory; sight reading foreign languages are mandatory. It was clear why Taki served as their representative. He thanked Walt for the compliment and said he had been a linguist and a translator during the Korean War.

This caught Harry's interest. "I wonder if our paths crossed?" he asked.

Again, the two men exchanged looks, and to Luke it seemed like the stares of men who had engaged each other in another time.

"I never saw military action," said Taki. "I was in the intelligence service."

When they arrived at the hotel, Taki remained in the limousine. The other Japanese got out escorting the Americans inside.

"I'll call you at eight tomorrow morning," said Taki. The window went up and the limousine pulled away.

The Americans went into the hotel and were registered by their Japanese hosts who insisted upon handling all matters. They found their luggage already being moved into a suite of large rooms, the appointments modern and Western. Harry was impressed, prowling around rather like a curious child, thought Luke.

Once unpacked, already bored, they stared down several stories to the darkening heavily traveled streets below. The neon lights of downtown Tokyo were beginning to display their lurid nighttime gyrations. They turned on a large television set, but the language barrier soon eliminated that diversion. Mark proposed that they get a taxi and go to a sauna before dinner. Walt objected at first but when pressed a little, he agreed.

Luke's command of Japanese served them. The others listened, but did not comprehend, a prolonged conversation between Luke and the cab driver before they got into the taxi.

"What was that all about?" asked Harry, when they were underway.

"I asked him to take us to a public bath, away from the tourist strip."

"How come?"

"We want an authentic bath."

"What's the difference?"

"Quite a bit. Sauna is dry heat, Finnish style. We want *Toruka*."

"What's that?"

"Turkish, you know, plenty of steam."

What they found, or rather, what the taxi driver delivered for them, was a plain establishment. No frills, not much business, low rates. The water was steaming, the baths large and already occupied by mixed bathers who watched the Americans with curiosity, the faces expressionless but the eyes riveted on the white strangers. Walt, with his big belly and shriveled little penis, came out naked from the steam room, almost crimson. He slipped into the heated pool with embarrassed haste, anxious to hide. Harry, a better physical specimen, but not much more endowed than Walt, went in more casually. The younger men, Mark and Luke, had nothing to hide. They were soon splashing and enjoying themselves, boisterous enough to drive the Japanese bathers out of the pool in a short time.

"Now, this is the only Japanese import I could approve of," said Harry.

Walt, soon tired of the water, wanted to know where they would eat.

"I've got something in mind," said Luke.

Harry wondered if Lucas had been in Tokyo before.

"No," said Luke, "my first time. But I think I know what you guys like."

"Maybe you can get us some women," said Harry after a while. Luke didn't reply.

"You're too old for that stuff, Harry," said Walt. "What would your wife think?"

"For Christ's sake. I'm not going to tell her."

"This is a business trip, not a convention," said Mark with pretended severity. For this remark, he earned Harry's wrath, who tried to put him under the water.

Sufficiently soaked, they got out one by one and went to the appointed cabinets for a massage naked. Luke spread himself out on a padded table, face down. He was about to doze off when he felt the masseuse begin to work on him. She had waited the usual brief time until the client was at ease, and then stolen in behind him. She commenced with oil, massaging his feet, manipulating his toes, gently cracking the joints of each, then the arches, then the ankles.

Strong hands, yet they were gentle, compelling, not unlike a lover's. Like purchased love, without affection, he thought drowsily, as she began to knead his calves. She arrived at his thighs, stroking them fully. By the time she had reached his back, he was riding an erection.

She kneaded his neck and shoulder muscles, then in a low voice said *daka*, pulling him by the arm. He rolled over, aware of the erect shaft in the dim light. His first sight of her added to the erotic pleasure. Small, comely, scantily dressed in a skimpy halter and brief shorts, her intimate hands aroused him the more. When she came to his thighs again, the torment had returned with greater force. Soothed by the woman's skillful hands, he heard her ask softly if he wanted relief. He knew the word. "*Hai*," he said. He could feel her anointing him with warm oil, then pulling him to a climax. She manipulated him until he thought the excruciating pleasure would be more than he could bear. The orgasm came without his expecting it, and he felt limp, exhausted, both physically and emotionally.

When he opened his eyes, the masseuse was gone.

Weakly, he sat up, and then got down from the table. He wrapped a towel around himself and went to get dressed. The others were already waiting.

In the cab, going back downtown, Harry's exuberance reasserted itself. "God, I've never had a woman handle me like that."

Mark laughed. "You've been married to the wrong woman."

"The masseuse I had was tiny," said Walt, "like a little kid."

"The Japs are small people," said Harry.

Mark agreed. "It's a little country. Everything is undersized here, little houses, little cars, little furniture."

A small laugh escaped Luke. "The Land of Lilliput."

They didn't seem to get what he said. "You know," said Luke, "Gulliver's travels, Lilliput, where this guy comes across people who are no bigger than his thumb."

Walt scoffed. "That's fiction. The reality is the Japs have a genius for making things small, tiny to the point of being invisible."

"That's fiction too." said Mark.

"Not really," said Walt, "that's why they're so good with microchips. They can miniaturize anything."

Luke thought the contrast between the two cultures, American and Japanese, was tremendous. "It's the case of a continental country like ours, a huge country, versus an island country, a tiny country."

Harry liked the analogy. "A giant versus a pygmy."

"The pygmy is winning," observed Walt.

"Like hell!" replied Harry. "We beat the bastards in war; we can do it again in technology."

"Times have changed, Harry," said Walt. "The days of big things are over. This is a new age when smallness and sophistication is the deciding factor."

Luke thought that was perceptive. Harry's bluff crude personality typified American culture, he thought, its naiveté and optimism. His large frame personified its bigness, its gigantic waste and inefficiency.

What did Taki represent he wondered. The antithesis of Harry?

It was a coincidence that Mark asked the same question about the time he thought it.

"What do you make of Taki?"

Harry picked up on that. "He's a sharp individual. But he doesn't look like a business man to me."

"He strikes me as the typical military man," said Luke. "Ramrod straight. Tough, behind that perpetual smile."

Walt thought he might be in charge of Tushimi's security operations.

Mark gave Luke a quick glance. "A company spy," he said.

"Sure," Harry said. "Industrial espionage."

"I think he slipped when he said he was once in military intelligence," said Luke.

"Me, too," agreed Walt. "There was just a flicker of annoyance on his face, as though he regretted saying it. I think Harry probably pulled it out of him by accident."

"Well," said Mark, "they'll get nothing from us. We're here to take, not to give."

Luke gave Mark a warning look, a frown, shaking his head. Shut up, he seemed to be saying. Mark got the message. Luke shifted the talk a bit. "I'd like to know what they've done with our microchip."

"It's revolutionary," observed Walt, "whatever it is."

Harry's big voice boomed. "They're like that. Whatever they steal, they improve on."

They had come into the inner city, and Luke leaned forward to engage the driver in conversation. The others listened with attention, understanding nothing they heard.

Nighttime in Tokyo is like a human beehive, Mark thought. They had come to Asakusa, the center of the city's fleshpot, where money flows like honey through strip joints, cabarets, adult movie houses, and unofficial bordellos that operate almost as freely after, as before the law of 1958, which banned legal prostitution.

Luke paid the cabbie and led them up a flight of steps to a second floor restaurant. A modest cover charge let them inside. A small, shapely hostess, wearing little, her face almost cosmetically disguised, met them at the door. She recognized them for what they were: slightly awkward, vulnerable Americans on the town, eager to see it all. It was voyeurism that had brought them, and they would pay the price. Her cute tinseled English tinkled as she led them to some seats.

Luke had chosen well, aided by a knowledgeable cab driver. They would sit along a counter where they might watch their meal being prepared, a feat performed by the chef that was not without artistry. They would drink and eat as much as they were disposed to, and watch a succession of women undress on a nearby stage.

The procession of strippers was without interruption, and went on long enough for them to recognize that some returned a second time. A small band, brassy and loud, concentrating on old American pop tunes, gave the women enough incentive to disrobe with vigor and some semblance of rhythm, even a suggestion that there is art in the matter of removing one's clothes.

They ate with gusto, clapping, competing with the band in their noisy approval of the performance. The lurid lights of many colors, cutting through the heavy layers of cigarette smoke, the bright naked bodies, the gaudy costumes, were a startling contrast to the well-cooked steaks that were coming off the grill.

Luke noticed with interest that there was a sprinkling of foreigners, mostly Caucasians, but some of Near Eastern complexion. Most were well dressed Japanese, inebriated and very loud. The foreigners were, by contrast, silent and staring.

Luke thought they looked like Arabs.

"Yeah," said Mark, "they seem to be everywhere since 9/11."

The meal was long; the show seemed endless. A little bored, Luke consoled himself with the thought he had given two old men a thrill. For dessert they watched a pair of couples come on stage and for a tantalizing brief time engage in sexual encounters. They fucked hard standing up for about a minute, and then ran off the stage. The band trumpeted the return of the strippers.

Harry, fascinated, had to be almost pulled out of the restaurant.

"What a town," he said when they started back to the hotel. "Any restaurant could make it with a floor show like that."

"Something to delight the senses," responded Luke cynically.

"It's a man's city," said Mark with a greater conviction.

Luke thought this was true. Japanese society, which revolves around the necessity of satisfying the needs of the male from infancy, would without doubt gratify all his desires in adulthood. For now, it seemed, sexuality and aggression found their outlets in pornography and commercial competition. Japan was up to date. He recalled a passage from a book he had read in college, to the effect that in the Japan of today, one sees the world of the future: congested, mechanical, plastic, vast numbers of people herded into work places and pleasure places, addicted to work and to pleasure. Driven to work in order to survive, they are driven to pleasure in order to forget why they work; a vicious cycle. Pleasure becomes for them a kind of work ethic, organized collectively for its accomplishment, as though the doing is more important than the result.

Sated with food and flesh, having seen Japanese society in its seams at the center of its commercial and industrial heart, they went back to the hotel. No wonder the suicide rate in this country is so high, Luke thought.

Chapter 3

Taki called at precisely 8:00 A.M. They were watching the morning news on T.V. while dressing, getting little from it, except Luke, who gave them the highlights.

Down in the lobby in a few minutes, they found Taki waiting for them. He was accompanied by a burly individual, powerfully built, the muscles sheathed in hard layers of fatty flesh beneath a rumpled suit. The shaved head, the ill-fitting suit, the protective manner, reminded Luke of a character out of a Hollywood B movie. Bodyguard, he thought.

Harry started to ask about breakfast but was assured by Taki that it had already been arranged. They would have breakfast with some Tushimi executives at the plant within the hour.

Luke went back to the desk to check his mail. The clerk gave him a plain unmarked envelope. On the way to the limousine, he opened it, spreading it just enough to see something like a ticket inside. It was not until mid-morning that he had a chance to take a look at it. Mark went with him to a restroom in the plant where they could have some privacy.

"What is it?" he asked.

"It's a ticket to a baseball game," said Luke. "This must be our contact."

"Jesus, they move fast. We just got here yesterday. What time? Is there a date?"

Luke examined the ticket again. "Today."

"Any idea who it came from?"

"Of course not." He reflected a little, looking down at the floor. "I imagine Taki's got things planned to the minute for the rest of the day."

"You're the one to go," said Mark. "You speak Japanese. The question is, how can you get away without raising suspicions."

"I'll tell Taki I feel sick. He watched us come in here. I saw him out of the corner of my eye."

"What's the matter with you?" asked Mark, almost laughing.

"I've got the G.I.'s."

"He'll believe you've got diarrhea alright. We've been here long enough."

Luke grinned. "I'll tell him it's the water we've been drinking."

Taki insisted on having his chauffer drive Luke back to the hotel. He also wanted the company's physician to examine him. Luke refused politely, but accepted the ride. He went up to the suite of rooms and stood by the window, watching until he saw the limousine pull away from the hotel. After that, he changed into casual clothes and went down to the hotel restaurant. After a cup of coffee and a few words with one of the waiters, he got the information he needed. The game was scheduled to start at one o'clock in the afternoon.

By then, it was nearly noon. He ordered a light lunch, took his time eating, then went out and found a taxi. He was surprised at the crowd coming into the stadium. He had not realized that baseball is so popular in Japan. If anonymity had been his contact's purpose, he thought, there couldn't be a better place than a ballpark.

He made his way through a throng of people until he found the right row. Before the second inning was over, all the seats in the vicinity were occupied, except the one to his immediate left. He had no doubt now as to what had been planned. It was just a matter of time.

Three innings were played, and still nothing had happened. By this time he had gotten interested in the game. He was suddenly aware of someone passing in from of him to take the empty seat. Bare feminine legs obscured his view momentarily; the subtle fragrance of a perfumed woman was the next sensation. When she was seated, he looked into her face. The features were Eurasian, not flat and round, but rather sharp, almost heart-shaped.

The more he studied her profile the more familiar she seemed to him. Where had he seen her before? Or was it his imagination? After a little while, he turned and flashed her a smile. She returned it with another brief stare, and then went back to watching the game.

She sat that way for half an inning. Luke called a vendor and bought a bag of peanuts, silently offering her some from the bag. She shook her head, looking straight ahead.

Luke tried some English. "Good game," he said.

She stared into his face briefly, saying nothing. Abruptly, she got up and started to leave. Passing him again, she dropped a small card into his peanut bag.

Luke watched her go up the steps and disappear, a mixture of emotions on his face. It was the woman's figure more than her face that jarred his memory. He had seen her in Honolulu some years ago.

He picked the card out of the bag and put it in his pocket, stayed for another inning and then left the ballpark. When he was in a cab and felt safe from watching eyes, he read the brief directions: a street address, an apartment number, and a time: 4 p.m.

He checked his watch. It was about three. He gave the taxi driver the address and settled back for a drive that lasted about thirty minutes. They drove into one of the better districts on the outskirts of the city. Ultra modern apartment buildings arose on both sides of the street. It was as though they had left Asia behind and entered an affluent section of San Francisco. For the length of a block, there arose an island of opulence. On one side stood cheap blighted buildings. In the other direction, a long block away, stood the seedy structures of Tokyo's commercial margins.

He had the driver slow down so that he could read the numbers on the apartment buildings, difficult in a city that does not post its numbers in many cases, and offers no consecutive system of enumeration. The cab driver knew where they were going.

Locating the building finally, Luke told him to head back toward the downtown district. He paid him off when he saw a taxi parked across the street. He got into the cab and went back to the vicinity of the apartment. By this time he had about ten minutes left on the hour. He got out and sent the taxi on its way, confident that if anyone had been tailing him, he would know it. He walked down the long block slowly and came up to the apartment right on time.

When he pressed the button under her apartment number, he got an immediate response. She hadn't indicated a code or password, so he gave the seat number and said "baseball." The security doors began to buzz, and he pushed his way into the building and took the elevator up to the third floor.

She opened the door at once. He went past her into the room. A young blonde woman was sitting on a sofa, saying nothing, just staring at him. The Eurasian woman sat down next to the blond, crossing her long sleek legs. He realized more fully now that he knew her from a previous time. He judged from her expression that she recognized him. There are exchanges like that between strangers who are not quite strangers.

In Honolulu she had a reputation for being an expensive call girl. When he first saw her, he was intrigued and aroused. She had been out of his reach, however. They had moved in the same circle, the edge of the underworld, but on different tracks; he, the police officer, she the companion of rich men whose business often touches upon crime. Luke chose to take the legal side; she had just as surely chosen the side of crime.

He wondered then if the desire she had aroused in him had been due to her erotic reputation; or was it simply beauty: the features chiseled sharp and appealing by Caucasian genes. Her figure was taunting, almost voluptuous, her aggressive personality was challenging. The lithe movements of the trim body, the nice uplifted breasts were accentuated with her stylish clothes. Men turned their heads for a second look. But he imagined there was no soul behind the perfect face, the smart brain, the quick tongue. She was a hustler, sharp and well connected. Now, in Tokyo, encountering each other for the first time in personal terms, they were on the same side. She was his contact, and his passion for her was no more than the fantasies he had entertained seven years ago. She knew him; he could tell. Or, at least, she knew of him from the Honolulu days. But there was a game to be played now, in this world of deception and theft. She pretended they were strangers, and so did he.

"What's your name?" he asked.

"Call me Kiah," she answered.

It was an alias, he thought. She had gone by another name in Honolulu, Joy, a phony name, appropriate for a high-class courtesan. She was asking if he wanted a drink.

"Sure."

"What would you like?"

"Anything."

She went to the bar, setting out glasses. "Anything but rice wine, right?" She laughed slightly.

"Or French champagne," he said.

"How about scotch?"

"All right, make it neat with a little ice."

Kiah looked toward the blonde girl. "Megen?" her voice a question.

Megen, remained silent, shook her head, refusing, then said, "Well, maybe."

Kiah had been rude, letting Luke and Megen stare at each other without introductions. It was the first English Megen had spoken, meager and defective, far from fluent. He realized that she could not have been educated in the West. He concluded that she was not Eurasian to be sure, possibly of European origins, but reared in Japan without doubt.

He took a seat facing the blonde girl. "Are you our contact?"

Megen nodded slightly as if to say no, still not speaking.

"Is this your place?"

"Why do you ask?"

"Just curious."

"I live here with a friend."

Kiah brought him a drink, keeping one for herself. She sat down with the practiced grace of the man's companion. The expensive dress slipped above her knees as she crossed her legs again to reveal a fine expanse of saffron flesh. They sipped their drinks in silence.

"Don't you speak?" he asked Megen finally.

Both girls laughed. "When I find it necessary," said Megen. Her English was colloquial with a foreign accent, but he couldn't figure out which country.

There was more silence. "Can you get it for us?" he asked.

Kiah nodded. "It's in two parts."

"Ah," said Luke. "You're both contacts."

"We work together," replied Kiah. "It's our system."

"How do you want to be paid?"

"You can have shares in your company assigned to us."

Luke was surprised by this. "You want to be stockholders?"

"Not exactly. We want to convert the shares into American dollars later."

He thought about it for a bit. "I can arrange it. How many dollars are we talking about?"

"Five hundred thousand."

Luke whistled softly. "Be serious."

It was obvious that Kiah was going to do the talking. Her face turned hard. "We know there's a market for what we have. Millions."

Luke buckled under immediately. "Okay. Let's work out the details. The information is in two parts?"

"Yes."

"What form?"

"Two discs, from the Tushimi computer banks."

"Banks? In one place?"

"No. In two computer banks, in different parts of Japan. Megen has one, I have the other." A slight smile came, a hint of triumph on the hard sharp face. "Theoretically, the information is unstealable and unusable the way we have it."

"Where in Japan?"

"Does it matter? You only want the formula. Right?"

"We want the information, and we'll pay for it."

She gave him a hard look.

"Where?" he repeated.

Kiah shrugged. "Two banks, one in Kyoto and the other in Sapporo."

Lucas was patient. He handed her his glass, and she went to the bar to fill it again. Megen remained silent, the face gentle, the soft eyes on his most of the time. Kiah came back, handing him his drink, and sat down, giving him another view of her fine legs. This time the skirt slipped up higher.

"Are you girls employed by the Tushimi Corporation?"

Kiah hesitated. "In a manner of speaking."

"You have access to the company, I take it."

"We have access to the executives of the company."

"Ah!" said Luke, a broad smile coming over his face.

The girls laughed. "Ah!" said Kiah. "You're beginning to see the light."

Luke grinned. "I understand Japanese gentlemen have a yen for beautiful western women."

Kiah was amused. "Yen? Is that supposed to be a pun?"

"Look," he said. "Let's say you furnish us with the discs. You know we would have to validate them."

"How much time would you need for that?"

"We've brought a couple of experts with us. I'd say it would require only a few minutes."

"All right."

They were still sparring. "When do you expect to have the information?"

"How long will you be in Tokyo?"

"A couple of weeks."

Kiah got up. "We'll let you know."

She got up and started toward the door. It was the sign for his dismissal. He followed her.

"How will we know?"

"The same as before. You will find a ticket in your mail."

They were at the doorway. Luke found himself moving into the hallway. He turned to look at the beautiful face again. "I think I saw you in Honolulu some years ago." It was a question rather than a statement.

Kiah was impassive. "It could be." she said.

He took that for a yes. "It is possible that we met there at one time."

This time he received a slight smile. "Perhaps."

She was closing the door with that, his last sight of her the sphinx-like smile.

Chapter 4

He left Megen's apartment with mixed feelings, satisfied to have made a solid contract, but unsettled at the same time. Kiah had given him a look as he went out the door. There was a sign of recognition, a suggestion of interest in her eyes. The old desire for her, never completely stilled, welled up again. Like unrequited love, it hurts.

He got back to the hotel a little before six, just in time to catch the evening news.

"How did it go today?" asked Harry as he came into the room. Luke was caught off guard and stared at Harry for a second. Mark intervened quickly. "I guess you got over your diarrhea."

Luke had forgotten he was supposed to be ill. "I'm feeling better," he said. He looked around at the others. "I think I'll skip dinner tonight, though."

There was some more desultory conversation, the kind that is interrupted by periodic attention being given to a TV show in progress. Taki had arranged for a trip up north to Sapporo the next morning. Luke looked toward the TV disinterestedly, absorbed by the conversation. The screen showed a body, wrapped in a white sheet, being taken on a stretcher from an apartment building. The entrance to the building looked familiar to him and caught his attention. The television narrator's voice began to seep into his brain.

"Keep it down," he said roughly. He grabbed the remote and raised the volume. By this time the stretcher had been placed in an ambulance. The picture shifted back to the news reporter. Luke listened while the others, unaware of his concern, watched silently.

A commercial came on the TV and Luke turned away from the set, feeling a little weak.

"What's was that all about?" asked Mark.

Luke turned the volume down and whispered. "That was the woman I met today."

"What happened?" asked Harry.

"She committed suicide, they think, overdose."

"Did they say why?" asked Walt.

"No."

Luke and Mark exchanged glances. As soon as he had a chance, he took Mark into an adjoining bedroom.

"I thought you looked funny out there," said Mark. "Who is the woman?"

"Her name is Megen. I was at her apartment a couple of hours ago."

"Was she our contact?"

"Yeah, one of two. We're dealing with two women."

"She committed suicide?"

"That's what the news commentator just said, but it doesn't add up."

"How come?"

"I was there between four and five o'clock, less than an hour ago. Why would she take pills so early in the evening?"

"Strange," agreed Mark, "I mean, that her dead body would be discovered so soon, almost as soon as she took the pills."

"Foul play," said Luke, softly.

"Do you think you were seen there?"

"You never know."

Mark wanted to know what Megen had to do with Tushimi.

"I think she was the girlfriend of one of their big shots."

"And she was going to deliver the information?"

"Part of it, but she didn't say much of anything. A Japanese woman did all the talking."

Mark walked around the room, a little nervous. "Don't you think that Harry and Walt should know about this? Especially if it looks like we'll be involved with a police investigation?"

"No."

"Why not?"

"Because it's company policy to keep the old guys out of the loop. Anyway, I don't trust Harry. He may be a genius when it comes to microchips and that's the only reason he's on this trip."

"How old do you think he is?"

"I heard he's in his late seventies, seventy-eight, maybe eighty."

"My God," said Mark. "He should have been retired a long time ago."

"He was, for about ten years. Then they asked him to come back because he is the principal author of the stolen formula. It was his baby. I think that may be why he's so bitter. He takes it personally."

"OK," said Mark, "so what's our next step?"

"We wait. That's all we can do."

The next morning Luke was not surprised to find a plain, unmarked envelope waiting for him at the front desk, or to see a ticket inside. There were, besides this, a few letters from the home office. Mark came up to the desk as he sorted through them, and Luke showed him the ticket.

"Another ball game?" asked Mark.

Luke glanced toward Taki and the ubiquitous bodyguard waiting near the entrance of the hotel.

"No. A little culture this time."

Mark's eyebrows went up perceptibly.

"I'm going to be introduced to *Kabuki*, it appears."

"What's that?'

"It's classic Japanese drama, a style unchanged since the eighteenth century."

"When's the show?"

"Tonight."

Mark heaved a sigh of relief. "That's good. You won't have to invent an excuse for avoiding Taki's tour of the day."

They went out and got into the limousine with the others. On the way to the railroad station Harry brought up Megen's death.

"Suicide's not the American way," he said at one point.

This evidently challenged Taki enough for him to turn around in his seat and confront Harry. "It is a death not without honor in Japan," he said evenly. For once there was no smile on his face. The eyes behind the steel-rimmed glasses were more penetrating than Luke had seen so far.

"It's a waste," replied Harry in his big voice, "and it's cowardly. In my country, men and women deal with their problems. They don't just lie down and die like dogs."

This produced a long silence, and no one wanted to break it. Finally, Taki turned around again and his voice seemed to hiss, "The news reports she was an American."

Harry squirmed with this. "Well, she could have been murdered," he said roughly.

Taki couldn't let that pass. He didn't bother to turn around this time. "The reports are the woman took an overdose of sleeping pills."

Taki had the last word. They rode the remainder of the way to the station in silence. The strain was great. During the trip to Kyoto Walt was able to steer the conversation back to shop talk. At the station, two junior executives joined them. Although not as fluent in English as Taki they were more westernized, very breezy, slangy, and friendly. Taki had recovered his composure, and Harry seemed to find the two young men diverting.

Mark and Luke took seats apart from the other.

"Harry is sure doing his part," observed Mark.

"Yeah," replied Luke. "Making us look like barbarians."

"It's all to the point, perfect cover for us."

Luke was troubled. "The way Harry and Taki snipe at each other revives something I thought was buried half a century ago."

"What's that?"

"The national and racial rivalries of the nineteen thirties."

"Ah," retorted Mark, not impressed. "That was ages ago."

"You don't sense it?"

"Apparently I don't."

"Maybe it's my background," said Luke, "you know, second generation Nisei." He hesitated. "I may be super sensitive."

"Sensitive, to what?"

"Harry is too American for me. Taki is too Japanese. I mean, the one is boisterous, crude, naïve. The other one is cold as ice, correct and calculating as a snake." He hesitated, looking at Mark's puzzled face. "They're both out of the past."

"They're old and feisty," agreed Mark.

"They're anachronisms, throwbacks, like they might crank up World War Two by starting World War Three."

"Now what does that mean?"

Luke reflected. "I don't know exactly. It's weird, as though systems of thought, the old values and hatreds of another generation, are being reborn just now."

"Maybe," said Mark laconically. "But Harry and Taki reflect their own times, not ours."

"I wonder," replied Luke after another long pause.

They joined the others. Pessimistic philosophy gave way to shop talk. The young Japanese executives, enthusiastic, statistical extroverts, with their command of sales and production figures, carried them on a wave of conversation to the Kyoto station, and thereafter through the Tushimi plant for the remainder of the day.

Back in Tokyo that evening Luke went out after dinner and rented a late model Toyota sedan. At eight P.M. he parked and walked a block or so to the theater. He was surprised to find Kiah already in her seat. It was, he thought, as he sat down beside her, almost like a prearranged date. There was on her disciplined face a suggestion of a smile as she turned to him. Gone were the implacable stares he had encountered the day before.

The house lights dimmed as he was getting settled.

"What about Megen?" he started to say.

She laid a hand on his arm. "Later."

The claques introducing the first act drowned out her words. The curtain rose. Luke could not resist a second question. "Don't we know each other?" he asked, leaning over to make it a whisper.

She squeezed his arm and said in a low voice, equally soft, "Yes."

The tone of her voice was enough. It was friendly. He felt the old surge of seven years before, but it was stronger now, a pounding in the pit of his stomach. How many men had been seduced, he wondered, by the provocative body and the challenging eyes? The play on stage, stylized eroticism, built his lust even more. This time Kiah did not leave him, but remained seated to the end.

At its conclusion, they arose together, without speaking, and went to the lobby. She took the lead. He could only follow. At the door, people streaming around them, she turned, her face lifted up to his. Her hand went into his coat pocket and came out again as he looked down.

"I have a car," he said.

Kiah laughed a low mocking laugh. "So do I. Follow my instructions. They're in your coat pocket."

She disappeared almost at once into the crowd leaving the theater. Luke went to his car and by the dome light was able to read the note she had left him. A time for their meeting was not specified. It said only "right away." There was an address, the name of a motel, its street number, and the room number. He was to knock three times in rapid succession, twice more slowly.

Luke took a tourist's map from the glove compartment and searched for the street address. It was on the south side of Tokyo. He took the freeway and got there in fifteen minutes. Garish lights of commercial establishments cast a pulsating color and shadow over deserted streets beginning to glisten from a mist hanging in the air. The motel, its lurid lights flashing a block away, sat somewhat apart from the other business places.

He remained in the car for a few minutes with the engine idling, listening to soft rock music on the car radio. An occasional vehicle going by at high speed on the freeway above disturbed the calm of the late evening. Satisfied after a few minutes, he cut the engine, turned off the headlights and got out of the car. He locked the doors and started down the street toward the motel. Apprehension stole over him as he walked, but at the same time a sense of urgency, the need to confront the woman again.

He found the number almost at once. Looking around, seeing no one, he started to knock, then changed his mind. A half dozen cars were parked in the lot. He walked to them and almost unerringly chose the one he judged was hers. It was a late model sports car, expensive enough to belong to her and no one else in the motel. He took a small jimmy tool from his pocket and picked the door lock without difficulty. A penlight gave him enough illumination to open the glove compartment. Her registration papers were there. He copied down her address and put everything back. Now he knew more than he was sure she would want to tell him.

In a couple of minutes he had returned to the door. He knocked three times rapidly, then twice more in slow succession. The door opened immediately, and he saw Kiah standing in the doorway. Suspicious, he went by her quickly, checking out the place. It was a love motel, typically Nipponese in the field of Japanese copulation. In a country too crowded and space too limited for most, a love motel offers at hourly rates and a moderate price as much room and time as needed to satisfy the hunger for the flesh.

Luke had to smile. He wondered if they had thought of drive-in whorehouses yet. The bathroom, western in style, was no more than a closet. A western style bed, also small, quite low, was the only substantial piece of furniture in the room. It looked like a Japanese futon with tiny legs. He wondered if it would bear his weight. On a small table next to the bed, the proprietor had placed besides the complementary matches, with evident thoughtfulness, a package of condoms.

He went back to face her, realizing that she had changed into a tight sheath dress of chartreuse silk, very oriental, with a high collar. Buttons running down the front, it clutched her figure, ending at her knees. The black hair framed her heart-shaped face like a picture. She had switched to high heels that brought her head almost level with his.

Their eyes were in contact for a moment. She finally moved away to light a cigarette.

"Any trouble with my instructions," she asked.

"No. I made sure I wouldn't be tailed."

Kiah paced, dragged nervously on the cigarette.

"What happened to Megen?" he asked.

"Suicide they say."

"About what time did you leave Megen's apartment yesterday?"

"A few minutes after you did."

"Do you know who discovered her body?'

I read in the newspaper that a cleaning maid found her."

He knew all this. "Have you thought how little time passed between the time we last saw Megen and when her body was discovered?'

Kiah was sober. "I thought about it, naturally. That's why I think they murdered her."

"Who are they?'

Kiah seemed surprised by this. "Don't you know? The Tushimi people."

He didn't say anything and she seemed surprised. "Don't you know who you're dealing with?'

"One never knows. Who are we talking about?'

Now they were at an impasse, Kiah displaying some signs of uncertainty, Luke puzzled.

"Do you want to deal or not?" she asked.

"Have you got the disc?"

That brought a long pause from her. "Yes," she said finally.

"Well, let's see it."

"We'd better talk price first."

"We agreed to five hundred thousand dollars in company stock."

"We can't cut that deal now."

Luke was beginning to get irritated. "Why not?"

"Because Megen's dead. I don't know where her disc is."

"She didn't get her half of the information, is that it?"

"She did, but I don't know where it is."

"Do you think it's still in her apartment?"

"I have no idea."

"So what have you got?

"My half."

"Half the information is of no use to us."

She started pacing again, lighting another cigarette. "It must be worth something."

"How much?"

"Let's say two hundred grand."

He meditated. "In company stock?'

"No, in cash."

"American dollars?"

"I want it in Japanese yen."

"That's a pile of cash."

She stubbed out the cigarette. "Take it or leave it."

He wasn't going to argue with her. It was peanuts for getting information worth millions if he could get the other half of the formula.

"Alright. Let's round if off. The whole deal for four hundred grand. But we want some leads to Megen's half of the formula."

"I can't help you with that." She had become very firm, staring down at the floor.

She seemed to relent. "We can deal. I have connections but I'll need some time to get Megen's disc. I'm sure I can find it."

"Who is this *they* we're talking about?"

"I can't tell you that."

"Why not?"
"Because no one really knows."
"Is it a secret organization?"
"Obviously."
"Criminal?"
"They have connections with Japan's underworld. That much I know. But that's just a fact of life."
"What's their connection with the Tushimi Corporation?"
She had become terse again, almost savage in response. "I don't know! I'll tell you this. They run the country."
He didn't believe that. "This is a democratic country."
"So they say. Think what you like. I've told you everything I know."
Luke laughed ironically. "Which is nothing. What makes you think they killed Megen?"
"They must have found out she robbed their computer bank in Kyoto."
"Industrial espionage seldom leads to murder," objected Luke.
"You don't know who you're dealing with," she said stubbornly.
He was getting exasperated. "You're really scared, aren't you?"
Kiah raised her head defiantly. "If they murdered Megen, what do you think they'll do to me?"
"Can we help you?" he asked gently.
She shook her head vigorously, proudly he thought. He decided she was being sincere. And if that was true, he was getting into something heavy. A little sense of alarm stole over him.
Kiah got up again, moving about restlessly. "I can take care of myself. Look. Have we got a deal?"
Luke hesitated. "OK, but first a few questions. Was that Megen's apartment we were in yesterday?"
"Yes."
"Who was keeping her?"
"I don't know him by name. Megen said their boyfriends use code names. You know, nicknames. She told me the name; but I can't remember it now. Something like Salanka or Sugoya."
"Is he a big shot?"
"He's high up in the Tushimi Corporation."
"Were you living with Megen?"
"Of course not. I have my own place."
"Why are we meeting here then?"
"I've moved out of my apartment."
Luke was satisfied that he had gotten everything he could out of her. He asked her where they would make the exchange.

"Meet me at the Central Tokyo Station one week from today."

Luke calculated. "The seventeenth of May. And then what?"

"I'll give you the disc. My half."

"Where and when exactly?"

"At six p.m., under the big clock in the center of the station, the lower concourse. I'll walk by and you can follow me."

Luke didn't like that too much. "After that, what's to happen?"

She had come up to him by this time. "That's as much as I can tell you now. Be there. I won't let you down."

That was it. They were finished. He felt emotionally drained. Some strange pressure seemed to be at work on him. Maybe it was the lateness of the hour, the sense of crime in the air, apprehension of danger. Megen was dead, Kiah was obviously scared. She alluded to a sinister force that could not be known.

They had concluded their business coldly, as hostile bargainers might. The little warmth she had displayed earlier in the theater seemed to have gone, his desire for her dissipated by their business. He started to turn toward the door but stopped, seeing something in her face. It was woman's mystery, both a questioning look and an invitation. Again, the intensity of their eyes in contact generated the old feeling. Did she know he wanted her? Was it to be the cement for sealing their bargain?

"There is something between us," he said, hesitating, not knowing why he said that, or what it meant.

"Yes," she said, and her voice was soft again.

He didn't want to kiss her. The hard symmetrical face did not ask for his lips. Her expression promised him more. She brought her hand slowly across her bosom, that fluttering which tells a man what he wants to know. His eyes followed her fingers as they came to rest on the buttons of her dress. His mind swirled, he reached out and began to undo them. She looked down with sober intensity, the fragrance of her perfume a powerful aphrodisiac. He slipped the dress from her shoulders, exposing the fine breasts. In the vortex of his emotions he realized that she had arranged for this moment. Without undergarments, she stepped nude from the dress, prepared as her trade required. Proud, she gloried in her body and wanted him to see her. She stood still for a moment while his eyes ran over her, then walked on high heels to the bed.

The sight of her slender back and long legs dazzled him. Bending down, she removed her shoes and slipped onto the bed, her smoldering eyes, commanding him to come to her.

Her eroticism drove him wild. He wondered how many men had assaulted that perfect body and been subdued by its energies. He tore his clothes from himself while she watched. Her face was hard with fascination, demanding haste. Oblivious of all but the oldest instinct, he went to her. She took him with quick passion, relentlessly seeking relief. He felt himself being drained, dominated as she knelt over him, absorbed by her mastery of him. The frenzy was brief. Groaning, he spent himself, and she collapsed upon him, the sound of her climax in his ears. A heavy sleep overcame them at once.

When he awoke, he was alone, feeling chilled and weak. He got into his clothes, slightly depressed, and went outside. A light rain further dampened the aftermath of a desire finally gratified, yet strangely unfulfilled. There had been no feeling, only an animal appetite satisfied.

He wondered if she was a nymphomaniac. Her lust had been as great as his. Driving back to the hotel in the silence of the early morning, he reflected on sex and money. Kiah symbolized, in fleshy terms, his lust for money. He decided that serving the lucrative business of industrial piracy was no different than serving a sexually aroused woman. Both were insatiable; both had the power to draw him. Were not all men engaged in seeking power consumed by the two: sex and money? He knew the world of big business a little better now.

Chapter 5

"What do you say we spend the weekend with the cream of Japan's industrial elite?"

Taki had made the invitation, and Luke conveyed it to the others when they got back to the hotel after an all day excursion.

"I'll pass on that," grumbled Harry, slumping down in a chair.

"What's the deal?" asked Mark.

"Taki says one of the Tushimi executives, Baron Akada, wants to entertain us."

"No kidding," said Mark. "Baron? A nobleman?"

"I thought titles were abolished during the Occupation," said Walt.

Luke tried to remember. "I don't think so. Actually, social privilege, which set the nobility apart from Japanese commoners, came to an end in the nineteenth century."

Harry was skeptical. "So what does a title mean anyway?"

"Prestige in Japan, the same as in Europe," Luke replied. "The European nobility keep their titles, hand out their cards when you meet them. They live a separate life, as though they're better than the common run of humanity. I imagine the Japanese nobility feel the same way."

Harry scoffed. "Titles! Like registered livestock."

Luke thought that was true. The Japanese aristocracy is inbred, evolving over a long period of time. After the Americans opened up Japan to trade in the eighteen fifties the Samurai class entered both the military and industrial sectors of the society. It was the Japanese equivalent of the military industrial complex that Eisenhower warned against in his time.

"I think we should go," Walt said suddenly, changing the subject.

"Hey," replied Mark. "I don't think we have any choice. Anyway, we've seen the cruddy bottom of Japanese society, the strip joints and the massage parlors. Let's see the top of their culture."

Harry kicked off his shoes. "Sure. We can go. I want to know how these bastards are spending our money."

Mark lost his temper. "Why don't you let up on that? We've yet to prove they stole our formula."

Mark threw up his hands, as if defeated.

Walt intervened. "What's his purpose?"

Luke frowned, not quite understanding him. "Whose?"

"The baron's. Is it business or pleasure?"

"It's a show of hospitality, I suppose. You know how polite they are."

Harry had spread himself out on one of the beds by this time, staring up at the ceiling. "I know how polite they are. They smile in your face and stick a knife in your back at the same time. You want to know about their culture and their national character? Consider this: we walk around with our heads in our hands; we're so guilty about bombing Hiroshima. "Forgive us," we say, and they act as though they deserve our pity. But what have they ever said about their attack on Pearl Harbor? Do they walk around guilt stricken? I guess not. How about what they did in China, during the 1930's? A crime so great that world opinion was disgusted. They bragged about their murder and their raping. Has anyone in Japan to this day apologized to the Chinese? How about Manila in 1942? A free city, defenseless, unarmed, without a military target in sight. They slaughtered the Philippine civilians. How about Indonesia? Do they admit their guilt? Do they apologize? They're without conscience."

Walt interrupted him. "They've paid for it, and they're still paying huge reparations for those atrocities, conducted by their military rulers, not by the Japanese people."

Harry sneered. "The people! Those fine people cheered them on, because they were winning. If they're still paying reparations, it's because they were beaten into the ground."

"No," said Walt mildly. "They're doing it voluntarily."

Harry's skepticism couldn't be dampened. "If it's voluntary, it's so they can improve their business deals in those countries. They're calculating; you know that. Invest two dimes in charity, and get back a dollar in profit."

Mark couldn't listen any more. He went to another room.

"That old man has a one track mind," he said to Luke a little later.

"Yeah. He gets more bitter every day."

"Do you think he's jealous of what he's seen in the Tushimi plants?"

"Could be. I don't blame him. Frankly, I'm impressed. I didn't know their robot technology was so far advanced in the computer field."

"Invisible workers," breathed Mark. "Who would believe robots could be microchips?"

"I would. Their industrial establishments interlock at the top. Technology in one sector of their economy flows like water into the next. We have nothing like it."

"I think the Brass were right," said Mark. "Tushimi has at least a five year lead on us."

"And we're only going to close the gap by getting some of their information."

"Any word from Miss Baseball?" asked Mark.

"You mean Kiah?"

"Yeah."

"No. I imagine she'll send me a ticket in the mail."

"Say Luke, what do you think the Baron's party is all about?"

Luke laughed lightly. "I'm not as paranoid as Walt. I think it's kind of like industrial diplomacy. P.R., that's all it is. They want to impress us. You've noticed that they're showing us their newest plants. Now, I suspect we're going to meet their best management, the chiefs of their operations."

Mark snickered. "All graduates of M.I.T. and the Harvard Business School, speaking English with a New England accent. My, my. Clever the way we train our competition. So, when are we privileged to attend?"

"Around one P.M. tomorrow. We can sleep in for a change."

For once, the punctual Taki did not arrive the next day to give them the courteous service they had come to expect. About one o'clock the chauffeur telephoned them in his slow, precise English, and they went down to the lobby to meet him.

The drive began on the elevated freeway and started southwest toward Note, the district of the rich and famous in Japan, the Yamonote hills overlooking the city.

"This is like driving over Chicago," said Harry, looking down below them onto the streets.

The contrast was starker than the likeness. Chicago's elevated expressways give the driver a view of the commercial city below. Tokyo's elevated roadways run over the residential areas of the city, combined pell-mell with the oldest and the newest of the financial and commercial establishments. The driver looks down upon a bewildering succession of stately townhouses, ultra modern business structures, standing side by side with wretched hovels, flimsy business establishments of paper and wood. The city has little conception of zoning ordinances, no convenient way to segregate dwelling places from business establishments, modern structures from those most blighted and old. The maze of narrow streets and alleys appeared from some height to be like the tracks of captive animals. Those who live there give up their privacy to those who drive over them. The

Americans stared into the rooms of dwellings as they rode, receiving in return the blank stares of the occupants. It was a new voyeurism, as provocative and at the same time as intriguing, as the views they had entertained of Tokyo's nightlife on their first arrival in the city.

"This is what the futuristic novelists write about in their darkest moment," said Luke.

"It's already here," said Walt.

"Future shock," said Mark.

The chauffeur drove to an exit ramp, leaving behind the multiple confusion of decay and modernity, the future and the past, which is Tokyo. Thereafter it was like going into the hills on the north side of Los Angeles, thought Luke: affluent, quiet, and discreet; yet there was a difference. A Mediterranean climate cannot produce abundant and verdant vegetation, the natural cover that gives to each rich resident the means for privacy, the sense of having retreated from the world. Note is lush, a hilly paradise, removed in time and space from the mad confusion of wealth and poverty; a sterile cleanliness amidst filth; the one piled on the other in Tokyo.

Winding roads, retaining walls of stone, trees and shrubs, presented a labyrinth, not troubled nor disfigured by the innumerable signs the westerner thinks necessary for streets and avenues. After a time of circuitous driving, they came out on the upper reaches of the hills. Stone walls and iron gates opposed them. The gates gave way as they approached, closing almost immediately, once they had entered the grounds that were groomed something like a park.

At the back of the park, through cryptomeria cedars, they saw a house distinctively Japanese, a rich man's retreat. Low walls, a tiled roof, covering a large area, rambled along the brow of the hill. In the warm afternoon of early summer several of the sliding doors had been pulled back, allowing the interior of the house to communicate with the lawns and gardens outside.

A westerner would have thought a circular drive was in order, and for that purpose might have removed perhaps one-half of the intervening cedars. The driver passed in a serpentine fashion among these obstacles, however, bringing them to one side of the house where a raised terrace served as a rampart to support the house on a precipitous slope. They stopped, a panoramic view suddenly presented to them: sprawling Tokyo far below and far away; and, beyond the megalopolis, Tokyo bay shining in the afternoon sun.

Half a dozen expensive cars were parked near the house. Servants, dressed formally in western attire, came down the terrace to greet them. They were without words, smiles and bows aplenty, as they led the Americans up the steps to the house. Their open countenances told Luke that the Japanese are a polite, warm, hospitable people. He glanced in Harry's direction. There was a stern expression on his face, almost a scowl. He knew what the old man was thinking: these were obsequious, cunning, hypocritical, treacherous people. The inscrutable Japanese smile conceals a malevolent nature.

A retinue of servants awaited them just inside; and again bows and smiles invited them to cross the threshold. Luke hesitated, thinking he should tell the others to remove their shoes. He looked down at the feet of his hosts. They were shod in expensive western footware. A glance at the room told him why. It was furnished in the western style. Sofas and chairs were stationed about an enormous room, a heavy carpet on the floor. Tables with lamps, tables with books, and tables with ornamental objects, racks of magazines, and the paraphernalia that the westerner considers essential for living were casually distributed around the room.

In the center stood a long table, dressed in a white linen cover, loaded with food, western varieties, the innumerable snacks that the westerner likes to wash down with a quantity of liquor and gossip. At the far end of the room a bar had been set up. Two boys, in black trousers and white tunics, waited to mix drinks upon demand.

Open doors at the end of the room gave a view of the expansive house, revealing the great contrast between civilizations, perhaps betraying physically the split in the Japanese psyche. The rooms beyond the open doors were virtually devoid of furniture. Tatami mats covered the floors, some cushions for those who might wish to sit on the floor. He could see a small stand in one room, a vase upon it, in which a solitary Iris appeared, somewhat like a distant exclamation mark, a splash of brilliant blue against the drab walls of gray.

There was opulence bulging in the western room they were about to enter; and a sparseness, almost ascetic emptiness, in the adjoining rooms. Luke wondered if the Japanese hosts considered the contradiction into which they themselves had entered. It divides their lives, in order that they might meet the West on the one hand, yet on the other they cling to their natural, native ways.

He had come to realize that the Japanese are not a philosophical people, but practical, mystical and religious. Philosophical questions are seldom raised, therefore never considered, except by their professional philosophers who have no public to communicate with in any case. Too obtuse are the questions: What is wrong and what is right? What is shame? What is guilt? The subtleties in values that allow for a distinction between a guilt society like the United States and a shame society like Japan are not of a kind to draw or long hold the attention of the Japanese thinker. Is the West the one, guilt ridden, and Japan the other, shamefaced? In such a case, could there be a convenient or lasting relationship for two neurotic societies? Could such a rivalry, irrational at base, ever be resolved? Would not a natural conflict last forever?

There were about a dozen Japanese to greet. They fell into line with sudden precision, startling to Luke, as though an unspoken command had been given. Low bows were followed by limp handshakes. Always in Japan, Luke had discovered in just a few days, individuality, seemingly strong at first sight, disappears with grateful surrender into collective actions.

The principal host, proprietor of the house, was a middle-aged man who spoke in a heavily accented but effective English. There was not a female present. Luke judged that Tushimi's leadership at the top was all male; it seemed no women graced the boardrooms of this multinational corporation.

As Luke came to the end of the receiving line he came to a face with features that were not oriental; unmistakably they were those of a Middle Eastern individual. The face did not smile; the eyes seemed hard and penetrating as they shook hands. Unable to catch his name, Luke asked for it again. It was still not quite intelligible, sounding something like Hussein Bin Laden. It appeared as if the Middle East had penetrated the Far East, at the highest levels and in some significant way.

Intrigued, Luke began to move among the Japanese guests. He discovered that most of them had received part, if not all, of their education in the United States. The talk centered more on American topics than he had expected. His questions on Japan were invariably shifted to American topics. Bored finally, he edged toward the open doors and went out on the terrace to get some fresh air, to take another look at the long view, Tokyo in the far distance.

Mark was already there, leaning on a balcony.

"That's really weird," he said.

"What?" asked Luke.

"They're holding the reception in a room that looks totally western. But the other rooms are practically empty, practically no furniture."

Luke nodded. "That's how the upper classes make their concession to western ways. They outfit one room with western furniture and never use it, except to entertain foreigners; *caijin* they call us."

They looked down from the ramparts of the terrace to tumbled hills that fell away to the immense spaces of Tokyo's flat land.

"This view makes me think of *Madame Butterfly*," said Mark, "when she looked down on the bay from a hilltop, waiting for her sailor boyfriend to arrive."

Luke couldn't suppress a laugh. He didn't expect so much culture from Mark. "She lived in the Nagasaki hills, you know."

"Yeah, *Madame Butterfly* is the only thing I can think of that's appropriate to Japan, except for Michener's *Sayonara*, and I don't know how that novel would fit in to this scene."

"I would say they both are stories about East meeting West."

"And never the twain shall meet."

"But the two do meet," countered Luke. "We're living proof of that, and I'm the best example."

Mark changed the subject. "What do you think will follow the reception?"

"I imagine we'll be treated to a gala Japanese banquet this evening. You know, squid, seaweed, half a dozen kinds of fish and oysters. Rice and plenty of saki."

"I'd settle for steak and potatoes."

"I think we'll get a little culture on top of the seafood."

"Meaning?"

Luke looked over the edge of the terrace to the drive below. "I caught a glimpse of a limo when I came out here just now. Half a dozen geishas were getting out and going into the house."

"I've never seen one in the flesh. That'll be a treat."

"It may be a bore. We'll see how the ugly American handles it."

Mark laughed. "You know Harry, he'll be his usual suave self."

"He'll probably proposition one of them."

"Do they put out?"

"Are you serious?"

Mark grinned. "I said that in jest. But what's the truth? Are they just entertainers, or do they really entertain, if you know what I mean?"

"I understand that if you spend enough time with them and establish a good rapport, they may consider becoming your mistress."

"You mean after months of foreplay, right."

"I mean you would have to cultivate a relationship. It could be friendship or love; it would depend."

"That's not what I had in mind," said Mark.

"They're not whores, I'll tell you that."

"I get it, no sex."

"Forget the carnal angle. That's secondary. They're totally feminine. They've been trained since they were young girls to be social creatures, according to what I've read. They play the role of companion and confidant, radiating intimacy, sharing interests, admiration, attention to the customer's whims, all those psychological things a clinging woman does to perfection. Rich men, who can afford them, fill up many hours in their company. Business men hire them to decorate their parties, like living flowers."

"In other words, the geishas are substitutes for their wives."

"Exactly, only better than wives, because there is no jealousy among the geishas, or so I understand. They are strictly professional. Also, they have talent. They will sing and dance if you ask."

"I'm getting excited," said Mark.

"You'll enjoy them so much you won't even get aroused. It'll be just like spending an evening with your sister."

That sobered Mark a little. He wanted to talk about something else. Why they hadn't seem Taki so far.

"I don't think we will," said Luke. "He's at the bottom of this particular food chain. This is a different Tushimi crowd. I'll bet the top Brass from all over Japan have come here this week, plus the Arab sheik we saw in there."

"We should feel honored," said Mark sarcastically. "What do you make of Taki? Second echelon man maybe?"

"It's a puzzle. He obviously has some authority."

Mark agreed. "But that body guard always hovering around him. That's unusual, to say the least."

"I thought so too, at first. But he's not the only muscleman on the payroll. I noticed two more when we arrived, almost copies of Taki's protector. Beefy, hard, bald heads like bowling balls."

Mark grunted. "Yeah, built like a brick shit house, and they probably smell the same."

"It makes me think of a godfather situation," said Luke.

Mark reflected on that. "You mean something like a crime syndicate?"

"In a way, yes. This could be an extended family, IE, a House, as the Japanese call it. If they are multi-millionaires, they would have to protect themselves against abduction and demands for ransom. Like in the U.S., crime is a way of life in Japan."

There was a jeer in Mark's voice. "What do you mean, if they're multi-millionaires? They're multi-billionaires. They own half the world already."

"You're right. They are super rich. But it's interesting to reflect. Look at this setting. It's modest by American standards. They haven't put much money into it. Like all rich people in all the poor countries of the world, they don't invest any more than they have to in their own society. Japan has a meager system of welfare for its poor. They build only a minimal infrastructure out of their huge profits. They'd rather invest in foreign countries."

That was a puzzle to Mark. "Why?"

"I have a notion. Two in fact. As conservative capitalist elite, still bound to their traditions, Japanese entrepreneurs are half-hearted about modernizing this country. Secondly, the more they create a consumer society, by virtue of their commercial successes abroad, the more they tend to lose that invisible control they traditionally hold over the policies of the government. If you think about it, these two motives really reinforce each other. In one way the Japanese elite is like our elite. They are satisfied to have their country be democratic, but they want to stifle democratic action because it threatens the established order of things."

Mark whistled. "Where did you get these ideas?"

"I used to read a lot. Anyway, I'm half-Japanese. I have more than a passing interest in this country."

"There's a third possibility," said Mark, "and not so intellectual."

"What's that?"

"They're salting their money away in different corners of the world, against the day when things break down in this country."

Luke was surprised by the thought. "Like the Arab rich class. Sure, I didn't think of that."

"See," said Mark, grinning, "you don't have to read books. The big shots just sit up here and get richer by the day, then ship the money out of the country."

"And they also remain powerful," said Luke. "It's always been like that."

He pointed to an imaginary line below them. "See where the hills end and the flat land begins? That's been the physical division between wealth and poverty, the aristocracy against the plebeian, for centuries. The lower classes have lived and worked on the flat land generation after generation. The wealthy living up here have managed them, siphoning off the profits. Naïve westerners think all this started in the nineteen fifties. It's really been going on for centuries."

Mark was skeptical. "More books."

"Yes, but common sense also. A textbook of history can give you an outline of events, the skeleton of history, so to speak. But to understand it you need to see the flesh that covers the bones. Standing up here in a Japanese mansion, I feel as though I'm looking down on history, as though all of this has happened before. I can see that the wealth and the power have always been on top of these hills."

"I could go up into Beverly Hills and get the same impression," said Mark, "by just looking down on Los Angeles."

"But there is a difference," argued Luke. "Here in these hills wealth and power are joined to the state in an organic, for all we know, in a familial way. That's another line of continuity in Japan that I think constitutional reforms, imposed upon the Japanese by the Americans during the MacArthur Occupation, did not interrupt. Do you know what I mean?"

"No."

"I mean this country is still run by extended families, at every level. Concentrated wealth and centralized political power in their conjunction, has always commanded the Japanese people. In appearance, Japan is democratic, a pluralistic society, rather like the American society. In fact, it is a homogenous society, collectively organized, and responsive to commands from the top, whether the authority figure is a Shogun, an Emperor or a Prime Minister."

Luke had worn Mark down, he could tell. He decided he wasn't too sure he knew what he was talking about anyway. There was the urge to understand a country, to which he seemed to belong in a biological and a permanent way, but words failed him. His ideas were so abstract finally as to have no relation to facts.

They went back inside, got another drink, and talked shop some more. They encountered Akada again. Gregarious, the Baron was unusually verbose as the day wore on. Liquor loosens the tongue. By sundown the Japanese had become animated, the Americans expansive. The Arab sheik seemed out of place. He sat in a chair alone most of the time, a magazine in his lap, seeming to stare at the distant wall across the crowded room. Luke was becoming more and more curious about the man from the Middle East. He certainly looked like the proverbial sheik from Araby, around 1500 let's say.

They were sobered up by being subjected to the tea drinking ceremony. Removing their shoes and coats, taking gowns from attentive servants, they were escorted to another room. It was empty for all practical purposes with only mats on the floor and a series of low tables lined up along one side of the room. Cushions had been arranged along the length of the tables. Small neon lamps affixed to the walls cast a subdued light over them as they began to sit down.

Akada took his place at front and center, the host sitting on his haunches, erect and staring to his front. The others arranged themselves to his left and right along the length of the tables. Whether by plan, or by chance, the Americans were separated and distributed amongst the Japanese hosts.

A sharp clap of the hands by Akada and a geisha appeared, bearing a ceramic work of art: a large hibachi. She knelt gracefully and sat it before him. Withdrawing, she was replaced by another who carried a teapot, a brilliant enameled piece that Luke judged to be another work of art. This too was gracefully presented to Akada who received it, as he had the hibachi, with a deep bow.

The ritual continued until finally the powdered tea, a stirring brush, and the cups had been distributed. The six women, having delivered the means for drinking tea, then seated themselves, at intervals along the tables, facing their hosts.

Years of work along the raw margins of American society had served to make Luke, if not a cynic, a skeptic. Still, it was not enough to prevent him from admiring the charm and grace of the ceremony as it proceeded. The exquisite manners of little women who seemed like painted, animated dolls, gave meaning to an elaborate ceremony that under other circumstances might have been thought of as contrived and artificial. The meaning to Luke was civility, an aesthetic pleasure in seeing fine things handled with grace. The tea, when finally served, was neither hot nor warm. Boiling the green powdered tea, it is said, takes away its flavor. Hot water, just hot enough, which depended on Akada's judgment, allowed for the maximum flavor. The guests pronounced it perfect and sipped the bitter, foamy drink, while a geisha, at a sign from Akada, stood to sing. Another left in that remarkable manner of moving without apparent haste, yet flying, to return almost at once with a *samisen*, in order to furnish her accompaniment.

A haunting love song, *China Nights*, a Japanese soldier's lament for his lost sweetheart, was followed by a dance, restrained yet erotic.

Dinner commenced thereafter, much longer than the tea ceremony, not so ceremonious. The bland food, not filling, came in courses, and was interrupted by the periodic performances of the geishas. Cups of the flat and somewhat tasteless sake before, during, and after the meal, restored the earlier inebriation. Luke noted that the Arab sheik was not present, not surprising to him; Arabs, if faithful to Islam, abjure alcohol.

Around midnight, the Japanese men started drifting away, one by one, to go outside and urinate or vomit. The beauty and precision of the tea drinking ceremony, a stylized art form, epitome of Japanese aesthetics, had become reduced to a drunken orgy. A heavy blanket of cigarette smoke hung in the air, a reminder for Luke that the Japanese, a stressful people, drink and smoke to excess.

The geishas had disappeared about the same time that the men had begun to leave. Where had the women gone? Did he read too much, Luke wondered. Had he given Mark another phony lecture? Another false set of ideas picked from the pages of a long forgotten book? He felt pretty drunk, pretty stupid and a little nauseous. His legs were cramped from hours of sitting on them. One foot had gone to sleep and seemed to buzz painfully beneath him.

Akada was starting for the doors, looking as though he might throw up. Luke got up with difficulty, stamping his dead foot back to life. He saw Harry sprawled out on the floor, drunk, simpering, and his head rolling about foolishly. This was as drunk as Luke had ever been.

Harry got to his feet. "Where the hell are the whores?" he demanded.

"Busy getting laid," said Mark, trying to get on his feet. "What do you think?"

Harry giggled. "Let's get a little nookie."

Luke heard Walt's old refrain. "Harry, you're too old for that sort of thing."

Luke guided the three of them toward the door. A servant, waiting attentively in the next room, seemed prepared to lead them somewhere.

Chapter 6

Luke woke up early, feeling groggy, a little punchy, his head half way buried between two pillows. He had heard that a sake hangover is painless and brief. His vision cleared. He wondered how he had gotten to this particular room. He was still dressed, face down on the bed. He looked around, seeing western appointments, beds, dressers, tables, lamps, plush carpeting; it might have been a hotel room in any western country.

Harry, still dressed, was lying on a nearby bed. He concluded that Mark and Walt had ended up in another room for the night.

What he desired, more than sleep, more than life itself at that moment, was a cup of coffee. He went out of the bedroom and started back across the empty rooms, looking for the reception room.

It was changed from the previous evening. The serving table and bar had been removed. The several coats and shoes of the Japanese men were gone. His coat, as well as those of the other Americans, had been neatly folded and placed on chairs.

He heard a slight sound behind him. It was a servant. They seemed to be everywhere, never in sight, but suddenly in view when needed. Luke straightened up, a question on his face. "Coffee?"

The boy responded at once, "*hai*," and disappeared just as quickly.

Luke hoped he understood. He'd had enough tea. He dropped into a chair and checked his watch. Eight a.m.

The house was silent, as though all had left. He went to the open doors and looked out over the terrace. The half dozen cars had disappeared. He came back into the room about the time the boy was returning with a tray and on it, an American breakfast: a pot of coffee, ham and eggs, toast, and two kinds of condiments: one fig, the other a berry.

After breakfast he started thumbing through some magazines, a little old and worn. He found Japan's equivalent of *Life*, really more like Paris *Match*.

He came across one with an arresting title: *Tradition. Japan's Yesterday*. Its articles had a scholarly character, a serious treatment of medieval armor, a short article on *Bushido*, the code of the Samurai warrior.

He went out on the terrace finally. Tokyo far below seemed almost lost to sight in the morning mist and the eternal smog that rises like a miasma from the great city, as one imagines vapor might steam from a monster.

He was aware of an irregular sound suddenly, disturbing the considerable calm. It had begun about the time he came on the terrace and continued thereafter at intervals. It sounded like a shot from a small weapon, he thought, but then it could also be likened to a small axe being buried in hard wood. Curious, he went down the steps and into the crytemoria cedars, the slight reports giving him direction. As he came closer, he heard something like a whiplash, then distinct vibrations of a bowstring. He knew before he got there that an archer was at practice.

When he came out in a small clearing, he saw Akada about to pull the bow back, an astonishing sight. He was dressed in a fashion that Luke could only guess was medieval Japanese regalia. A stocky man with heavy shoulders and big arms, Akada suffered from the physical defect common to Japanese: bandy legs, the limbs short and bowed, often the consequence of being carried in a sack on the mother's back for the first few years of their life. Endowed with normal legs, Akada would have approached his height, Luke thought, about six feet. Akada's frame was bigger than his, the musculature for a middle-aged man, well developed and well preserved.

Akada must have sensed him standing there, silent, watching. He turned and smiled, that enigmatic Japanese smile. "*Ohio gomenasi*," a very good morning.

Luke responded in Japanese without thinking. He had kept his knowledge of the language to himself, without exactly knowing why. Akada had not tested him this way the previous evening. Now it was out, and they exchanged some pleasantries in Japanese.

"Perhaps you wish to speak English," said Akada after a few minutes.

Luke shrugged. That was his preference.

"I practice English when I have the chance," said Akada.

He held out the bow to Luke. "Try it."

Unsure, Luke shook his head. It looked formidable.

"Go ahead," the baron said.

He took it and attempted to string the arrow. He had never held a bow before.

"One moment please," said Akada. He pulled off the leather gauntlet and slipped it on to Luke's wrist.

"The string will cut you."

Funny, Luke thought. He would have said to a novice, "the string will hurt you." Was that a difference in their culture? To be cut is to be hurt. The Japanese don't think of being hurt. They're hurt so much anyway. They abuse themselves so much.

He pulled back the bow, surprised at how much strength was required. He was in good condition, but the wrong muscles were being called into play. He could feel his arms trembling, needing all the strength and will power he could call upon to send the arrow so far. He missed the target entirely.

"Try again," said Akada, handing him another arrow.

Luke got off a second shot and considered himself lucky to have hit the target. He surrendered the bow, somewhat against Akada's will.

"Try another."

"I should begin with a lighter bow," said Luke.

Akada gathered his arrows and they walked back to the house together.

"What is your sport?" he asked.

"I really don't have one," said Luke.

"How do you keep fit?"

"I practice karate." It just came out, another secret pulled from him he thought.

Akada was evidently impressed. All Japanese men admire physical skill. They take knowledge of karate as a compliment to their culture.

"Do you have a belt?"

Luke decided not to tell him he was a champion, wondering even as he thought about it, why the secrecy? Why did he feel compelled to conceal little things just now? He thought he had already divulged too much about himself. He looked at the stolid Akada walking beside him. Was his imagination working overtime? He sensed a rival in Akada, more than that, an unspoken enemy. The baron was gracious, generous, but he was alien. It wasn't race, or culture, or nation. It wasn't even corporate rivalry. It was something else, a contest almost pristine and irrational. Of noble descent, Akada was something out of the past, an anachronism. What was a twentieth century chief executive of one of the world's largest corporations doing on a Sunday morning practicing archery in medieval dress? It was an anachronism beyond explaining.

Akada was saying that he would like to work out with Luke sometime. He had a small training room. He was talking about his jui jitsu training as a boy. He wanted his American guests to see his ancestral estates. Luke caught most of this while lost in his own thoughts.

They came up onto the terrace and found Walt, Harry and Mark eating breakfast. A servant had brought a table outside for them. Akada excused himself with bows and smiles, the slow and gracious manner of the cultivated host taking leave of the commoners.

"That's a beautiful looking weapon," said Mark, when he'd gone.

Walt nodded. "I've read that the Japanese gentleman practices the martial arts. It's part of their tradition."

"I hear they learn how to write beautiful letters with a brush and arrange flowers," said Mark sarcastically.

Walt, always serious, wondered if this could still be true with a modern Japanese man.

"I know this much," said Harry. "They can drink like hogs. I was out by midnight."

Luke laughed. "We all were."

"Who got the geishas?" asked Harry, a grin on his face.

"The ones still on their feet," said Mark.

Walt laughed. "That wasn't us, as I remember."

"Luke has a theory," said Mark. "The geishas are to look at and not to touch."

Luke was embarrassed. "I was talking about the traditional geisha."

Mark scoffed. "I have the impression those broads were not professional geishas. But they were professionals, if you know what I mean."

Harry groaned. "Whores! I should have stayed sober the whole night."

Walt uttered the usual: "Harry, you're too old for that sort of thing."

Mark changed the subject. "What's on the agenda for today?"

"Akada wants to drive us to his family's estate somewhere near Mount Fuji," said Luke, "give us a tour of a medieval fortress."

Walt wondered again why they were receiving so much attention. Luke repeated his earlier opinion: It was Japanese hospitality.

"Maybe he wants to hire us after Tushimi buys us out," said Mark.

"Just another job interview," said Harry. "Is that it?"

They all laughed at that.

The limousine arrived about noon. They had forgotten how small Japan is, how mountainous the terrain. New highways, cutting long grades through the mountain passes, eliminates distance by removing obstacles. By car and by train one begins to realize how cramped the country is. If freeways in the U.S. have annihilated distance, in Japan distance has been more completely dissolved by a similar system of high speed roadways. What used to be an excursion of several hours by train, from Tokyo to Fuji, is now a swift transit, measured in minutes. From Note they ascended the ranges that lie below the mountain, passing through heavy timber, crytomeria groves and bamboo forests. Fuji's brilliant cones appeared periodically as the road turned to ever-higher levels, so close in appearance that they felt they might reach out and scoop up snow.

The early summer heat dissipated rapidly, a consequence of the higher altitude. The semitropical condition gave way to an alpine setting. They entered a region that Luke reckoned to be level with the base of Fuji. A thousand years ago great lava flows had spread out, drowning small lakes, dividing larger ones, leaving smaller ones, shining in the new volcanic soil abundant with vegetation.

They passed villas, the mountain retreats of Japan's nouveau riche, and came shortly to great iron gates and the usual protecting walls. Electronically operated, the gated opened then closed behind them as they entered a park, vaster than the one at Note. Some time was required to traverse a tamed woodland, maintained as carefully as a garden might be. At the end of the road, through the fading parkland, they encountered a fortress of considerable dimensions.

Typical of Japan's medieval keeps, it sat on a sloping stone foundation, rearing up for several stories, roofs on roofs, slightly curved, partly crenellated in the style of Chinese military architecture: but not as severe, a distinctively Japanese architecture.

An expansive man, Akada, had related his noble lineage during the drive from Note. The Akada were Samurai. Having arrived, he gave a brief account of the military keep they were about to see: its origins, its recent history. In doing so he revealed more of himself than he might have intended. The castle had no dramatic history to recall. It had been constructed by his grandfather at the close of the nineteenth century, commissioned and built to imitate what was imagined to have been the typical medieval fortress.

"Of course," said Akada, "the Samurai did not carry out their warfare in these isolated mountains. In those days they served the great lords, the *Daimyo*, on the coasts of the country. Unfortunately my family became *ronin* in the eighteenth century; men of honor but without a patron."

Puzzled looks from the Americans required that he define the term *ronin*.

"The Samurai served a great lord, the *Daimyo*. They depended upon him; he depended on them. It was mutual obligations with honor, fealty very much like European feudalism. If the *Daimyo* should fall from power, lose his estates, and thereby end the means by which his retainers were supported, the Samurai became men without means, rootless, men on the waves, which is what *ronin* means. My family, having become destitute Samurai, was *ronin*. Two centuries were required for the recovery of the Akada fortune.

Entering an immense central hall, Akada led them to a sitting room. Seated with the Americans, he seemed pleased to tell his family's story, proud to relate it. "I think you know how it began. Yes?"

An exchange of looks between the Americans suggested that they did not.

Akada laughed again, the big chest heaving. "We went into business in the western way; at your suggestion I might say."

There was still silence, as though that was a joke without a point.

"Your Admiral Perry arrived here one day in 1853 and invited us to trade with you. We've been doing so ever since. My grandfather found a way to make a lot of money in a short time." The baron paused for effect, evidently waiting for a response.

There was none then, Luke finally said, "How's that?"

"Tobacco, the vile habit, as one of the English kings called it. You Americans introduced us to the habit, and it was popular."

Akada chuckled. "You turned us into nicotine addicts." He laughed again. "Better than opium, I think."

They had to laugh at Akada's humor, amused by his story telling. Akada took out an ornate silver cigarette case and opened it, offering them a cigarette. He produced a silver lighter and they lit up all around, suddenly feeling companionable.

"My family's brand," said the baron, letting the smoke escape from his nostrils.

Again he waited for a response. There was pause and Luke filled the void once more. "I saw the brand the other day," he said. "Wings isn't it?"

Akada nodded. "You may have noticed that the package has a picture of a bird in flight, the national bird. It is part of our family crest. My grandfather began with the pipe, then cigars. When cigarettes became popular he captured the market in Asia. There wasn't a single competitor at the time."

Akada settled into a more comfortable position. "My family's first success in business tells the story of the success we have had since the last war."

Once more he waited for a response. There being none Luke supplied the necessary question. "How's that?"

It was apparent Akada enjoyed these exchanges. "We're a little country, Mr. Sullivan, with hardly any natural resources, not enough arable land to feed our population adequately. For centuries the mass of our people have lived on rice and what we can take from the sea. We lived, but we did not prosper. We could not. The tobacco trade tells the story of our eventual national success. We imported cured tobacco leaf from several countries, shredded and blended it. The market was inexhaustible. It made my family, and a few other families, rich. But the trade did not enrich our population. We remained a third world country, always living close to the subsistence level. That's why, for good or bad, we moved our operations into Korea at the end of the nineteenth century, then after that into Manchuria, then

China. The Imperial government followed the trail we laid out in business operations."

Harry finally had something to say. "Yeah, we know all about your trade. After Southeast Asia then the Pacific Islands. If you could have had your way, Australia and New Zealand would have been next; raping and murdering, killing all the way."

Harry had gotten to his feet, almost shouting. Walt pulled him down. Akada seemed impassive, his disciplined features unchanged. Finally he said, "There were reasons enough. We were a starving nation, a threatened nation. Your country was content to let us starve." His voice had started to rise.

"Why do you say that, Baron?" asked Luke.

Akada leveled a stare at him. "Why do you think we agreed to trade with you, not so long ago, in 1853?"

Walt spoke for the first time. "So why did you?"

A small smile escaped Akada's stern face. "Because we were watching what the western powers were doing in China and the rest of Asia, the Pacific regions generally. We did what we had to do in order to protect ourselves. We were determined not to be occupied, swallowed up by European colonial powers. We used force because force was required in our national interest."

Walt realized what the baron was driving at. "Like the force we used against Hiroshima and Nagasaki. Is that it?"

Walt's remarks produced another period of silence.

Akada's features were fixed in a frown; his eyes seemed baleful.

"Now you are a disarmed people," Luke said finally, almost gently.

"By our own choice," Akada replied quickly. "We want it that way. We don't need nuclear weapons and a standing army. In 1941 we had a Navy equal to yours, probably a superior one. We have no need for a Navy now. We have cargo ships and tankers. We trade in commodities; we haul the world's resources here and manufacture what the world wants and needs. Your policy is to change the world into something it cannot be. Our policy is to accept the world as it is and to profit from it. You won the war in 1945. Now you are losing the war."

"No more wars," said Walt. "Is that it?"

"It depends on what you mean by war. A war is going on now. This is still a world in which everyone struggles for survival. The war now is economic. Through economic warfare my country is today the second richest nation in the world. Why is that so?"

"You tell us," said Harry belligerently.

Akada seemed almost to heave a sigh. "The success we have today in Japan is the same as my family's success before. Without resources, we went abroad and found what we needed. Today we buy it, own it, ship it home, and transform it into products that are wanted around the world. One day we may be the richest country and your country will take second place. We are in a new revolution; the outcome no one can say, or even guess. Some call it the third industrial revolution. It is really a technical revolution that will transform the relations of those states already industrialized. The world will become divided between those who have the technical competence to find and exploit diminishing resources, even if far beyond their borders; and those who, in the absence of technical efficiency, will become consumers, obliged to live off a fraction of what their natural resources are really worth."

The baron's remarks sounded like a challenge and a threat. He was describing a new, a future condition, of the oldest capitalist phenomenon, Luke thought. There was a producing elite and an uncritical consuming mass. Some things never change they only assume different shapes. There would emerge in time a new technological minority. As always, the mass consuming society would depend upon this creative minority. Richly endowed countries, such as the United States, might fall into the consumer class; find it necessary to sell their resources in order to survive in a relentless competition. A small, poor country, like Japan, having mastered the secrets of the new technology, would take those resources, transform them into valued products and skim off the main profits.

"We thrive on competition," Akada said, as though his Americans guests would agree with him. It was their own rhetoric they heard. They had attempted to export it abroad for the past half century. The Japanese had listened and learned its lessons well. Akada talked more like a teacher than a host. Akada got to his feet, as if to indicate the lecture was over.

"Have you thought of it?" he asked. "It has been only a little more than a century since we first entered into competition, not a long time for us. A hundred years in three thousand years is but a breath of time. We are an old and indestructible people."

Thereafter, Akada walked them through what seemed interminable rooms. All were virtually empty, in that uncluttered and exquisite fashion of the Japanese, a stand here, a vase there, medieval weapons on the walls. In so much space, there was a paucity of things. Harry remarked on the craftsmanship, the fine woodwork, highly polished to reveal the natural grain; the enameled and decorated panels that served discreetly to relieve the drabness of unpainted walls.

They came, finally, to the room which Akada has reserved for the end of the tour. He opened large double doors and Luke was surprised. They were the first western doors he'd seen, hanging on hinges. They had entered a room that almost startled them. Big game, North American and African specimens filled the immense space.

It was incongruous, thought Luke, that in an imitation Japanese fortress, all the rooms almost devoid of furniture, that one should be crowded with stuffed animals. On the polished plank floor laid a massive tiger skin, the head complete to tongue and glaring eyes. A magnificent elephant head was mounted on one of the paneled walls. Goat, sheep, bison, a half dozen prey animals from the African veldt, festooned the walls.

"My father's collection," said Akada simply, as they walked about, inspecting the trophies. He walked to the end of the long room. "This is my contribution."

They looked up to see the massive head of a brown bear.

"Kodiak bear," he said.

Akada had finally earned Harry's respect. "What caliber rifle did it take to bring that fellow down?"

Akada evidently savored the moment. "Two arrows," he said.

Luke watched Harry's face, a mixture of disbelief and admiration. He had seen Akada practicing earlier in the day and believed him.

"I didn't know that big a bear could be hunted with bow and arrow," said Luke.

"The Ainu of Hokkaido have always hunted the bear this way," replied Akada. "However, they poisoned their arrow tips, and their bows were inferior."

He went to the display case and took out a bow, handing it to Harry.

"Try it."

Luke remembered the same words, addressed to him that morning, a challenge and a taunt. Harry gave it a pull, struggled a little, pulled more determinedly, and managed to bend it about half way. Akada took it back from him and planted his feet, pulling the bow into a half circle without apparent strain. The Americans gawked a little.

"Archery requires practice," Akada said, going to put the bow back in its case. "The American guide on the Kodiak expedition thought I was mad. I told him to stand with his rifle and cover me if I should miss. I placed one arrow in the beast's throat. When he reared up to claw it away, I sent the second arrow into his heart." It was a simple story of skill and courage, and the Americans were impressed. They went back downstairs and out to the waiting limousine without speaking.

"I shall remain here with my family for a few days," said Akada, leaning slightly into the limousine. "The driver will take you where you wish to go."

It was not a goodbye, but a dismissal; careful, charming, the *noblesse obliges* which the titled class affects in the presence of commoners. The chauffeur started the limousine and drove back through the park toward the gates.

"What was that all about?" asked Harry.

Walt laughed. "And we thought we were being scouted for positions in a multinational combine."

"I think he just wanted to show off," said Mark.

Harry, still smarting from the humiliating test of strength, grunted meanly. "The little bastard intended to put us in our place. You got his message, didn't you?"

"I don't know," said Mark. "What was it?"

"He brought us up here to challenge us in his polite way, with that shit eating grin. Time is on their side, he thinks."

Mark disagreed. "I think he has an inferiority complex. It turned him on to show us his family heirlooms."

Akada was more complicated than that, Luke thought. But he couldn't put his finger on the common denominator that would explain the man's complexity. Beneath the western facade, Luke thought he detected those imperishable qualities, gallant and callous, of the Samurai. Behind the careful smile, the perfect manners, was a strength one would have to call brutal, perhaps merciless. Harry seemed to typify both the strength and weakness of American character. Akada personified the best and worst in Japanese character. In one man, Luke thought, he had discovered the Japanese stereotype. The social contrast was uncomfortable to contemplate, the one noble, the other plebeian.

Chapter 7

The problem for Luke was simple: he needed Harry's expertise, but he wanted to keep him ignorant of what was going on. He and Mark worked out a strategy. Harry and Walt would meet Mark at a bar in the Tokyo Station at 5:30 P.M., just off the main concourse. About a quarter to six, Mark would excuse himself and go to the vicinity of the big clock where he could watch Luke. From that point, things would develop according to what Kiah did, or didn't do. Harry would be nearby to check the disc on his laptop.

Luke got into position about six P.M. He carried the cash in a small briefcase, yen in packets of $10,000. The rush of passengers was greater than he had expected, and he realized that had probably been Kiah's plan. They would become swallowed up in a sea of humanity when she approached him. Mark would have to be nearby in order to follow.

He wondered where Kiah would lead him. Where would the exchange take place? She had only said, "I'll walk, and you can follow me."

Luke saw her. She was coming towards him through the throng of people, her face fixed without emotion, her eyes fastened on his; not a sign of recognition, not a shadow of feeling. She went by him at a moderate pace. He fell in behind her, dodging passengers, struggling through the crush of people to stay behind her. He wondered if Mark had been close enough to keep up.

She was heading toward one of the escalators, and he concluded that there would be some kind of involved evasion outside the station. Then suddenly she turned off into a corridor, leaving the main stream of the crowd. Storage lockers lined both sides of the hallway. Luke figured it out as the crowds began to disperse. He caught up with her as she slowed down and stepped before one of the lockers. There she turned to face him. It was as though they had come out of a river of people into a quiet eddy.

They were still without words. Kiah looked down at the briefcase in his hand. He lifted it up, waist high and snapped it open, lifting the lid for her to see. She stared at the stacks of bills for a few seconds, but it seemed longer. A slight nod of her head, and he closed the lid. She started to reach for it, and he shook his head silently. She understood and began to rummage through her clutch purse. She brought out a key and handed it to him. He took it and let her have the briefcase. She started to move away.

"Don't you want to count the money?"

"No," she said, and began to move again.

He caught her by the wrist. For once he elicited an expression from the disciplined face, a sign of alarm. He held her while he put the key in the lock. Opening the door, he found a large envelope. He took it out with one hand. Mark appeared at his side at the same moment, taking the envelope from him. They couldn't have rehearsed it better.

"I'll get this to Harry," he said, and he was off at a pace close to running.

Kiah was upset. She was twisting and pulling a little, trying to get free, but his grip was like a vice.

"This wasn't in the deal," she said, in a low angry voice.

"You know we have to authenticate the data," he said.

They stood there awkwardly. She was angry, he was uncomfortable. She would not look at him now. Some of the spirit seemed to go out of her, and he felt sorry for her.

"It'll be just a few minutes," he said gently.

She didn't answer. The time seemed long as they stood there, shifting their weight from one foot to the other.

"Why did you leave me the other night?" Luke finally asked.

Kiah looked up, stared at him, refusing to respond.

"Let go of me," she said finally, harshly. It was a command, but more than that, a challenge that he should recognize her code of integrity. He released her.

She stood still after that, looking away.

"Why?" he repeated.

"I don't always do that," she said at last.

Luke was almost inclined to laugh, but he really didn't know what she meant.

"You mean stay afterwards?"

"No, you know what I mean."

She had closed the avenue of discourse between a man and a woman that is most guarded, more difficult to enter than the mere mingling of their bodies. Luke remembered his jovial grandfather's admonition long ago. "Women will do it son, but they won't talk about it."

So profound had the recollection become that Luke nearly forgot that Kiah stood beside him willingly. Willing to stay, she was unwilling to speak. Perhaps she had made him a gift that night, and he had received it badly. Over Kiah's head he saw Mark suddenly appear at the corner of the hallway, his thumb up in a sign of victory, a smile of triumph on his face. Luke felt his heart quicken with relief.

"Kiah," he said softly.

She frowned at his tone, puzzled.

"You can go."

She started to turn away, hesitated, seemed to want to stop.

"Will I see you again?" he asked.

Her eyes searched his face for a few seconds. "Maybe I'll send you a ticket."

She moved away with the lithe athletic movements Luke found both appealing and disconcerting. The old feeling she inspired in him returned.

Mark had come up to him now, a broad smile stretched across his face. His hand went out to take that of Luke. At the same time, he was curious, anxious to ask questions.

He looked in the direction Kiah had gone, then back to Luke.

"Do you know who that is?" he asked.

Mark's tone startled him. "I think so. I recognized her from the time when I worked in the Honolulu division. Do you know her?"

"Not personally. But she had high visibility in Honolulu's business circles, one of the sexiest broads in town. She was available. There wasn't a guy under eighty who didn't want to get in her pants."

"Did that include you?"

Mark laughed. "I'm normal." A short silence. "No such luck."

They got into Luke's car and started back to the hotel.

"I wonder how a high class whore got into this." Luke said suddenly.

"Beats me."

"You set up this operation in the beginning, Mark."

"Not exactly," said Mark defensively. "I arranged it through a third party."

They drove a little way in silence. "Let's analyze this," Luke said finally. "Who's the third party?"

"A distributor of electronic parts, operating out of Jakarta."

"What's the connection?"

"Legally speaking, the Jakarta firm is an independent distributor of Japanese products. For the past year their hottest item has been a computer, assembled by a virtual slave labor force."

Luke smiled, skeptical. "You mean low wages?"

"I mean subsistence wages, just this side of starvation."

"What's the situation exactly?"

"The trade talk is that it's actually a Tushimi subsidiary, hiding under Indonesian paper, enjoying all the privileges which go with that status."

"God! How can we beat something like that? They steal our technology, buy foreign franchises, and employ skilled Asian labor at a low level no one in the world could match."

Mark was thinking on another wavelength. He snapped his finger, the light of inspiration coming on his face. "Have you considered that Kiah might be a double agent?"

"No," said Luke. "How could I? I'm being filled in just now."

"So am I. I didn't know she was our contact. You didn't tell me that you knew her. All you said was that she was a Eurasian woman."

Luke was embarrassed. "I didn't know her personally. I recognized her from another time. She was as visible to me as to you."

Mark laughed, almost a titter. "Were you one of those horny guys under eighty?"

Luke grinned. "Touché. I'm normal too."

It was apparent that Mark was burning to ask the question. "Did you score the other night?"

Luke hesitated to answer. "Yes," he said finally.

"You lucky bastard."

"It wasn't that good."

"I'd love to be the judge of that."

It occurred to Mark that intimacy brings knowledge, little disclosures. "Did she tell you anything?"

"No," said Luke sharply. "No," he said a second time, more carefully, recalling the sterile encounter. "She's impenetrable."

Mark laughed uproariously at that. "Is that a joke?"

Luke frowned. "You know what I mean. She's sexy, but cold as ice. Inscrutable."

"Is she cool enough to be a double agent?"

"I'd say so. What's your theory about her?"

Mark shrugged, sliding down in his seat. "Here's what I think. Kiah was laying up with important Japanese businessmen in Honolulu. Her power over them was sex and that gorgeous body. Why couldn't she have served as a conduit to take our information to Tokyo, for a price? And then, being connected with the Tushimi people after that, why couldn't she sell their information to us, also for a price? You know, she did just that less than an hour ago. In other words, isn't it possible she has become her own dealer?

"The second half of your theory is proved," admitted Luke. "About the first half, who knows?"

"She would get rich. There's a sufficient motive. She's not so young for her line of work anymore. She may want to retire."

"That's right," said Luke. He had first encountered Kiah seven years ago. That would give her some mileage.

"How old do you think she is?" asked Mark.

"She might be mid-thirties." Luke's face became grim. "That raises the question of Megen's so-called suicide."

He shot Mark a quick glance. "Would Kiah have killed Megan in order to get the other half of the formula?"

"If she did, then why didn't she sell it to us when she had the chance?"

"I don't know. Maybe she still has it. Today's trade may have been bait. If she has squirreled the other half of the information in another locker, we will hear from her. She'll want plenty for it."

"Do you have any way to contact her?"

"No. She said she might arrange another rendezvous. When I get a chance, I'll get into Megen's apartment and see what I can find."

He waited a couple of days before he had some free time. He hung around the apartment house until a tenant opened the security doors, allowing him to go up to Megen's apartment. A small jimmy tool forced the lock open in a few seconds. Inside, he found the draperies drawn. The light was dim, but not too much for the search he was prepared to make. Putting on thin gloves, he went through the place systematically.

The rooms were crowded with expensive furniture. Evidently occupied for some time, the apartment had become a storehouse for trivial objects. He went through books, magazines, piles of papers, seeking the telltale slip or note that would tell him something. He found nothing.

Drawers were crammed with the innumerable objects women with money dote on. Patiently, he searched this considerable volume of litter. Letters, notes, and a diary but found nothing of any consequence.

He had decided to quit when he discovered an old and worn photo album in a kitchen drawer. It seemed an odd place to be kept, and he examined it carefully. It was evidently a keepsake of Megen's, going back to her teen years. Faded photographs were carefully mounted on each page. He judged it to be a vain woman's record of her amorous conquests. The first pages contained a gallery of young men, some posing alone, others photographed in company with her. Further along, the males became older, paunchy, and balding.

As he progressed through Megen's love life, he saw that she became more stylish, better dressed, and more sophisticated in her appearance. The signs of wealth and grooming were self-evident. Luke concluded that the album was a graphic proof of how a beautiful woman who elects to sell her charms can make a large profit.

At the end of the volume he found a small bundle of photographs, bound with a rubber band. Sorting them out, he found four that interested him. Throughout the album, Caucasian men had been Megen's consorts. The four photographs he selected were middle-aged oriental men, Japanese businessmen without a doubt. He put the four photos in his coat pocket and replaced the album in the drawer.

After finishing the search, he went to the door and started to go out when he heard the elevator coming to a stop. He ducked back into the room and closed the door to wait. Almost immediately he heard a key turning in the lock. He could hear the voices of two men coming into the apartment. Looking about for a place to conceal himself, he saw a louvered door closet. He slipped in, pushing the clothing down the rack to make room. He could hear two men walking through the apartment, speaking in Japanese, barely audible. The sound of their voices became louder as they came into the bedroom, and then faded as they returned to the living room. The front door closed. Silence followed.

Luke felt himself relax. It was the manager taking a potential customer through the apartment. Assured, he straightened up to leave the closet. His head struck the shelf above sharply. Reaching up to nurse the bruise, he felt a thin metal chain close to his head. He looked up to see it dangling, glinting in the dim light. He gave it a pull, and a heavy object fell into his hand.

In the bedroom he examined what he had found. It was a large medallion on a silver chain. On one side there was a raised impression of the rising sun, the rays spanning the circumference of the medal; on the other side a cloud in the shape of a mushroom. A row of characters were embossed on the margin of the medallion. He put it in his pocket with the photographs and left the apartment.

As soon as he returned to the hotel, Luke took Mark into a bedroom to show him what he had found. Mark examined the medallion curiously.

"What does the character mean?" he asked finally.

Luke took it from him. "The words on one side are: Kan Pai, which means to drink or to toast."

He turned the medallion over. "On this side, the word is Nichi, which means day."

"Toast the day," observed Mark.

"Or drink to the day," said Luke.

"There's a rising sun on one side," mused Mark. "On the other side, I'd say a mushroom cloud, like atomic, if you know what I mean."

"I know what you mean," said Luke.

"The atomic bomb, right?'

"It's too distinctive to be anything else."

"I wonder what it could mean." Mark asked, more to himself than to Luke.

"It could commemorate the bombing of Hiroshima and Nagasaki," said Luke.

"But that doesn't sound Japanese to me," said Mark. "They want to forget that disaster, not celebrate it."

"Not entirely Mark. There are the breast beaters, the pacifists, who still look upon the bombings of World War Two as a just retribution for Japanese militarism. They decided never to arm again and keep the memory of Hiroshima and Nagasaki alive as a reminder of the consequences of atomic warfare, or any war."

They had reached a dead end on the meaning of the medallion. Luke had the nagging feeling that he had seen the characters before.

"Since we've been in Japan?" asked Mark.

"I believe so."

"Maybe on a billboard?"

Luke tried to think of what he'd seen in print for the past week: restaurants, public baths, and theaters, daily tours of Tushimi plants, dinners, public and private. He knew the words, Kan Pai Nichi, had at some point stood out enough to enter his subconscious, then retreated without leaving a tangible context for him to recall.

Mark picked up the photographs and laid them out on the bed. The blond girl had posed with a different Japanese man in each picture.

Luke pointed to one of the photos. "This one is interesting. It has an unusual background."

Megen and a Japanese man had posed together before a white limousine. Behind them, a castle, constructed in the gothic style, nestled in a wooded valley. Mountains, of considerable proportions rose behind the castle.

Mark thought it was a European castle, or maybe Swiss. Luke had doubts.

"I bet this picture was taken in this country."

"We should have the photo blown up, so we can see the details."

Luke agreed. "If you get a chance have Walt look at these photos without Harry knowing."

"Why?"

"I want to find out if any of these people are with the Tushimi Corporation. Walt may have noticed them during the tours they've been making of their plants."

"How about Harry?"

"The less he knows the better."

Chapter 8

Harry's curiosity could not be stifled. He wanted to know how Mark and Luke had gotten the disc.

"Is it Tushimi's?" he asked.

Mark lied. "We don't know. We're looking into it."

While they were getting ready for the flight to Sapporo, Harry kept badgering him. Mark manipulated the old man's questions. He wondered if Harry could project the rest of the formula from the disc.

"Get serious," said Harry. "I got my Ph.D. fifty years ago. There's been a lot of water under the bridge since then."

Mark persisted. "Is there anyone in the American universities today who could complete the formula, you know, some sort of extrapolation?"

"No," said Harry emphatically. "I wasn't entirely straight with you a minute ago. There isn't a brain, human or mechanical, that could do it."

That surprised Mark. "Why not?"

"Because the code is interrupted, and it's been done intentionally. There must be a second disc."

"Can you explain that in terms a layman could understand?"

Harry started getting into his clothes, talking at the same time. "What I think they've done, to preserve the integrity of their formula, is to weave the math into two discs, something like a key or a code. They've converted our formula in some way to make it their own."

Mark laughed. "Clever, these Japanese."

Harry reached into his pocket and pulled out a passkey.

"Look at the irregular edges of this key. They're designed to enter a lock and spring the tumblers. Now, if I remove the ridges, some of the tumblers will be unaffected. The lock can't be opened. That disc you have is exactly like that in principle. There has to be a second disc. If you had it in your possession and superimposed it on the one you've got, all the information would dovetail. It would be like laying two partial keys on top of each other, making a single composite key with all the information."

"That's believable," said Mark, seeing the analogy. "But why can't you deduce the missing information by some system of extrapolation?"

Harry laughed. "I just told you, the possible combinations are infinite. You could program the best computer in the world from now until doomsday and never achieve the integrated formula."

Mark walked into the bathroom and muttered to Luke. "We spent millions of yen on a worthless piece of information."

Luke's eyes caught Mark's in the mirror. "It's better to have that disc in our possession than someone else's."

The telephone rang. It was Taki, punctual at eight, to tell them the limousine had arrived.

"I can't get used to this royal service," said Harry.

Walt couldn't get over the regimentation, the discipline, of the Tushimi's management and staff. It seemed military, more athletic than commercial. Organized calisthenics every morning were like drill exercises.

"I'm waiting for the day when Taki organizes morning calisthenics for us in the lobby," said Mark, laughing.

Luke thought it was the right time to tell Harry and Walt. "Mark and I aren't going to Sapporo with you this morning," he said.

Walt seemed more surprises than Harry did.

"What's up?" asked Harry.

"Nothing," replied Luke casually. "I talked to the Brass in L.A. and they gave us an assignment to do while we're here."

Harry laughed, more boisterously than before. "I'll bet it's got something to do with that disc you picked up."

They wouldn't give him an answer. He was insistent.

"There's a second disc, I know it."

By this time they were going out the door.

Taki met them at the elevator when they came out into the lobby. Luke told him immediately that he and Mark couldn't make the trip. After that, he went to the front desk, half-expecting, half-hoping to find a ticket from Kiah. There was nothing. There were some messages from stateside, and he perused them quickly.

Mark came up to talk privately.

"I've got a feeling Harry is going to blow it on the way to Sapporo."

"I know it," said Luke.

"He's got to be told. Otherwise he won't be quiet."

"This is all screwed up, Mark. If we could have gotten both discs, we would have been able to square with him and Walt right away."

"On the other hand," said Mark, "he and Walt have every reason to be curious, and as far as that goes, they would be justified if they were sore as hell for the way we're deceiving them."

"We'd better fill them in," Luke said.

"Taki and that bodyguard are on top of us. How are we going to do it at the last minute like this?"

"We can't. As soon as they get back from Sapporo we'll level with them."

After the limousine left for the airport, Mark and Luke went into the hotel coffee shop for breakfast. It was a modern, western ambiance catering to a foreign clientele, mainly American. They ordered the usual: ham and eggs, toast and coffee.

At a nearby table two young Caucasian women were talking to a couple of Japanese men. The women were fair, vivacious, obviously in control of the situation. Mark and Luke watched with frank curiosity.

"How long have we been here?" asked Mark.

"About a week."

"I'll bet I've seen a dozen European women in here in that time."

"Probably most of them are American women, not European, and on the make."

"These Jap guys will fall over themselves to get to them."

Luke grinned. "And don't think those women don't know it."

"Pathetic," said Mark. "Those guys are little, timid. You can see they're scared to death. The two broads are half again as big as they are."

"The Japs have the equalizer though," observed Luke, "the money they're willing to spend on those hustlers."

"That reminds me of Kiah."

"I was thinking the same thing." He leaned forward, a little quiet, confidential. "We've got to get into her apartment."

"I thought you said she moved out."

"I did. But I want to see what she left behind. We need clues, and I can't think of another place to go."

He took the medallion from his pocket and swung it idly by the chain. "I wonder if there could be a connection."

"Between what?"

"Between this medallion and the formula."

Mark shrugged. "There are a lot of possible connections. Drugs, international embezzlement. It might even be a political scandal. You know, maybe a government minister is, or I should say was, involved with Megen."

"You see," said Luke, "we're in a swamp of motives. We've got to get something concrete."

"Do you have Kiah's address?"

"I've got it."

They paid their bill and drove over to Kiah's apartment house. It was another expensive modern high-rise building, about a mile from Megen's apartment. They waited for someone to go in, and then followed quickly, getting by the security doors. Luke picked open the door in just a few seconds. Mark couldn't conceal his anxiety.

"They would put us away for a long time if they caught us breaking and entering," he said.

"They would lock us up and throw away the key," said Luke, "and they have no sympathy for foreigners."

The apartment was tastefully furnished in the western style. The empty drawers and closets gave evident proof that Kiah had left for good. Luke slipped on gloves and looked in all the unexpected places: behind pictures on the wall, under shelves, seeking that one place where something of value might be secreted; perhaps taped beneath a table. He attempted to remove the legs from the furniture. This took some time, and Mark, losing interest, finally dropped into a chair.

"How could those people make Megen's death look like a suicide?" he asked.

"Easy. In her case, the diagnosis was an overdose of sleeping pills. I imagine a couple of thugs held her while another guy poured barbiturates dissolved in water down her throat through a rubber hose. If they were careful to leave no bruises, the police are left with no conclusion to draw except suicide."

"If that's true, we're involved with cold blooded killers."

Luke grunted. "That may be the tip of the iceberg. I think there's something bigger at stake here than industrial secrets or the death of a beautiful tart."

Mark got up to walk around. "Frankly, I'm getting a little nervous. Maybe we should bring the police into this."

"Are you kidding? We can't even tell the L.A. Brass. We only have some suspicions so far. Besides, our job is to get the other half of that formula."

He'd finished with the search and went to sit down. "This place is clean. All we have is half the formula, which is worthless by itself. We're out of luck and out of leads."

"What did you do with Kiah's disc?" asked Mark.

"I put it in a bank safety deposit box and mailed a copy of the key to L.A."

He reached into his pocket and took out the medallion, studying it briefly, and then hung it around his neck, tightening his tie again.

Mark watched, curious. "What are you doing that for?"

"I'll wear it for a good luck charm." He laughed. "I don't want to lose it and I don't want anyone to take it from me without an effort."

"Do you expect some violence?"

"I think we ought to expect anything. As Kiah said to me the other night, we don't know what or who we're dealing with."

They got up and left the apartment. It was about noon when they arrived downtown.

"We've got the rest of the day to kill," said Luke. "What do you want to do?"

"I don't know, go sightseeing? Pretend like we're tourists?'

"That's not for me," said Luke.

"If you're thinking of a museum, count me out. I don't dig culture, Japanese or otherwise."

"How about sex and violence, Japanese style?"

"Luke, you're turning me on."

"I saw a couple of likely movies advertised over in the Asakusa district last week."

"I don't know the language," said Mark

Luke gave him wink. "I think you'll understand the plot, Mark."

"A little porno, huh?"

"Yeah, and then we'll get a massage."

After the movie, a double feature, artistic enough to satisfy the male's normal needs, they went to a sento, soaked, got a rubdown and relieved; and after that found a Sushi restaurant. They got back to the hotel about six-thirty.

Luke turned on the T.V. and took off his coat, then went into the bathroom. The news began, and Mark dropped into a chair to watch. His expression changed from boredom, to interest, to concern. The camera was panning a mountainous terrain. He had the distinct impression that the announcer was talking about a disaster. He got up and ran to the bathroom door, calling Luke.

Luke came out in a hurry and went to stand in front of the T.V. Mark could tell it was bad news. The picture on the screen dissolved, and a commercial came on. Luke went to a chair and dropped down weakly.

"What did they say?" asked Mark.

Luke didn't answer at once. "They're dead," he said finally in a low voice.

"Harry and Walt?"

"All of them, Harry, Walt, and the Japanese businessmen."

"That would be Taki and his body guard."

"Right."

"My God, what happened?"

"Their plane crashed in the Hokkaido Mountains, south of Sapporo."

Mark sat down. "I can't believe it."

"It's believable alright," said Luke dully. "It's just bewildering. One suicide, now four accidental deaths."

"Did they say why the plane crashed?"

"No."

"I mean bad weather, or something like that."

"No. Nothing."

Luke raised his head to stare at Mark. "Are you thinking what I'm thinking?"

Mark nodded. "No suicide and no accidents. All killings."

"Somebody must have sabotaged that plane," said Luke. "But why?"

"Well," said Mark, "at least this eliminates a suspect I've been considering."

"You mean Taki?"

"You bet. He seemed suspicious to me. Too cool, too professional."

Luke agreed. "As Harry said, hardly a business man."

"But now Taki's a victim as much as Harry and Walt. I told you I was a little nervous this morning. Now, I'm scared shitless."

Luke didn't respond.

"Don't you think it's time to tell someone?'

Luke got up from his chair. I'll phone the Big Brass. But face it; they're going to know about this already. Tushimi is big. When they lose people, the world learns about it."

"I think we should report the whole thing to the home office."

"It wouldn't do any good," said Luke sharply. "The truth is they don't want the details. They want results. That's the nature of this business. And believe me; they're not going to do anything to disclose their espionage activities. Don't forget, we are the appointed scapegoats."

"So, we can't go to the police, and we can't tell the company officials. What do we do?"

"Nothing for the time being," said Luke. "We'll wait. Patience is the name of this game."

"We just sit?"

"Right. I've gotten into the habit of sitting in a hot bath with naked Japanese. Are you coming along?'

"No thanks. One bath a day is enough for me. I'll find me a broad tonight," Mark said, as he checked for numbers on his cell phone.

Chapter 9

It took almost a week to identify and claim the bodies. Although badly burned, the corpses were recognizable. After the somber duty of identifying the remains, arrangements were made to ship the bodies back to the United States.

Luke and Mark, silent, each lost in his private thoughts, rode in the hearse with the coffins to the airport. It was their unspoken agreement to honor in this way the two old men who in some sense had died for a cause. Exactly what that cause was, Luke could not decide. It certainly would not be a topic of conversation in Los Angeles. He was sure of that.

The coffins were placed aboard a commercial jetliner. They watched the grey metal boxes go up the elevator and disappear into the belly of the plane. Buried in this fashion, Harry and Walt were gone, as surely as if they had been shoveled under six feet of dirt. Mark and Luke turned away and took a taxi back to the hotel. They talked in language almost monosyllabic, a little dull, and a little depressed.

"What did they say was the cause of the plane crash?" asked Mark.

"The official report is mechanical failure. Four passengers and the pilot dead."

"Did you call L.A.?"

"This morning."

"What do they want to do?"

"Nothing. They accept the report as stated."

Mark stirred with that. "What are we supposed to do now?"

"The Brass wants the other half of that formula, that's all. You might say Harry and Walt were expendable."

"So are we."

"True. That's why we're so well paid."

Mark's spirits were rising. "Soldiers of fortune. We know our duty."

"I think we should move out of the hotel," said Luke suddenly.
"Why? Tushimi's footing the bill."
"I know. But I don't feel comfortable there now."
"I can agree to that, and we don't need all that space."
"It's got some bad memories," said Luke.

The driver dropped them off across the street from the hotel. Traffic was light at mid-morning. They stood looking up at the hotel for a minute, both silent, both having some private thoughts, and then started across. They heard the squealing of tires and the high pitch roar of an engine. In that space of a few seconds when one considers that automobile noise in a city is not unusual, then the intellectual reflection that some sounds are abnormal, the total cognizance that it is dangerous, they turned to see a car bearing down on them. They threw themselves out of the way, sprawling on the sidewalk. The speeding car barely grazed them. It went up on the sidewalk, tires whining, spitting; narrowly missing a pedestrian, then went back onto the street. Crazily, it raced off down the block, dodging an oncoming truck.

Mark and Luke lay there, watching the disappearing car, turning to look at each other, bewildered. They got up slowly and brushed themselves off. Luke had skinned the palm of his hands, the result of diving into the sidewalk as if it was a pool of water. Mark was a little shaken. He had thrown himself into a forward roll, banging his head on the pavement.

"Jesus. If I had any doubts before, they're gone now. Somebody is after us."
Luke was equally stunned. "Another accident! And we're supposed to be it."
They went into the hotel in a hurry.
"We're on somebody's list," said Luke.
"Did you bring a gun with you?'
"Yeah, shoulder holster type and from now on, I'm going to wear it."

They got on the elevator and went upstairs. This time they came out in the hall cautiously, looking both ways before going down to their room. Inside, Mark waited at the door while Luke checked out the baths and bedrooms.

"I can't believe Tushimi would orchestrate a multiple murder plot," said Mark, coming away from the door.

"It may not be the company *per se* that we're dealing with, if you know what I mean. There are so many layers in a multinational corporation."

"Yeah," said Mark, "the right hand doesn't know what the left hand is doing."

Luke got out the little evidence they had and laid it on one of the beds.

"We don't have much to go on. A few photos and a medallion with a rising sun on one side. That's got to be the symbol of Japanese nationalism, right?"

"I would say so. Land of the Rising Sun. And on the other side an atomic mushroom cloud."

"What does that signify?"

"Pacifism. We can't rule it out. I understand Japan still has its Ground Zero fanatics, after all these years."

"OK," said Mark. "I'm guilty, a war monger. But what about the inscription: Kan Pai Nichi?"

"To The Day," said Luke. "What day? What for?"

"Hey!" he said. "Maybe we're reading too much into this medal."

Mark shrugged. "Hell, we haven't read anything yet. That's the problem."

Luke arranged the four photographs in a row. "Anybody of any importance connected with Tushimi that we've seen do not bear any resemblance to the men in these pictures."

Mark summed up the facts. "One suicide and four accidental deaths."

"Five, if you count the pilot," said Luke.

"As far as I'm concerned, the pilot is the only accidental victim. The others were murdered. But wait a second; Taki is one of the Tushimi big shots. Who would want to kill him?"

Luke grunted. "After that little episode on the street ten minutes ago, I don't know what to think."

"So what do we do?"

"We begin by finding another hotel."

"OK, but I don't think we can hide."

"True. And we've got to stay in touch with Tushimi, act like nothing exceptional has happened."

He stared hard at Mark. "We've only got two choices. We can get the hell out of this country now or we can keep moving around."

"We're moving targets," said Mark. "I need a gun."

"We'll get you one. How's your karate?"

That brought Mark up short. "Fair, but rusty."

"Hah!" Luke took a position of defense. Mark assaulted him. They sparred, kicked, spun, leaping from bed to chairs around the room. Mark was good, but Luke had the speed and the moves. He took him down in a few seconds.

"I quit," said Mark breathlessly.

"You're dead if you do," said Luke laughing, pulling him up.

They moved into a smaller hotel nearby. Two rooms seemed adequate. It was a Japanese establishment strictly, no westerners. Luke called the Tushimi people and gave them the new address, and then got in touch with the L.A. office.

"How is Kiah going to contact us now?" asked Mark.

"She'll find us if she wants to. Count on it."

"She's got to. She's our only contact."

That raised a question for Mark that had been on his mind for a while. "Don't you have some family connections here?"

"In Tokyo, you mean?"

"Anywhere in Japan."

"I don't know. I don't even know my grandmother's maiden name."

"Didn't she keep in touch with the home folks after she married your grandfather?"

"Yeah, but I was never told anything."

"You know what? I think I'll call Grampa."

Mark's face brightened. "That would help. Who knows? Maybe you're related to the Emperor."

Luke ignored the joke. "Up to now, I haven't really wanted to know about my origins, my roots as they say. It's funny."

"Funny?" asked Mark.

"Strange. It's as though a mental block has been lifted. I really want to know."

Luke phoned and the old man's voice came through loud and clear. "Hi Grampa. I'm calling from Tokyo."

"When did you get there?"

"About 10 days ago. Look, I want to see if I have any relatives here. What can you tell me?"

There was silence with that. Finally, the voice came back, sounding a little weak, a little hesitant.

"I don't know if it would help you Luke, to have your grandmother's maiden name."

"Why not? I could probably locate her relatives through a provincial prefect, or maybe the Tokyo police."

There was another long pause. "Do you need it right now?"

This puzzled Luke. "Well, sure. I just made up my mind to call you a few minutes ago. You know how impulsive I am."

The voice on the phone was silent for a moment. "Can't you tell me anything now Grampa?"

"I'd rather not. I need to get my thoughts together. I'll send you a letter right away."

Luke gave him the hotel address and hung up.

He waited for the letter with more impatience than for any other communication. Each day he checked with the desk clerk, almost eagerly. Forgotten now was the prospect of receiving a ticket from Kiah.

After a week the letter came. He tore it open at once and scanned it rapidly. After that he went upstairs and read it more slowly.

Dear Luke,

In many ways your grandmother and I were closer to you than our own son. In one respect there has been a wall between us. If you had not gone to Japan, perhaps the wall would have remained standing. First, I must tell you that your father was not born in Honolulu. Your grandmother gave birth to him in 1946 in Japan. I was shipped back to the United States that year, not knowing she was pregnant when I left.

We were not married. The non-fraternization rules that applied under the military occupation rules did not allow me to marry her, nor could I bring her back to the States with me. It was my shame that I had to leave her in Japan, without my protection. When she wrote me later that she was carrying your father and in distress, I arranged to take a position with the Honolulu police force. My MP background during the war made that possible.

With the help of the Japanese community in Honolulu, I arranged to have her and our son smuggled into Hawaii. That was easy to do. Papers were forged to legalize our marriage and your father's birth. In short, I committed a crime while a police officer. I am not proud of what I did, but I don't have any regrets. I loved your grandmother and I loved our son.

Your grandmother was married and had a daughter from that marriage. Her first husband died during the fire bombings in Sendai and your grandmother was badly burned. It is possible that the cancer your grandmother eventually died from was the result of those bombings.

Her daughter's name is Niani Hayashi. Until my retirement, I sent money to help support her. The village you want to find is somewhere on the Izu peninsula. I don't know the prefecture. After all these years, I had forgotten and couldn't remember it when you phoned.

All my love,
Grampa

Luke read the letter several times; trying to squeeze out all the meaning the few lines could give him. He felt close to crying. It was as though a part of his grandfather's soul had been written on paper. He brushed away the small tears that lingered in the corners of his eyes. He did not know whether he felt sorry for himself or pitied his grandfather.

He tore the letter to fine bits, went to the toilet, and flushed it away. Now a mixture of compassion and curiosity demanded that he look for something tangible that would connect him to a country still strange to him. Suddenly, it seemed to be his home more than he had realized.

Chapter 10

It took him way back, Luke thought, although the situation was reversed. Ten years ago he would have been in the inner office, calling people in, one by one, for the usual grilling. Now, he was one of them, waiting for his name to be called.

Mark was apprehensive. He had never been in a police station.

"It seems like I've spent half my life in them," said Luke. "My father was a cop, so was my grandfather. Even my university education was directed toward law enforcement."

Mark chuckled. "Now look. We're on the edge of the law, close to breaking it."

Luke had not been surprised by the early morning telephone call, rather expecting it. The Japanese voice, a little hoarse, a little cracked, struggled with bad, slow English. "Detective Masuro. So sorry. This is formality. We would wish to talk about death of your friends."

Luke pitied the man's halting English, felt inclined to go to Japanese to spare him, but thought better of it. The less he said the better.

He set an appointment to meet the detective in the afternoon. Masuro invited Mark to come along, and that didn't surprise Luke. So many accidental deaths in so brief a time, all seeming to touch the Tushimi interest, could not be less provocative to the Japanese police than to himself. He looked at the others sitting in the room. They were silent; stolid Japanese, all men, waiting their turn. He'd heard from the old days that Japanese police don't labor under the disabilities of western standards of investigation. The Miranda rule is unknown. You don't have the right to remain silent. You face the distinct possibility of being intimidated and kicked around. Cuffing, punches, a little mental torture, threats against the family, make Japanese police efficient. And, if all this is only a parcel of common rumor, it serves the police nonetheless. They are respected by the average citizen, if not feared.

"I wonder if they have anything that would tie you to Megen's apartment?" said Mark.

"I doubt it. I didn't leave any fingerprints. I made sure of that. I can pass for Japanese, so I don't see how anyone could have thought to identify me as having been there."

Mark laughed. "Now, that's an advantage of being a Eurasian mongrel."

"Right. Half Irish, half Japanese."

They were evidently going to get favored treatment. Last to arrive, they were among the first to be called. Masuro came out, looking like all cops, a little frazzled, his coat off, eyes hard. He'd been westernized it appeared. Maybe he'd watched too many American movies. He wore a white shirt with short sleeves. A watch gleamed on one of his tan, hairless arms. A neat black tie fell down his chest. He was short, beefy, round shouldered, with a bit of a paunch from sitting behind a desk for a long time. Luke imagined the bandy little legs inside the blue trousers. All the ominous signs of the tough little cop were belied by the round face that lit up when Luke responded to his summon.

"Mister Luke Sullivan."

"Here," said Luke, getting up from the bench. Mark stood up at the same time.

They went in and took seats around the desk. Masuro spent some time getting into his swivel chair. He had to go into his files, and then make a phone call. After that he took some more time to go through the dossiers on his desk, an occasional "ah hah" as if he had discovered something.

Luke knew this act. In Honolulu they called it "the warm up." The suspect was the "client." They put a fire under him by letting him guess how much was in the portfolio on the desk. There was power in these theatrics. Luke had played that game many times.

Masuro finally looked up, a toothy grin on his face. "You are acquainted with Miss Alistaire?"

Luke must have betrayed his surprise. Masuro had really caught him off guard. He didn't know the name. He supposed they were going to talk about Harry and Walt. That would bring them closer than he wished to the subject of industrial espionage. How much did the police know about this operation he wondered.

"I don't know the name," said Luke.

Mark shook his head. He didn't know it either.

Masuro let that settle, with a little pause. "Miss Megen Alistaire."

Another surprise for Luke. So, we don't all look alike, he thought. How the hell had they found out that he'd been in her apartment?

"She is a Swedish citizen," Masuro was saying. He held up her visa. "Living in Japan for two years, employee of Tushimi Corporation."

Luke stared, playing dumb.

"You visited her, I believe."

Luke decided a brief honesty was best. "I went to see her friend, someone called Kiah."

"On a matter of business, perhaps?"

Luke had a sudden inspiration, a beautiful lie forming for him.

"No, a personal matter. I'm looking for a relative."

Masuro's expression told him that he didn't expect that. "You have relatives in Tokyo?"

"An aunt, but I don't know where she lives. My grandfather gave me an address to contact while in Tokyo."

Masuro frowned.

"Her name please?"

"Hayashi. I don't know her first name."

"And the friend of Miss Megen Alistaire. What is her relationship to your aunt?"

Luke relaxed. Masuro had taken the bait. He could spin family relations out of the air all day now. "I understand they were friends and that she might help me find my aunt."

"What did you say her name was?"

"My aunt?"

"No, the friend."

"Kiah."

"Did she say where your aunt lives?"

"She wasn't sure, maybe a village on the east coast of Honshu."

Masuro had run out of questions. Luke seized him in this span of indecision, an appeal to his generosity and good will.

"Can you help me? I have no way to find her."

Masuro was hooked. "You know only her last name?"

"Yes. That's all, except that she lives in a village."

Masuro brightened. "Ah, yes, but not very definite." He swiveled out of his chair and went to a wall map. "North or South of Tokyo? Do you know?"

Luke decided to be truthful. "The Izu Peninsula, I think."

Masuro made a note and handed it to Luke. "The office of the prefect in this prefecture could perhaps assist you."

Luke displayed a great disappointment. "Would that require correspondence? I will only be in Japan a few more days."

Masuro seemed touched. "I think you could telephone, yes?"

"I speak so little Japanese, I don't know." Luke hesitated, a helpless look in his eyes. He tried to see if Mark was keeping a straight face.

Masuro went back to his desk. "We would like to help you find your aunt. I shall telephone."

He was getting up from his desk again, escorting them to the door. He said goodbye, shook hands, and bowed almost at the same time. They were dismissed.

"Damn," said Mark as they went down a long flight of steps to the street. "How could you lie like that?"

Luke felt like laughing. "They're dumb as hell. They can't help letting themselves be flattered. Its part of their conceit and at the same times their sense of inferiority. To help a foreigner, especially a westerner, is something ingrained in their nature. Masuro got so involved in my personal problems he forgot his investigation. Pride won't allow him to go back to it. I'll bet you I get a call from him about my aunt within twenty-four hours."

He was right. Masuro called the next day, very friendly, very obliging. He had located two Hayashi families. Luke took down the information. Masuro was off the phone almost at once. "No problem. Glad to help out."

"What have we got?" Mark asked when Luke closed his phone.

"A trip to the Izu Peninsula. Do you want to come along?"

"You bet," said Mark.

They rented a car and left early in the morning. The freeway over the flat coastal plain south of Yokohama made the trip relatively short. Tabara, the village Masuro had located was on the coast. They got off the freeway and drove over roads that were more like raised dikes across the vast paddy land.

"Mosquito heaven," said Mark, looking out over the inundated landscape. "They must breed by the million trillions."

"They're a parasite in a perfect ecosystem," said Luke. "These paddies are nothing less than cesspools under water."

"What do you mean?"

"I mean agriculture and sewage is hooked up in a symbiotic way. My grandfather was an M.P., stationed in Sendai during the occupation. He told me the Japanese farmers carry shit from the towns and villages out into the paddies all winter long. In the spring the stench is unbelievable, until they flood the paddies with water. The paddies are about ninety percent shit. The shit turns to silt from ages of accumulation. The rice grows in the shit, the people eat the rice, turn it into shit, the farmers carry it back to the paddy and plant more rice. It's an endless cycle: rice, shit, people, rice, shit, people, without end, for centuries, maybe forever."

"No shit," said Mark, laughing, "Very efficient, I call that the ultimate recycling."

Periodically, they passed through tiny villages standing like islands in the paddy land. They were approaching the coast. Luke pulled the car to the side of the road and looked on the map. Tabara appeared to be one on those marginal villages that, with its hinterland, the *Mura*, draws together the rice culture of the farmers and the fishing culture on the coast.

Luke studied the intersecting roads on the map. They were far from being a grid work, but wandered across the ancient system of canals and embankments without design or purpose, contrived by man and nature for ages. Water management dictated the course of the roadways.

They drove more slowly until finally the long arc of the sea began to come into view, and far down the road a town of modest proportions.

"That must be Tabara," said Luke.

The road they traveled became an unpaved street, running through the town, consisting of unpainted buildings on each side for a distance of perhaps a quarter of a mile. Beyond the two lines of buildings were some scattered small huts and modest dwellings. A maze of paths, trees and shrubs suggested the existence of a scattered town population.

Luke pulled to a stop when he saw a constable's sign. He got out, leaving the motor running. He came back in a few minutes.

"I located the *joika* Headman."

"Who's he?"

"*Joika* is the elected communal council. I'll talk to the Headman and see if he knows anything. If my aunt doesn't live in this village, we'll have to go on to the next one."

They drove to the end of the town and Luke parked. Mark waited while Luke started along a path. He encountered two young girls on the path and engaged them in a brief conversation while Mark watched. After that he disappeared and didn't come back for half an hour.

Mark settled down, eyes closed, about to doze when Luke got into the car.

"What did you find out?" he asked.

"She's well known here. She has a business about a mile from here."

"Did you get her name?'

"Niani. That's the name my grandfather gave me."

He started the car and began to drive toward what seemed like an estuary, the tide out, the lowland exposed. Seagulls rose and fell in squadrons, beating the air and searching the tidelands by turns.

The salt air, sharp in their nostrils, tinged with the oily smell of fish, became increasingly strong. The road angled off to the shoreline. Half a mile, and they came to a small village.

"I bet this is Tabara," said Luke.

He felt depressed. The buildings were shacks, lining the road, a mean poverty on all sides. Fishing nets hung on the walls of the hovels or laid out on drying racks. A few children, half-naked, ran up to the car when they stopped. Adults came to the doors, to lurk there and stare without leaving their houses.

"I thought the town we just left was Tabara," said Mark.

"I was mistaken; this is Tabara."

Mark could not contain his cynicism. "Welcome home."

Luke got out and went to one of the houses to talk to a man who had just emerged. He came back in a few seconds and started the car again.

"He said Niana lives down the road about a quarter of a mile."

The road turned off toward the sea again. They soon came to a small stand of evergreen trees, dwarfed, and severely warped by the coastal winds. A small house stood in the lee of the trees, surrounded by picket fences and hedges. Within the stockade they saw a considerable expanse of young trees, plants and shrubs.

"Looks like nursery stock," said Mark.

Luke nodded. "I understand that's her business."

They got out and started toward the house, then stopped when Luke saw a woman standing in the nursery, almost concealed by the shrubs and plants around her. Quite still, she seemed to be straining to hear. They walked toward her, the sandy path making their footsteps almost noiseless. Her expression told them she heard them approaching, yet she did not see them.

"I think she's blind," Mark said softly.

Luke felt moved, pity combined with disappointment, a feeling strange to him as though he should know the woman. "Niana," he said in a low voice, almost doubting.

She didn't reply.

"Niana," he repeated.

"*Hai*," she said, turning toward him.

He knew she wouldn't know him. He said his grandmother's name. Her blind face registered a puzzled expression, a sign of anticipation. He told her he was the grandson of her mother.

A small cry escaped her and she went slowly toward him, arms opening. He embraced her, and her hands came up, anxious fingers exploring his features. Her face had become a mixture of joy and disbelief.

Mark had watched, first fascinated, then moved, then embarrassed by the intimacy of the meeting. He began to edge away, idly examining the blooms in the garden. Out of the corner of his eye he saw Luke start toward the little house with the blind woman. She picked her way slowly but surely through the maze of plants and soon they disappeared. He went back to the car to wait, turning on the radio to find some music.

He dozed off. When he awoke, Luke was getting into the car.

"What did you find out?"

Luke held the wheel in both hands, staring straight ahead. He turned to Mark finally. "I have more relatives than I expected."

He paused, giving Mark the impact of his stare. "A blind great aunt, and she has a daughter."

"Really?" said Mark. "How about that."

"What would our relationship be?" asked Luke, starting the car.

"Whose?"

"My great aunt's daughter and me?"

Mark thought a second. "She'd be your cousin wouldn't she? Maybe she's a cousin once removed, whatever that means."

"Uncommon." agreed Luke.

"How old is she?"

"Who? My great aunt?"

"No, no her daughter."

"From what I can gather, she's in her late twenties."

"How about your great aunt?"

"Surprisingly older than she looks. Late sixties I would guess."

Mark looked around as they started back, slowly driving through the shanties lining the streets.

"No offense," he said cautiously, "but I can see why your grandmother went to America."

"No, you can't," retorted Luke in a low voice, a little resentful.

He was immediately sorry for the outburst. "It's more complicated than that. I'll explain it to you some other time."

"Are you going to look up your cousin?"

"I think so. Yes. I want to."

"What's her name?"

"Midori."

"Does she live here?"

"No. She lives in Tokyo but Niani doesn't know where."

"That's a little strange isn't it?" asked Mark.

Luke felt like exploding. "Everything is strange. Niani said a couple of time Midori has passed; Midori has passed."

His voice was strained. "I'm learning a lot. Do you know what nigger means?"

"Sure. Who doesn't?"

"A white man doesn't, that's who! It means contempt, it means rejection, and it means ostracism. You know our country's history!"

Mark was puzzled. Luke had become increasingly somber, half angry. "I don't know what you're driving at," he said finally.

"Nigger is a slur, a dirty word, an ethnic put down. A white man may say the word nigger, but he doesn't feel the pain of it. When Japanese say Eta, they're saying nigger, to one of their own. Figure that out."

"What's Eta?"

"It means outcast."

Luke looked back saying "Niggers live there."

"Is it a ghetto?"

"Sort of."

"They look like Japanese to me."

"They are, but they're outcasts. That's what Burakumin means, or the slang word Eta. It's a community of segregated people."

"Well, I'll be damned. I never heard of that."

"Me either, until today. I just got a lesson on Japanese social history from my great aunt."

Luke's face had become pained. He looked into Mark's eyes. "I'm an outcast. This is my grandmother's village. This is where her life started."

They rode in silence for a while.

"I thought my father was born in Honolulu until I telephoned Gramps last week. He said in his letter that my father was born in Japan and my grandmother joined him in Honolulu later."

"Where does your great aunt Niana come into this?"

"My grandmother had been married before. She and her husband had a daughter, Niana. Her husband was killed at Sendai in 1945 during the fire bombings and my grandmother was badly burned. I sometimes wondered why her skin was so pale, especially for a Japanese woman. Now, I know."

"Burned all over?" asked Mark curiously.

"Evidently. Her husband's remains were never found. My grandmother was treated at a missionary hospital, that's where she met Gramps, so far as I can tell."

"That's a tragic story," said Mark.

"The burns probably caused cancer in my grandmother's later years. I just learned Niani became increasingly blind as she got older."

"Can she see at all?"

"She says she can make out the shape of things. Apparently everything is a gray world for her. In the States she would be considered legally blind."

Mark was curious about the Eta. "Why are they segregated?"

"I don't know. Niani is an uneducated woman. I really didn't get much out of her other than a little family history."

"That's what you came for," Mark said gently.

"I want to know more," Luke said determinedly.

They drove back to Tokyo. All he had to go on was a name, Midori Hayashi, and her occupation, school teacher. He telephoned Masuro.

"No problem," said the detective. "If she is a teacher, she will belong to a union."

Masuro suggested two federations, Japan Teacher's Union and Japan Teacher's Association, and gave him a couple of numbers to call.

Luke called the first union and got nothing for his trouble. He called the other, *Nikkyoso*, and found that Midori was a member. But they wouldn't give him her address or telephone number. Back to square one, he thought.

He called the patient Masuro. "I should have thought of that," said the detective. "*Nikkyoso* is very careful about their members."

"How can I locate her?" asked Luke.

"At what level is she certified to teach?"

"I don't know."

"It would help to know. Ask *Nikkyoso* if they will tell you that much. Then you can call the schools."

"Thanks," said Luke, and started to hang up. He caught the last of Masuro's words. "She may not be teaching. It is summer."

"The school would still have the information on her," objected Luke.

"You are right. You could go to city hall and look at *koseki*, her family file."

Luke was a little surprised. "Can I do that?"

"Of course, why not? Families are registered, as required by law. It would only cost you . . . ." Masuro seemed to be calculating. "It would cost you about fifty cents, American money."

"Can anyone do this?"

Masuro laughed. "No. No one can, but everyone does. It's the way our system works. We are an open society."

Luke went downtown and tested the open society. Masuro was right. For a small fee the girl at the counter went for Midori's file. He marveled at Japanese bureaucracy, wondering if he had paid a small bribe without knowing it. No one's privacy could be secure under such a system. But then he was deeply disappointed. The clerk came back to tell him that Midori had no file.

Luke called Masuro later in the afternoon and realized the detective's patience was wearing thin.

"She may have changed her name," said Masuro.

"But she's registered with Nikkyoso as Midori Hayashi."

"She may be married now," said Masuro.

Luke thanked him and hung up. He called Nikkyoso again and was gratified beyond expectation. They gave him Midori's professional level, the high school she taught at and a phone number. He had even more luck, Midori was teaching the summer session.

He phoned the high school. Midori came on the phone, surprising him with only a short wait. It was a sweet voice, finely modulated, very precise. He stumbled over his words at first. Their communication had started so suddenly, he had not thought of what to say.

"This is your cousin."

She didn't respond at once. Fluent in Japanese, he had to wonder if his American accent could be detected.

"Taka?" she said after a moment, her voice disbelieving.

"No, my name is Lucas Sullivan. I'm from America."

Again, there was the sound of silence. He tried another tack.

"Do you speak English?"

She did. It was very formal, as precise as his Japanese. He told her they were related. This news invited another long pause. When she spoke again, she reverted to Japanese, and her voice sounded withdrawn, hostile it seemed to him. He asked her to meet him, and she was evasive. Finally, they set a time and a place, a park across from the school where she taught, the next afternoon.

Luke hung up the phone, aware that she was not pleased. The most he could think was she had obeyed giri, a Japanese tradition, the obligation which requires one relative to honor another.

Chapter 11

Luke had forgotten to ask Midori for a means of identification. This bothered him a little when he arrived at the park the next afternoon.

It was a pleasant setting: small, as with most things Japanese; immaculately groomed, always the Japanese character; charming and secluded, by the manner in which shrubs, swept sand, rocks and moving water under hoary trees are combined to produce a sense of privacy in a public place.

The suburb was obviously middle class, "new middle class", the abode of the salaried man, *sarari*. Neat paths led to small houses, each with its own character, each different, yet all varieties of a single specimen; fragile structures of light wood and oiled paper, ensconced behind walls or fences; embraced by shrubbery, vines and flowers in bloom.

Here nature embraced humanity. Luke thought it remarkable that he sat in such rustic surroundings when he considered the larger circumference of the environment was industrial and commercial Tokyo, the megalopolis. At this hour of the day, the men and most of the women in the neighborhood were at their work places; most in downtown Tokyo, he suspected.

A mother or a nanny with children passed by occasionally. Otherwise, he was alone. From across the road, the sounds of students at work and play came to his ears. Singing briefly enlarged the pleasant babble of childish voices.

A young woman emerged from the building and he stood up. Intuitively he knew it would be Midori. He was surprised by her western style of dress. Somehow, he had seen enough of this regimented society, working, playing and studying in lockstep to think she would be in uniform, as without doubt her students were.

She wore a stylish blouse; open at the throat, trousers resembling designer jeans and thronged sandals. A bright red scarf was loosely tied around her neck. Her hair, black and straight, cut in a pageboy fashion framed a moon shaped face. In it, he saw his grandmother's visage, as he imagined she might have been as a young woman. The body was reminiscent of his grandmother also, small and comely, fashioned for strength and endurance, the bearing of babies. The full breasts that the blouse accentuated were typical of oriental women, expansive rather than obtrusive.

All this Luke absorbed with a mixture of aesthetic appreciation and the acute personal interest a stranger entertains when encountering a relative for the first time. Midori had arrived by this time, coming toward him without hesitation. She had seemed to give him as much scrutiny as he had to her in the span of a few seconds. Her hand went out to him, and he took it, surprised with her unaffected manner, so western. He had expected, perhaps without thinking about it, a more subdued, more thoroughly oriental woman. In another time and place, they both would have bowed deeply to each other, the space between them precise, as if measured. Their hands would not have touched.

They still had not spoken. She withdrew her hand and sat down on the bench. He dropped down beside her. Their faces turned and eyes came into contact for what seemed to Luke to be an uncomfortable amount of time. She was studying his face with her eyes.

He spoke English and wondered if she would follow him or, as yesterday, revert to Japanese. Her features were sober, perhaps curious.

"I want to know you," she said simply, as if a confession.

He was surprised by this since she had seemed so remote when he talked to her on the phone. Now, there was that consanguine sense of knowing each other although strangers, as if relatives have a special antenna for their own kind.

"What can I tell you?"

"Are you here for a visit?"

"Sort of. It's a business trip."

"You're a businessman?"

"Not exactly. I'm salaried. I work for an American electronics firm."

Awkward, without words, they seemed to have run out of polite exchanges immediately. Luke proposed they walk together.

"You're English is excellent." he said.

"Thank you, I teach it."

"Do you expect to teach at the university level some day?"

"No," she replied. "That opportunity is closed to me."

"I don't understand."

"I chose Normal School Training."

Luke nodded, pretending to understand. He wanted her help and tried to think of a way to raise the subject.

"I'm very ignorant about Japan," he said after awhile. They had come to another bench and sat down. He removed the medallion from around his neck. She took it from him, examining it curiously.

"Have you ever seen an emblem like that?"

"No," she replied. "It is unusual. Where did you get it?"

He lied. "I picked it up in the Ginza, as a souvenir. I have an American friend who thinks it might be a symbol for members of a peace movement; advocates of an anti-nuclear policy for example."

"I think I would know about that, if it were true."

"Are you involved with the peace movement?" she asked.

"Generally, yes. Presently we still support Ground Zero, although the end of the Cold War makes it seem to be a movement without meaning."

Luke replaced the medallion around his neck and adjusted his tie.

"I take it you belong to the Left, in political terms."

Midori's eyes narrowed, her words stern. "I am on the Left in all ways."

"Is there any kind of right wing movement, equivalent in strength to the Left, operating in Japan today?"

"Not that I'm aware of. There are several small rightist clubs and associations, but they are notorious for their feuding and disunity."

"What about a secret right wing movement?"

"She reflected on that for a moment. "I doubt it."

"Why?" asked Luke.

"I think the mood of the country is liberal, favorably disposed to what the Left believes in."

Luke felt challenged by this. "Could there not be an extreme Left, as secret as the Right?"

"There could be, but I don't know of any, except for the Communist Party, and it's very public in all ways."

Midori was puzzled. "What exactly are you looking for?"

Luke had to be honest. "I honestly don't know."

He thought the time had come to fulfill the promise he had made to Niani.

"Your mother wants you to come and see her," he said abruptly.

Surprised, Midori seemed to freeze, her expression troubled.

"You've been to Tabara?"

"Yes, a few days ago."

Midori got up. He thought she might walk away.

"I don't want to go there."

Luke went to her and without quite realizing it; he was putting his arm around her shoulder. She started to wrench away, then submitted.

"How long has it been since you were there?"

Her head was down. "Six years," she said dully.

"Your mother wants to see you."

"I can't go there."

"I know your mother paid for your education. I just learned of it two days ago."

"I am grateful to my mother," she said softly.

"I also learned from my grandfather that the money came from my grandmother. She sent it to your mother."

Midori seemed to tremble. Luke could sense a convulsion of silent weeping within her. He pulled her into his arms and stroked her back until she had composed herself. He led her back to the bench and they sat down.

"Why don't you want to go back to Tabara?"

She raised her head, her eyes a little red.

"I've cut my ties," she said harshly. "I had to."

His puzzled expression told her what she had suspected.

"As you just said, you don't know Japan."

She hesitated, staring into his eyes.

"Do you know what it means in this society to pass?" She stressed the word pass.

Luke shrugged. "I'm not sure. It means to succeed or fail, I suppose."

"No, nothing so simple. Eta can succeed and still fail." Her voice broke. "I am Eta."

Luke put his arm around her, comforting her. "I know. Your mother told me something about it. She said you had passed but I didn't understand at first."

"To pass means one who is Eta has escaped from the previous condition of being dirty and segregated, and has become clean and acceptable to Japanese society. I have arrived there. I can't go back."

Luke was shocked. "It seems so medieval. I thought Japan was a modern country."

"It's a social condition as old as Japanese civilization. The outcasts are those who have been segregated for centuries. Even after laws were passed to eliminate Eta, it has persisted. They are *Kumuru*. They cannot enter Japanese society as equals. Failing to be accepted, they eventually fall back into their villages, ostracized as before. They remain Eta."

"I never knew such a thing could exist."

"You have it in America. Aren't there minorities who are oppressed, restricted to ghettos?"

"I don't think it's the same," he objected. "Segregation in the United States ended a generation ago. In the U.S. today ghetto is simply slang, meaning a poor, run down area in one city or another."

"Do not the minorities in your country also fail? Failing to pass, do they not also fall back into their ghettos, their run down areas? Do not American Indians prefer to stay on the reservations assigned to them, rather than live among the white dominated society which surrounds them?"

Luke had never considered that before. He thought there must be a difference, but he couldn't quite make up his mind.

"How does one pass in Japan?" he finally asked.

"Sometimes by schooling, gaining a high degree, and sometimes by marriage, if one is fortunate." Her face became sad. "I was engaged to be married. Last year my fiancé's parents learned that I was Eta. They made him so miserable that he finally renounced me."

Luke felt disgusted. "He couldn't have had much character. You're probably better off."

"I didn't blame him. When others learned that I am Eta, our marriage would have become increasingly unhappy. He had an obligation to his family."

Luke had to think about the ease with which he had been able to look up Midori's family life. It explained a great deal about social control in Japan. In Japanese society, there are no secrets. He told her of his attempt to locate her file and she didn't seem surprised or offended.

"If you have no family to trace, family in which to take pride, you cannot advance in Japan. If you have family that is in disgrace, you cannot pass. You become ostracized in society as an individual, just as whole communities of families, the *buckram*, become ostracized."

Midori got up, hesitating, seeming ready to leave.

"We've just begun to talk," Luke said, reaching out for her hand.

Midori was determined, pulling away. "I must go back."

He followed her. "Will I see you again?"

She wouldn't reply. He watched her as she crossed the road. Midori stopped and then turned momentarily. "Goodbye," she said, then went up the stairs into the school.

Chapter 12

Luke called the school several times, but Midori wouldn't respond. She was in class, out on a field trip, out to lunch, or off for the day. Luke cursed himself, he hadn't thought to ask for her home address and she hadn't offered it. If she had a cell phone she didn't offer him the number. Now she wouldn't see him. He drove out to the suburb and stationed himself in the park, facing the school, resolved to stay there until she came out.

He had purchased a worn paperback book in one of the shops on the Ginza. He didn't know exactly why he chose it, perhaps because the title was intriguing: *The Surrender*.

The book was set in his grandfather's era, the time when the U.S. and the Land of the Rising Sun had prepared for the Gotterdammerung. Would the Japanese people, devoted to their Emperor, subservient to the military class that ruled the country, exhaust their last resource, expend every remaining life to protect the homeland against the barbarians from the West?

Over this drama hung the threat of atomic bombs. Two cities had been flattened, scorched, hundreds of thousands killed and maimed; many more towns incinerated by fire bombing, leaving the civil populations of each obliterated or scattered. How many more cities would they sacrifice before yielding to an invincible power?

The book was fascinating to read. Two hours had passed when Luke reached the denouement, finding the conclusion more exciting than fiction. He had never heard of the plot prepared by a group of Japanese officers, the Young Tigers, determined to overthrow the Emperor, Hirohito.

It was not the details of the abortive coup that intrigued him, but the discovery that thereafter the plotters had escaped all punishment for what ought to have been considered a great crime, nothing less than treason. For their treachery, the Young Tigers had not considered performing *seppuku*, the formal disemboweling rite as atonement for their disgrace. They just disappeared.

Why had the Young Tigers been spared what might have seemed a just punishment? The simple fact was the ruling military circle of Japan had been found guilty of conspiracy to conduct an aggressive war against a peaceful country, the United States, thus a war crime. The plotters, outside the circle of power, had played no part in making policy. As far as the U.S. was concerned, the Young tigers had planned to overthrow the legitimate power, supplant Hirohito with a military figure, for patriotic reasons alone.

The reconstituted Japanese government had shown no inclination toward punishment, although one of the plotters, because the evidence was too blatant to be ignored, had been tried by Court Martial. He was acquitted. The rest of the Tigers vanished, slipping anonymously back into Japanese society. Some changed their names; some perhaps underwent plastic surgery, the better to preserve themselves from retaliation. The number of plotters could not be precisely known. Of those known, only four could be identified as still alive at the time *The Surrender* was published.

What had happened to the Young Tigers in the aftermath of the war? While the mass of the Japanese people suffered terribly from the effects of economic dislocation, they had prospered. Some had gone into business and succeeded brilliantly, as capitalists might. One became an author, a scholar of note, who made himself an authority on World War Two. Another rose high in the ranks of the Japanese Land Self Defense Force.

Who were the patriots then? Luke had to ask himself. And who were the traitors? The ruling military circle which had surrendered unconditionally to a foreign power? Or the Young Tigers who had wished to resist to the death, carry the nation down with them if need be?

He closed the book, bemused with the implications of these few facts. How many of the Young Tigers were still alive now? They would be middle aged, or older. He wondered if they, like all military veterans, communicated with each other. Japan, a country of gangs, clubs, societies, associations almost without number, would certainly have active veterans organizations.

Midori had said that she knew of no far right wing groups. If one existed, it would have to be secret. And so it would, Luke thought. He wondered if age tempers fanaticism. In their younger years they had been willing to sacrifice themselves and their country; indeed, to sacrifice the God Emperor (the two joined as one in their minds). Would they have found in their advancing years any reason to change their view of the world? Or their place in the world? Or Japan's place in the world?

He opened the book again. A collection of photographs had been reproduced and bound into the center of the volume. The faces staring up at him were old in some cases, others obviously young; all military men with the severe expressions of duty, discipline; perhaps fanaticism. He carefully tore a half dozen of the photographs from the book. There were no captions. He slipped the pictures into his wallet.

So preoccupied was he with the photographs that he scarcely realized that the students were beginning to leave the school. He watched with considerable interest, thinking of American high schools and the contrast was inescapable to him. The Japanese students filed out in lines, almost in formation. They were in uniform, speaking little, unlike their American compeers who would dally, chatter, skylark and take hours before dispersing. The Japanese students were gone in only a few minutes, they had marched away with almost regimental solemnity. The scene was again silent, the school seemed deserted.

A group of teachers emerged suddenly, Midori in their midst. They too seemed in lockstep, descending the steps with formality. Bowing, they parted, as quickly and silently as the students had a few minutes earlier. Midori remained standing alone.

Luke pitied her for her isolation. Knowing her plight, his heart went out to her. Still he sat and would not rise. He had decided it was not pride but principle that was at issue. He had come this far and waited this long. She would have to cross the road.

His eyes were on her, and she looked up to see him sitting there. She stood fixed, staring at him for a considerable time. His own stare was implacable.

She was dressed differently today, more on the order of what he had expected at their first meeting: a long dress, ending just below the knees, clutched around the waist by a narrow belt. A kerchief tied around her head framed the pretty face.

He wanted to speak, to call her to him, but he wanted her to yeild too; and for that she would have to cross the street. She came about the time he thought it, a quick easy stride. When she arrived, he was still seated, rudely staring up, presenting a harsh exterior he did not feel.

"I have received your messages," she said softly.

Luke affected a little sternness. "I left my cell phone number also."

She sat down beside him, fingering the book lying beside him, silent, her eyes on his.

"Midori, I don't want you to say goodbye to me again."

"I don't want to." She hesitated. "I didn't want to."

Luke reached out and placed his hand on hers. "Let me help you."

He could see the puzzlement on her face, the question. What could he do for her? He didn't know himself. Perhaps he wanted to help himself. He realized one thing with increasing clarity. The more he knew her, the more she interested him.

"What are you planning to do this weekend?" he asked.

"Nothing in particular. Why do you ask?"

"I want to drive around Tokyo. I need a guide."

She smiled. "Tokyo is so large. I know only the area around the university, and not even that very well. My apartment is within walking distance of the school."

"You would know Tokyo better for having seen it with me."

She wouldn't respond.

"Please," he said. "I have so few days left here. You have so many."

His appeal decided her. "All right," she said.

He drove her to her apartment, walked her up a flight of stairs and made a date with her. He stood there, waiting until she had gone in, then went bounding down the steps with the abandonment of a boy, an exultant cry close to his lips. The sophistication and maturity of a decade slipped away from him as he drove away.

By the next day the delight of a young man who has won the first round in the eternal engagement of male and female had faded a little. He was to pick Midori up Saturday morning at nine. The itinerary was for him to choose. From the beginning he had evolved a plan. He would drive around the eastern perimeter of the city until they had arrived at the south end. He got out a map of Tokyo and studied the streets. He wanted to pick up the freeway leading to the Izu Peninsula. Tabara would be their destination.

It came close to being abduction. He wondered how she would react to his deception. Would there be anger? Or resignation? He thought her true character would reveal itself.

He was not mistaken. He only misjudged her. Once out of the city, the signs proclaiming the kilometers lying between them and Yokohama, she turned to him with questioning eyes. He said nothing.

"You planned this, didn't you?" she asked. A little smile was on her face. Annoyance was not in her voice or the sound of surprise.

"I don't mind," she said after a while. "I want to see my mother."

They drove for quite a while, without speaking. But, vivacious, Midori could not be still for long. There was so much she wanted to know about America. And hadn't she said that she wanted to know him?

She had donned a blouse and slacks again, dressed as he had first seen her. He glanced her way, finding her more attractive than on first sight, and for the first time, provocative.

""Have you driven this way before?" he asked.

"I can't drive a car," she said. "I came to Tokyo by train six years ago."

"Your English is fluent. Where did you learn it?"

"I was educated by English missionaries until I was old enough to go to high school."

He thought Midori seemed to grow a little quieter, somewhat more tense with each passing mile.

"Who is Taka?" He asked suddenly. He remembered she had mentioned the name in their first conversation. That had to be cleared up he thought. Surely, she could have no brothers.

"He is my cousin," said Midori. "My mother has a brother, Yosh. Taka is his son." All was clear then.

He learned it was an extended family when they arrived. The news of Midori's arrival went over a grapevine almost as efficient as a telephone service. In a few minutes a crowd of kinfolk had assembled around the little house. His blind aunt came out in the slow but certain steps of those who see little, yet walk with confidence. Midori ran to her mother's arms. Both wept, the blind woman running her hands over Midori's face, the fingers doing for her what her eyes could not. Luke withdrew for a time, greatly moved by the emotion.

Tables were contrived from boards, benches and boxes. Food was brought out from the house. Sake was served and in about an hour, conviviality became high. Someone proposed a swimming party. They crowded into an old dilapidated pickup truck until it resembled more a moving mass of humanity than a vehicle. A stream of bicycles followed them as they drove about a mile down a sandy road to the beach. The sea, warm and nearly waveless, powerful with its fishy smell, assailed the nostrils. The hot sun, the earthiness of fish and salted air and the dark and heated sand under their feet, all was a confusion of the senses for Luke. Up to now, he had forgotten about the casual manners of the rural Japanese; but he had not known at all the mores of Eta, which by the standards of the urban Japanese, were considered scandalous. With easy grace the large family of bathers divested themselves of their clothing. The sake, the sun and the festivities had produced high spirits and laughter. The men, keeping on only a fundoshi, a single strip of loincloth, went plunging into the sea. The smaller children stripped themselves naked. The women, bare breasted, wore no more than brief pants.

Self-conscious, Luke was a long time in removing his shirt, then his shoes and socks. He let his trousers drop and stepped away in his jockey shorts, feeling exposed, vulnerable in the presence of a boisterous family still strangers to him.

Midori seemed to him shy as she removed her slacks and kicked off her sandals. She took off her blouse almost as slowly as he undressed.

His first view of her abundant breasts struck him almost like a physical blow. A sudden erection pained him at the same moment, a signal he could not conceal, and she could not fail to recognize. He didn't realize how much he desired her until just now. In panties, nothing more, she came toward him, eyes bright, her hand reaching for his. Together, they ran toward the water, her golden body making him feel dizzy.

Once in the sea, he was more at ease. She frolicked like an otter, he thought. Fisher people by trade, his relatives were as much at home in the water as the fish they caught. It seemed to him that Midori had returned to her natural element.

Slowly, they separated from the group and finally played alone. He had not suspected she could laugh with such abandon.

"You see how easy it is to return and want to stay?" she said in the midst of her laughter. Then she instantly sobered, looking at the others who were beginning to return to the beach. "They are happy here, happier than I can be for all my education."

They stood waist deep in the water. He had forgotten they were virtually naked and his desire for her. It was her soul on her face that he saw.

"You're trapped between two worlds," he said gently. It was more a statement than a question.

"Yes," she said, then laughed again, and abruptly broke free, diving away from him.

She was a powerful swimmer. Suddenly he felt her pulling him down. Underwater, she had a determined grip on him, half-drowning him. In his arms she felt like wet satin, supple and enticing. She released him, and he came up sputtering, weak and a little blinded. Giggling and joyous she led him out of the water and up to the beach. They went back and got into their clothes.

It had been a brief dip, an invigorating one. In a way it had been an initiation. They had seen each other's bodies without shame or curiosity. They knew each other, and he had become part of the family.

They all piled into the truck and drove back to the house. Part of my heritage is here, Luke thought, I have always been a part of this family. I've just been away for a long time. He put his arm around Midori and they rode without speaking.

In the evening the family celebrated Midori's return. Luke was honored equally. There was more food and more sake. There were stories, long tiring accounts as well as briefer ribald ones. Late in the evening much of the family disappeared. The nuclear family dispersed to the few rooms. Bedding was laid out on the floor in one room, and Luke slept with four others. He did not see Midori until the next day.

Sunday morning his aunt Niani and her brothers made their obeisance before the Kamidana, a tiny Shinto altar in the main room. Midori attended but was unusually restrained, it seemed to Luke. Later in the morning she said she wanted to visit the Christian missionaries who had raised her.

There were some perplexing, certainly intriguing questions for Luke to ponder, as he drove Midori some twenty miles to the mission.

The staying power of the Christians seemed remarkable to him, in a country that had for centuries persecuted all Christians, officially banned them until 1871; a country whose ancient religious affiliations, Buddhist and Shintoist, gave the Japanese what they needed: solid communion with the earth and their ancestral roots. Christianity, it appeared to him, could offer the Japanese nothing. He looked at Midori as they drove. What had she been given that was powerful enough to bring her back after an absence of perhaps ten years? He discovered the essential answer to that in the next two hours: she wished to return to the mission with love and gratitude.

"My mother walked this road to the mission, half-blind, with me in her womb," Midori said quietly.

Her remark, half to herself, dramatic and intense, seemed important.

"Can you tell me?" Luke asked hesitantly.

Midori turned to him. "There are things you want to know, aren't there?"

"Are you Christian?" Luke asked.

"Nominally, yes, but not in faith. My mother bore me in the Garden of Love. I was baptized but not confirmed in the Anglican Church. My mother and I owe the Anglicans more than we can repay, but neither of us became believing Christians. As you saw this morning, my mother adheres to Shintoism. It satisfies her needs."

"What is the Garden of Love?"

"They minister to the poor and to mothers pregnant out of wedlock. They operate both an orphanage and a small clinic."

"Where is your mother's husband?"

"No one knows. It is understood in Tabara that he passed into Ippan."

"Ippan, that means majority, right?"

"Yes. Ippan is majority. We, Eta, are the minority. We think of those who have passed as the majority. And they really are. They hold us in contempt. Among themselves they call us *yotsu*."

He didn't know the word.

"What does it mean?"

"It's untranslatable. It means a human being that walks on four legs, like an animal."

Luke could see the distress on Midori's face.

"You always speak of they and them," he said quizzically.

"That's true. They and we. Them and us. It is always an objective relationship between unequals. We are apart. We want to be together; we need to be separate."

"A community divided culturally and spiritually," he mused.

Luke was struck by her protean personality that could shift from somber reflection to an ironic humor not much different from cynicism.

"Why did your father abandon your mother?"

"They don't say to abandon or to desert in Tabara. He just left. He passed."

"That sounds like millions of American men who desert their wives and children, but refuse to acknowledge the word desert. They just leave."

"I've read about that. But in the case of the Tabara women, it has made them more independent. It is possible for the men of Tabara to leave, but almost impossible for the women. Consequently, they are more independent, equal to men. Did you notice that yesterday?"

Luke had realized the Tabara women were not the submissive type with downcast eyes he might have expected. When he met them, he encountered a sense of equality. Instead of the steeply inclined bow, there was the slight nod of the head and shoulders, a forthright expression in the eyes. It had struck him as almost American, not culturally feudal, as he had observed elsewhere in Japan. His aunt Niani was obviously the head of the house, her brothers and uncles subordinate to her. It had seemed to him like a matriarchy, on first sight.

"Why did your mother go to the mission house? Did her family reject her when her husband disappeared?"

"She was twenty-five, already going blind and was pregnant. My father had perhaps abandoned her for those reasons. I think she was too proud to go back to her family, to accept the degrading position for the rest of her life. She was without protection or money. She walked twenty miles to the English Mission. She knew her mother had been helped by the Garden of Love in another time."

Midori sighed, "Its fortunate for me that my mother had the physical and moral strength to do that. Otherwise, I would be just another Tabara woman, virtually uneducated and segregated." She paused for a long time. "I would be trapped in a Buruka village."

"The missionaries educated you?"

"Yes. My mother sent word to your grandmother. From then on the annual gift of money was sent to the Mission. Then the money stopped coming."

"That would have been at the time my grandfather retired," said Luke.

"The missionaries kept the money for my mother. It was quite a savings, I believe. When she was thirty-nine years old, and I was fourteen, she took the next step. She decided to return to Tabara to complete my education. By then she spoke a little English, not much more than she does now. I was fluent in the language."

Midori's eyes closed, a soft smile of satisfaction on her face. "I remember my excitement. My mother took counsel from the missionaries. They told her that I had an excellent mind and thought I could pass into Ippan, that I might be trained sufficiently to earn a high enough mark in high school to sit for the university examinations."

Midori's voice trembled. "If you could know how difficult the examinations are, or how desirable the success in passing them, you can imagine my mother's pride and hope. I could see resolve growing on her face. Nearly blind, staring over the heads of those who had befriended her, she said several times: Midori will pass."

"And so you did," said Luke, feeling moved himself.

"With her savings my mother was able to buy a fish drying business in Tabara, but it was already declining. The old way of fishing in small boats was giving way to capitalist enterprise with diesel boats, hired crews and expensive equipment. That is why my mother took her next courageous step."

"What was that?"

"She converted the fish establishment into the plant nursery you have seen. It was a gamble but today she is successful."

"Despite her handicaps," said Luke.

"Because of them," said Midori. There was pride in her voice.

He concluded that Midori was always argumentative, her bright mind and willful spirit never yielded.

They returned to Tabara around noon, Midori subdued by the emotional meeting with the missionaries. There was another party, another swim; for Luke another view of the enchanting Midori, nearly naked, gamboling in the water and on the beach. The barbarian girl and the intellectual woman were combined in a unique and appealing way for him. What did he like more: the smart brain or the neat little body? She was not the statuesque Kiah, athletic, inviting sexual competition with her erotic power. Natural was the word for Midori, he decided, natural goodness; but she was rootless, and he thought she was unhappy. It occurred to him that condition was his also. Half-Japanese, half-American, he really had no roots. Was he happy and fulfilled? He'd never thought about it until now.

They stayed late in the day. Midori wanted to leave, he could tell. Yet, she wanted to stay.

Her ambivalence remained when finally they started back to Tokyo. She wanted to talk about it and he was content to listen.

"I loved this visit," she said, stretching, a little tired but contented.

"Six years," Luke started to say not finishing the sentence.

"It makes me seem heartless, I know. But I've cut my ties with them. I can't go back. I am Ippan, they are Eta."

"But the pain for your mother. How about yourself? How can you stand a prolonged separation again?"

"It was my mother's wish that I should pass, that's all. She has devoted her life to its success. She is happy with it, happier than I can be."

"But she's alone," objected Luke.

"No," said Midori sharply. "Her brothers help her. She has her friends and her business. Her hours are full."

Midori became sober. "She will grow old, contented, die and dissolve in the soil of Tabara."

It sounded so materialistic to Lucas, devoid of feeling or religious sentiment. "And her soul?" he asked gently. "What of it?" He was really thinking of Midori's.

"She would say Kami, spirit, the elements of her being. Those will be gathered in death and restored with her ancestors."

"That's Shinto, isn't it?"

"I think it's universal, a feeling shared by all human beings."

They drove a while in silence.

"You can still visit Tabara," said Luke.

"No," she said determinedly. She reached out and touched his arm. "I'm grateful to you for bringing me. With you, I could leave. Without you . . . ." She let the words trail off in silence.

"Without me?"

"Alone, I might want to stay." She watched his profile, seeing his frown.

"You don't understand, do you?

"No."

"The Burukumin segregate themselves. There is every compulsion to do so. There is no law which binds them to the villages; yet they remain, in larger numbers than they leave."

That puzzled Luke. "I thought you spoke of the social sanctions against Eta the other day, as strong as any law on the books?"

"I did. But that's the excuse we all fall back on, to justify our self-imposed isolation."

She sensed his skepticism. "It's not unusual," she said. "I've read the Jews imposed isolation on themselves for thousands of years, living self sufficient lives in self-imposed ghettos. It's not some kind of hypocrisy, if that's what you're thinking."

"Then what is it?" he asked.

He thought she talked like a teacher, every ready to lecture. She was evidently thinking.

"The Burukumin don't want to change," she said finally. "They reject modern civilization with its stresses, its regulations, its codes of comportment. They want to be free. I understand. I want to be free. The desire for freedom sometimes almost overcomes me."

She had become passionate, her voice tremulous; then just as quickly subdued. He shot her a glance; at that moment her eyes were coming to his face. There was a smile, sly, almost roguish. "You didn't expect to see so much of me, did you?"

She had caught him off guard. He flushed. Her boldness startled him. "I didn't mind, I enjoyed it."

"I wanted to see you," she said. "All of you, or at least most of you. The rest I could imagine."

She laughed. "You see, I'm shameless, yaban."

He laughed. "Yaban, you mean barbarian, right?"

"Yes, civilization is only a veneer. I could strip it off like my dress and go back to Tabara. I don't like civilization any more than they do. The difference is they are honest."

Luke thought she was punishing herself. "Don't talk that way," he said sharply. "The difference is you gained an education. You know their world within, and you know the larger world without. That is why you are torn this way."

Midori was immediately conciliatory. "You're right. But I'm not bitter. The people of Tabara are unchanged since the seventeenth century, actually from a much earlier time, now that I think about it. They are rejected by modern Japan because their morals are too uninhibited, too natural. But you see the Bukurumin rejects modern Japan also, because of its rigidity, its machines, and its conventions which make life itself mechanical."

"I can understand that," said Luke. "I can see what you mean by self-imposed segregation, reinforced by disapproval coming from Ippan, the majority.

She sighed. "There are many Tabaras, little islands of Bukurumin, scattered all over the country, the last holdouts against modernity."

"Outcasts," said Luke soberly.

"Cast outs," said Midori with a laugh, almost a giggle, "rejects."

Luke suddenly didn't feel so sorry for Eta. The outrage he had experienced at his first visit had been dissipated by this visit.

Without his realizing it, she had slipped closer to him. Their intimacy now seemed stronger than their fleshy encounters on the beach and in the water. That had been the casual contact of virtually nude bodies at play in the midst of a family. This was the private union of ideas and values.

He felt aroused, a little excited.

"What did your mother say about me?

"She likes you."

"Had you heard of me before I called you on the telephone?"

"No."

"Your mother never mentioned my name?"

"No."

"Didn't she ever tell you that she had a family in America?"

"No, not until today."

It sounded almost brutal to his ears when he said it. "Your mother is my grandmother's daughter. Your mother is my aunt and you are my cousin."

Her silence told him she had been thinking. "I know," she said finally. "I talked to my mother about it, a blood tie."

She was silent again. He turned his head. She was looking at him. "Does it matter?"

Her eyes studied his, reading his mind. "No," she said finally, "It doesn't matter."

He let his hand drop to her lap and steered with one hand. She took it and they exchanged glances, almost shyly. They had an understanding, a need for each other. For the remainder of the drive she placed her hand where he wanted it to be, high on his thigh. It was a promise.

They arrived in Tokyo after midnight. Midori had fallen asleep, slumped down in the seat. Tired, Luke made a couple of wrong turns before finding her apartment.

Once parked, he nudged her. Midori awoke abruptly, startled, and then relaxed, still half asleep. He stared into her face in the dim light, and then his lips moved to hers, the soft mouth absorbed his. She got out of the car and he followed her into the apartment.

It occurred to him that they had not said a word to each other in several hours. There was really nothing to say. She turned on a small neon lamp, a subdued light, and came to him; no sounds but the rustle of their clothing as they undressed each other. Nude, she went to a cabinet and took out a futon, spreading it on the floor while he watched. When she had arranged the bedding and bolsters, she laid down for him with her arms outstretched. No words were needed.

He went to her, wanting to root himself, driving with all his power. She moaned, demanding more of him. Inflamed by her passion, he exerted himself until exhausted, resting on her breast. Sleep overcame him.

The next morning he awoke to hear the peal of birds' song outside the windows, then a slight movement in the room. He turned over to see Midori. She was dressed and about to go out. There was a soft smile on her face.

"Good morning."

She knelt beside him. "Will you be here when I get back?"

"What time?"

"I'll leave early. By three o'clock."

"I'll wait for you."

Her eyes went over him. "I wondered if you would be circumcised."

He looked down, half-embarrassed. "It's practically universal in the West by now."

"Most Japanese men are not."

He laughed slightly, annoyed with himself. "I didn't come last night."

She bent down and kissed his lips. "You will this afternoon."

When she was gone he went into the tiny kitchen and attempted to make a breakfast, after that he went to the car to get his cell phone. Mark didn't answer. He called back an hour later and Mark came on the line.

"How was the weekend?"

"Great," said Luke. "Look, I may be out of touch for a couple of days."

There was immediate concern in Mark's voice. "Any trouble?"

"No, no trouble. I just need a few days to myself."

"OK." Mark snickered loudly. "But if you're up to what I think, that's incest my man."

Luke hung up, annoyed. But he had to think about it. Was Midori too close to him biologically? It was academic, he decided, had no affect on his passions. Midori had responded with as much ardor as his own. He liked her and she was good for him. They were good for each other. Each rootless, in a different way, they had the need to nourish each other.

When she returned he heard the key turning in the door. He stripped quickly, enormously aroused, and settled on the futon to wait for her. Eyes luminous, she undressed before him, teasing him with the deliberate divestiture of her clothing, a piece at a time.

"Yaban," he said softly. She went to him in a hurry.

Chapter 13

Luke had an instinct about the Young Tigers and asked Mark to read *The Surrender*. A reluctant reader, Mark plowed through part of it, found it dull and laid it aside.

"Give me a verbal review," he said, when Luke came back to the hotel.

That was too flippant for Luke. "Damn it, I've been away for five days. How long does it take you to get through three hundred pages?"

Mark had picked up a bar hostess and his time had been profitably employed. "I skimmed the conclusion to the book, Luke. I still don't know what you want."

"I want your opinion," said Luke. He posed the same questions he had set for himself: was the medallion connected in some way with the Tushimi Corporation? Was Tushimi connected with the Japanese government in some political sense? Was a military faction, after more than half a century, still connected with government and big business? In other words, was Japan what it has always been: a state run by a military industrial elite; the democratic trappings just a sham?

Mark thought it was an imaginary scenario, too much out of touch with the times. "These people are disarmed, by desire. They're pacifists. All they want to do is make money."

Determined, Luke drew upon an historical precedent. "After World War One, the old military clique from the Kaiser's day joined with big business and the German government to restore Germany's supremacy in Europe. The result of that was World War Two."

"And you're looking for something like that in Japan?" asked Mark, skepticism in his voice. "Another dictator? World War Three? Come on, Luke."

Luke admitted to himself that it seemed like a fantasy when put into words. On the other hand, the world is full of surprises; the unexpected often becomes commonplace.

"You know there always are a few men who are disposed to plot," he said.

He let that sink in. "There are also many in the world who shut their eyes and refuse to believe the worst."

"I know." quipped Mark, "the price of liberty is eternal vigilance."

"Something like that," Luke replied. "Here's another quote for you: Those who cannot learn from history are doomed to repeat its mistakes. History does repeat itself; in parallels, never identical repetitions. Let me give you an example. That book that you find so dull gave me a word I didn't know."

"What word?"

"Zaibatsu. It means roughly speaking, a financial clique; a monopoly of the heavy industry and the finance capital of this country, controlled by a few magnates. It goes back to the nineteenth century. Three great companies controlled most of Japan's industrial might, and their top administration was locked into the highest echelons of the Japanese government. It combined industrial, military and political power. And you know how ambitious they became. They really believed they could take over the world."

"I thought we broke up that monopoly after World War Two," said Mark, but he showed interest for the first time.

"The U.S. tried, but no country can dictate to another for very long. The American Occupation lasted only seven years. The Zaibatsu is back, and has been for a long time. There's a new name for it, Keiretsu, but it's still the same old system."

Luke paced around the room. "Here's something else I learned. Tushimi is a changed name for one of the nineteenth century companies. It was huge before the war; it's immense today. No one can guess how much. It's investing in virtually every country in the world; it's into everything from pharmaceuticals to nuclear energy. When we talked merger, you can see why they jumped on it. They're ready to swallow us."

"You got all this from one book?" said Mark.

"Right. It made everything come together for me."

"Then it seems to me the opinion to consult would be the author of *The Surrender*."

Luke slapped his forehead, amazed at his own obtuseness. He picked up the book and checked the publishing date. "1970, nine years before I was born. Think of that: how much has happened since then. I wonder how we could find this guy."

"He may be dead by now," said Mark. "Say, didn't Midori graduate from Tokyo University?"

"Of course. I didn't think of that.

"There's your connection, Luke."

Luke drove out to the suburbs to see Midori. Mark, not unhappy with this, went to find his Japanese girlfriend.

He stopped at a shop on the way and bought Midori an armful of Iris, a deep purple bloom, shot through with white edges as though a light snow had dusted them.

He was sitting in the car waiting for her when she arrived at her apartment. She didn't see him, and was going up the steps when he slipped up behind her, catching her around the waist at the door. She squealed, delighted, and fished in her bag for the key. She brought out the futon and they were on the floor in a few seconds. The Iris lay in a bundle beside them, forgotten.

"God," said Luke a little later, "I missed you so much in just one day."

"I know. I could hardly concentrate on my classes."

Luke groaned a little. "I'm lovesick," and he let his head fall to her breast.

She raised his head and looked into his eyes. "I don't want to be in love again."

"You're right. We have important things to do. I can't concentrate on the work I'm doing."

"We've become too close," she said.

Luke laughed softly, suddenly teasing her. "Just because we're cousins?"

She slapped his ass so hard it hurt, and pushed him off her. They lay without speaking for a minute.

"Do you want to break it off?" she asked almost harshly.

The expression was so American, so idiomatic; he thought; he couldn't believe she'd said it.

"I want to take you back to the States with me," he said after some reflection.

It was Midori's turn to ponder. "We're too close," she said.

He knew what she meant. "You mean biologically?"

"Yes."

She turned over and started to play with him. "We can be lovers. I like that. But we can't be husband and wife."

He watched as she fondled him, his passion rising. How could they talk this way and caress at the same time?

"Midori, this isn't your first affair, is it?"

"I told you, I was engaged to be married."

"I mean, have there been others?"

"I'm an emancipated woman. What does that tell you?"

"Did you love him?"

"Who?"

"Your fiancé."

That puzzled her for a moment. "You mean was it miai-kekkon?"

"Yes, an arranged marriage?"

"Obviously not. It was ren'ai-kekkon."

He knew the term. "A love match."

"Yes. But ren'ai-kekkon doesn't necessarily mean romantic love. It means that a couple makes their plans independently, without the service of a go-between. The couple negotiate themselves with the families."

"Did his family approve?"

"Reluctantly they did, but not happily. I was a university graduate and I had a profession. I was a teacher. They could forgive us for following the demands of our hearts."

"What happened?"

She shrugged. "They found out I'm from Tabara."

"How?"

"I don't know. They learned I was Eta."

She trembled slightly. "He was weak. I told you he renounced me. That's not quite correct. He suggested Shinju."

"You mean joint suicide?"

"Yes. I refused. It is a detestable custom. It only satisfies the masochistic tendencies of those who watch. They glory in the tragedy of lovers drowning themselves, jumping off cliffs, or burning themselves to death in their own houses."

"Would I be going too far to say you didn't love him enough to die with him?"

She laughed softly, almost harshly. "He didn't love me enough to commit suicide alone."

"So, who renounced whom?"

"It was a double renunciation," she said quietly.

"The question still is, did you love him in the first place?"

"Yes." She hesitated. "Yes and no. I think it was infatuation more than love. I wanted to be accepted. I was alone. He had a good family, *sarari*, salaried middle class. I had nothing."

She seemed to muse. "Our sex was good." She began to stroke his chest, entangling her fingers in the hair.

"Like ours?"

"Not like ours. He didn't have your body. Yours is perfectly proportioned."

She stroked him as though he were a domesticated animal. "You should know that Japanese women adore Eurasian men. They're so hairy."

She stood up to look him over. "You're a blend of East and West, cousin."

He laughed. "A mongrel."

That offended her. "No. Eurasian. A fusion of physical traits. I wish the cultures of East and West could be mated so well."

Midori laughed, a slight taunt in her voice. "You are Ainoko."

He didn't know the word.

"It means crossbreed."

Luke stroked her inner thigh playfully.

"It's not complimentary," she said softly. "It implies an illicit relationship and an illegitimate issue."

Luke felt a little shocked. "A bastard? Even if the child is legitimate, the result of marriage?"

"Yes."

"You mean that there are racial overtones in Ainoko?"

"I believe so. The Japanese pride themselves on their racial purity."

"Then you're saying the Japanese are racists."

"As much as white men, perhaps more. The Japanese have always thought of themselves as more than a nation, rather, a race apart, separate from the Mongoloid, as from all other races. They're like the Jews. They think they're special people.

Luke could agree to that. The old expression, "they all look alike," had some validity when it came to the Japanese. "They are homogenous," he said, "as though they had been stamped into existence by one of their robot machines."

Midori had become quite still. "How do you feel about it?" he asked.

She rolled over and got on top of him. "I think you are aware of how liberal I am. I'm certainly not a racist."

She began to rough him up a little. She was hardly gentle in her play. "I told you, hairy men fascinate Japanese women."

"We could have a love child," said Luke.

"No, we couldn't. I've taken precautions. I take the Pill."

She had surprised him again. "You little devil, marry me."

"I have a profession and a cause. I don't want to think about marriage again."

He rolled her over, going between her thighs. "You need love, not a cause."

Her legs went around him. She sighed. He was relentless, driving into her.

"We're too close," she whispered.

"There are enough children in the world. I can be fixed. Say yes."

"Yes," she said breathlessly.

He strained. "Say yes again."

"No."

"We're too far apart," she said later.

"Lord," he said, exasperated. "First we're too close, now we're too far apart."

She was resting on his chest, her face reflective. "I mean, politically we are poles apart. I'm a communist in spirit and you're a capitalist in every way."

Luke laughed at that, thinking it was true but silly.

"Technically speaking, maybe I am. Right now I'm a capitalist's errand boy. Have you decided what kind of communist you are?"

"I know exactly what I am."

"Well?"

"A seraphic communist."

The term was only vaguely familiar to him. He thought of nineteenth century French communism, but nothing came clear. "What is seraphic?" he asked at last.

"Pacific communism, non-violent."

"Not Marxist?"

"In no way. Marxist-Leninist socialism was aggressive communism, brutal and authoritarian. The communism I favor can be advanced through education. In the long run, the training of minds, millions of young minds, will have a greater impact on society than the rhetoric and machinations of politicians and ideologues."

"Mind power," he said skeptically.

"There's more to it than that. Japan is on the way to becoming a corporate democracy, a planned society. That's really what Karl Marx envisioned, not the brutal dictatorships which so many have evoked in his name."

"Well," said Luke, "while you are enlightening, I would say conditioning, the minds of children, the authoritarians on either the right or the left will be running things for their own advantage."

She scoffed. "I don't see that. I don't see them running anything."

"You mean in Japan, don't you?"

"Yes."

"I have a theory. What if the Right is around today and can't be seen? Then what would you say?"

"I would say that even then they are so few as to have no power, no influence in this country."

"You don't think the Right can come back in Japan?"

"Anything is possible."

"I think they are around, and they are seeking power."

Midori got up and went to arrange the Iris for display. She knew the art of Ikebana. Kneeling on the tatami mat, she skillfully arranged the blossoms into a fan shaped bouquet. Finished, she came back to stand over him again, giving him the pleasure of tracing her figure with his eyes. She had a neat body, he thought, but not perfect. The belly was a bit too round, the thighs a little thick, the legs short, the feet too big, peasant's feet.

He pictured Kiah's body by contrast, the fine taut breasts, flat stomach, long shapely legs and small feet.

Why did he compare the physical attributes of the two such dissimilar women, he wondered, the one a whore; the other an intellectual? Kiah was athletic, ultra feminine, a professional sex machine. Midori was all mind, passion, reason and eroticism combined in fascinating proportions. He lusted after Kiah, a physical thing that dominated him; but he realized just now that he wanted Midori's love, the possession of her mind and body. That was quite a difference.

She reached for a kimono, slipping it over her shoulders, dropping another over Luke's head.

He pulled the kimono off his head and slipped it on. Midori went to heat water for tea. Luke got out the collection of photographs and spread them on the floor.

"Do you recognize any of these men?" he asked.

She glanced down at them. "No. Who is the woman?"

"One of their mistresses, but that's another story. Do you see any familiar faces here?"

She shook her head. "This sounds so mysterious. Why do you keep talking about the Right?"

Luke wondered if he should tell her. He decided he'd better not admit to being an industrial spy. He couldn't bring himself to injure her idealistic view of things. Besides, he wanted her respect as much as her affection.

"I'm trying to trace a leak in our company's security," he said, "and the trail might lead to some of these men."

That was general enough, he thought, perhaps true as well. It was a white lie.

She poured the hot green tea. They sat informally before a low table, he cross-legged; she in an unlady-like posture by strict Japanese etiquette, sitting on one foot, the other leg drawn up. She had set out chagashi, tea cakes, resinous and somewhat tart but delicious with the slightly bitter green tea.

"I have a question," he said, "really more like a hypothesis. All these men, with the possible exception of the four large photos that shows a woman, were officers in the Japanese army at the end of World War Two. I have read that one of them, if he is still alive, is an amateur historian. He claims to be an expert on military history, World War Two, that sort of thing. He gives, or used to give, public lectures. Does any of that sound familiar?"

She shook her head, sipped her tea, and searched his face with a serious stare. "Isn't there more here than you're telling me?"

"Yes," he answered, faking it a little, "more than I know or can tell you."

She didn't like his evasiveness. "What you're doing sounds like government work."

Luke grinned. "You probably think I'm with the CIA."

"Are you?"

"No, this is really company business. Can't you think of any clues or contacts that would help me?

Midori gave it some thought. "A professor at the university might know of an amateur historian, especially if he is socially prominent."

"Do you know of one?"

"Yes, I do. He was one of the few professors who took an interest in me."

Luke became eager at once but she cautioned him. Professor Iwata, the one she had in mind, might not be at the university during the summer months.

When Midori came back to the apartment the next afternoon, she had good news. Professor Iwata was not teaching but was in the city.

That evening they drove to his house. It was in one of the middle class suburbs near Tokyo University, tucked away behind a high fence overgrown with vines and shrubs. They were punctual in keeping their appointment.

Iwata's daughter, a dumpy middle-aged woman, had met them on her knees, sliding back the wood and paper latticed door. Midori mumbled polite expressions of greeting. They went down on their knees, bowing deeply, their hands on the platform before the door, then rose and took off their shoes before going inside.

Watching, Luke concluded that tradition had remained unbroken in the Iwata household. There was not a sign of western furnishings, the main room almost bare, typical of the Japanese home, and so sterile in the eyes of the westerner. The woman went to another door, knelt, and slid it back. Professor Iwata came into view at once. An old man, his pale, almost transparent skin was stretched tight over fine bones. The face was long, with a sloping forehead, a receding hairline and prominent teeth, all the clichés and stereotypes that serve to describe the oriental professor. He was sitting on his haunches before a low table, a kimono wrapped about his frail body. He bowed low, not speaking.

Luke and Midori went in and settled down opposite him. They exchanged smiles and polite words, the formulae of conventional greetings. Then Luke was introduced. The old man's keen eyes studied his face. The exquisite conventions of the middle class Japanese gentlemen did not allow for personal questions. Luke volunteered no information; he let Midori do the talking.

The subterfuge, which she had accepted with reservations, was plausible. Luke posed as a journalist, engaged in writing a popular account of the American Occupation of Japan from 1945 to 1952. He wanted to see it from the Japanese point of view, from the angle of one who had been there and remembered the events.

"I don't want to lie to Professor Iwata," Midori had said when he proposed his strategy. "He was one of the few teachers at the university who befriended me. I owe my position to him."

Luke felt pained to insist upon it. He didn't want to use her, yet he had no choice. He had kissed her, cajoled her and she had agreed with reluctance. Resigned to deceive Iwata for his sake, Midori performed well. Luke was free to play the role of the interested and ignorant, albeit intelligent, American journalist. He knew only English. That was the ploy. Midori translated for him. Iwata, once drawn into the complexities of the history of his own period, became engrossed as only a scholar might be. Luke took notes as a journalist should. Periodically, Midori turned and translated for him in English, a charade, but an effective one. They talked of the Young Tigers; of Seppuku, the honor of taking one's life when one has failed to serve the Emperor. They discussed nationalism, militarism, pacifism, traditional values in a world becoming rapidly modernized; indeed too westernized from the professor's point of view.

Luke was touched. Midori had returned to sit at the feet of her teacher. Her regard for the old man, his respect for her, was self-evident. Forgotten was Eta, her dirtiness, her barbaric origins.

Luke asked if the professor knew the book, *The Surrender*. Midori handed it to him, and Iwata perused it quickly with professional interest. He had read it and pronounced it a sound work.

Luke expressed his desire to interview the author.

"Unfortunately," said Iwata, "that would not be possible. He died several years ago."

It seemed the entire generation was falling away at a rapid rate, Luke thought. Disappointed, he took out the photographs and laid them on the table. He watched the old man carefully, and he thought he detected a sign of surprise, a slight emotion on his wrinkled face. The professor picked up one of the photos and looked at it carefully.

"This was my relative," he said, and laid it down.

"Was he a close relative?" asked Midori.

"He was not in the chain of my house. I knew him only slightly before the war."

Luke asked if he was still living.

"No," said Iwata. "He passed away several years ago."

Luke wondered if he might have been one of the Young Tigers and watched the old man's reaction.

"I do not know," he said carefully, his wise old eyes penetrating as he looked at Luke. "They did not reveal themselves openly, as you might suspect."

"Were they afraid of retribution?" asked Luke.

"Those who obeyed the Emperor in those terrible days of August could not forgive the Young Tigers."

Luke wondered if there had ever been a secret organization or a reunion of the Young Tigers from time to time. The old man didn't know, and Luke felt immensely disappointed. There was nothing more to ask, but then suddenly Iwata told Midori that he recalled hearing one of the Young Tigers speak after the war at a university seminar. The professor picked up another photo. "This is the one."

"Do you know his name?" asked Midori.

"No. I'm sorry."

Again, Luke was disappointed, but almost immediately Iwata said that he could find out.

"Did he give lectures only?" asked Midori, "or was he an author also?"

"I remember that he published articles for some years. I may have something in my files. If you wish to telephone me tomorrow afternoon, I can tell you."

Luke was delighted and made no effort to hide his pleasure. It was all part of the plan. Abruptly, Iwata clapped his hands sharply. They sat silently for a few moments.

"We shall have tea," said the professor.

The sliding door opened, and his daughter entered with a tray. She knelt and placed the cups before them. Luke hurried to pick up the photos, careful to place the two that had been identified in a separate pocket.

The tea drinking at the end of an interview, itself long, was somewhat ceremonious and lengthy. Luke slumped a little, his back beginning to pain him. His legs, curled under him had become numb. He wondered how he was going to get up. Midori and the professor, rigidly upright on their haunches, betrayed no signs of discomfort. He marveled at Japanese discipline.

Eventually, they departed after a few deep bows. Driving back to the apartment, Luke was effusive, gratified with the success of the visit. Midori was unusually quiet.

"I feel that I have betrayed the old gentleman," she said softly.

Luke hugged her. "You haven't harmed him. Believe me."

He hesitated. "Will you call tomorrow with any information you get?"

"Of course."

In the afternoon, when she had returned from school, Midori gave Luke more than he anticipated. She had the man's name and a fact of particular interest. He had retired recently, his last occupation the publication of a magazine with a small circulation, devoted to Japanese culture.

The title of the magazine, *Tradition*, caught Luke's attention. He had seen an issue at Akada's mansion. He wondered if that was significant, or just a coincidence.

The professor got us a lot of information," he said. "I wonder how he did it."

Midori laughed. "I wonder if you can guess."

"No."

"*Who's Who.*"

Luke was surprised, feeling a little stupid. "Really?"

"Yes. Professor Iwata told me so."

"It didn't occur to me that Japan published a *Who's Who* in the American manner," said Luke.

"Have you forgotten," Midori said archly. "We've been Americanized."

Luke went to the city library the next day and spent several hours in an alcove going through past issues of *Tradition*. He had carried with him a tiny, powerful camera. By the end of the day he had taken some notes and a number of photographs, among the latter, a picture of a gothic castle, identical to the one he had found in Megen's apartment. The brief article that accompanied the photograph of the castle described it as being a private museum on the island of Hokkaido. The article did no more than summarize and critically appreciate a large collection of medieval artifacts, mostly military. The castle's precise location, date of construction, means of access, museum membership: all these critical points of information were not given.

In examining the issues, year by year, he discovered that the publication began in 1955 and ran in quarterly issues without interruption until 1981 when it was suspended. The first quarterly issue of 1965 had instituted a new masthead. Threaded into each thereafter were diminutive intricate characters. As Luke read them, he felt the hair on his scalp prickled slightly with the discovery: Kan Pai Nichi. To The Day. He realized now where he had seen the motto for the first time, the nagging shadow of a memory that would not give up its secret. He had read it, perhaps subliminally, while sitting in Akada's mansion in Note. Was it coincidence? Or did it signify something important?

Chapter 14

"You're like a dog with a bone," said Mark

He was watching Luke toy with the medallion, swinging it like a pendulum, his lips pursed, brows knit in thought.

Luke didn't answer.

"It can't be that important," said Mark after a while.

"It's got to be associated with some clique, some group," Luke said finally. "Japan is full of gangs, some legal, some outside the law. They're called *yakuza*. Grampa told me when the American MP's wanted to trace someone involved with the black market they never went to the Japanese police. It was a waste of time. They located the *yakuza*. One lead took them to another. It was like layers of informers, gang after gang, interconnected like the strands of a spider web. I think if we ever get a solid lead, it will open one door after another."

"But what are we looking for?" asked Mark.

"We won't know until we get that first lead."

"Kiah could be it."

"Could be. But, number one, if she knows anything she's too scared to talk. Number two, she's stopped communicating with us."

Luke got up all at once. "Let's get an expert's opinion."

They drove around Tokyo until they found a jewelry shop that looked appropriate for their purpose. It was one of the older establishments that didn't cater to the junk set, the tourists with too much money, too little taste, crowding in for cheap jade and ivory carvings. This one was run by an old man with a wispy white beard, thick glasses, a round face and a perpetual smile radiating gold fillings.

Luke laid the medallion on the counter. Mark wandered around the tiny shop while Luke put some questions to the old man. Not much was said. The jeweler examined the medallion with a magnifying glass, pointed out a couple of things that Luke realized he should have recognized. He thanked him. The jeweler bowed deeply, following them to the door.

They came out into the bright sunshine, Luke looking at the medallion with a little more interest than before.

"What did he say?" asked Mark.

Luke unlocked the car door, and they got in. He pointed to the small loop at the top of the medallion. "See this? The old man pointed out that this loop is made of a different alloy than that of the medal."

"So what does that imply?"

"It appears that Megen, or someone, had a jeweler attach this loop so that it could be worn as a necklace."

"What do you conclude from that?"

Luke started the car and began to pull out into the traffic. "Obviously, the medallion was not cast originally to be worn as jewelry."

"Just as obvious, it had another purpose," said Mark.

"Ah, but to what purpose," said Luke with a pretense to gravity.

They drove through heavy traffic for a few minutes. "Damn!" said Luke. "I just had a thought. Serendipity!"

"What?"

"Serendipity. You know, finding something you're not looking for."

He shot Mark a quick look. "What if the thing they want so much, and is worth the lives of six people so far, isn't the Tushimi formula, but something else?"

"That's a riddle," said Mark. He thought about it. "You're saying they want the medallion."

"Or to protect whatever it stands for. It must represent something very important."

"Maybe it's like a cipher, you know, a key for unraveling a set of clues."

Luke was meditating. "That sounds pretty Mickey Mouse to me, but anything is possible."

"We have the photographs," Mark said hopefully.

They decided to have them enlarged and drove around until they found a photo shop, small, modest, with a humble patron to assist them. In half an hour they were back in the car with large glossy prints, big blow-ups. The details were distorted and grainy, revealing nothing to them.

"I keep coming back to this one," said Luke.

Mark agreed. "It's that castle. So western, so out of place in this country."

"I'm not talking about the castle," said Luke. "See that?"

He pointed to some numbers in the corner of the picture, barely discernible. The angle of the shot had caught the limousine from the left rear, capturing a corner of the license plate, just enough to reveal three numbers. They were still not quite legible.

"If that's a Japanese license number," Luke said, "we'll have a solid lead."

They went back to the photo shop and had the picture enlarged further. The numbers came out clearly.

Luke called Masuro and the obliging detective was able to tell him what he wanted to know. Luke closed his cell phone, a little excited.

"What did he say?"

"The three numbers are a prefix for a Hokkaido license plate."

"For sure?"

"No doubt about it. That limo is registered on the island of Hokkaido."

"Who's it registered to?"

"Masuro can't tell us."

"Why not?"

"He's not allowed to by law in the first place. In the second place, we have only three numbers."

"How did you con him into giving you the information?"

Luke shrugged. "I told him I'm looking for another relative in Hokkaido. He bought it."

As they started driving back to the hotel something flashed in Luke's mind. He hadn't told Mark, had forgotten himself, not considering it significant until now.

"Kiah told me that the discs came from two computer banks, one in Kyoto, the other in Sapporo."

"I know, you told me, and Sapporo is on the island of Hokkaido," said Mark.

"Here's another fact to recall. Walt and Harry were killed while flying to Sapporo on company business. Just a coincidence?"

Mark laughed ironically. "The world is full of coincidences. We should go to Sapporo."

Luke nodded. "You bet. But I think the first thing to do is to check out the editor of that magazine *Tradition*."

"What for?"

"We might learn a lot, providing we could find a way to get into his house."

Mark was dubious. "I hear the Japanese are very private people. You don't just call him on the phone and say. Hello there, I understand you are a former Young Tiger. Will you tell me about your past treason? I want to publish it in the newspaper."

"Spare me your sarcasm, Mark. You know we would have to do a number on him."

"What about Midori? She arranged the interview with the professor for you. That turned out to be gold."

Luke was interested. "What angle are you thinking of?"

"If Iwata believes you are an American journalist and Midori is willing to play go-between again, he might use his influence to get you an interview with the editor of the magazine, what's his name?"

"Sakomizu."

Luke considered it worth a try. He went out to see Midori in the afternoon, stopping to buy some oranges, California navels, and a bundle of roses.

He parked near her apartment. It was a long wait. Eventually, he slid down behind the wheel and dozed. He awoke with a start. She had slipped in the car, sitting beside him, enjoying his startled expression. He straightened up, pushed the roses into her lap and leaned over to kiss her, crushing the flowers between them.

It was a breathless kiss. Impatient, they went upstairs and undressed. Their bodies mingled. It was through her flesh that he reached her soul, touched the intimacy of her mind. She got up from the futon and went for the oranges. Kneeling beside him, she peeled one. The slender fingers, glossy nails like living knives exposed the soft fruit. She fed him, a slice at a time; one for him, one for herself, giggling, laughing. It slaked their thirst, consummated their love tryst.

He was beginning to think that she gave him more than her body. He could not decide which he admired more; her conversational skill or her adeptness in love. To possess her physically, and then enter her brain thereafter was a unique experience, erotic and cerebral. He could never make love to an average woman again, he thought. With Midori it was like intellectual pornography, a sharing of their minds and their bodies. Somehow, sophisticated conversation with the brilliant woman turned him on, carnal delight.

"I thought Japanese women were modest," he said teasingly, as he caressed her.

"They are."

"In the public baths they display themselves. They bathe naked with strange men around."

"But didn't you notice the barrier separating men and women?"

Luke scoffed slightly. "It's hardly a wall. I've been there."

"That's such a western attitude, Luke. It's a matter of decorum. Westerners stare, rudely I might say. We have a habit of looking past what we don't want to see, sort of like the eye sees but the brain does not."

"Uh huh. The proverbial blind spot."

She laughed. "Well put. I'm sure you are aware that when women are out of the water, they conceal themselves with a wash cloth, the tenugui."

"That's modesty?"

"I think so."

"They don't cover their breasts."

"Bare breasts titillate westerners. Not us."

"The woman's breast is a sex organ, Midori, as much as her genitals."

He nibbled at her nipples gently.

She pushed his head away, annoyed. "Westerners consider nudity of any kind, if not immoral, indecent."

"Not so much anymore. The West is changing. Public display of the genitals is common in the entertainment business."

"We Japanese would not go so far," said Midori, conviction in her voice.

He laughed. "Except in the striptease, Sutorippu. Believe me, I've been there too."

"Don't you have striptease entertainment?"

"More than tease, total nudity. But I was joking. You meant the urban Japanese, generally, didn't you?"

"Yes. The rural Japanese are more casual about nakedness and bodily functions. Like my people."

"Very much like the French," Luke said.

"Were you shocked by my family?"

"Probably not. Just embarrassed by my own hang-ups."

She giggled. "Aren't they barbarians? What did you think when I took off my blouse on the beach?"

"I thought you had perfect breasts."

"I noticed."

"What?"

"I noticed that you noticed."

"Say again?"

"Your erection. That made me think I wanted you."

Luke was flabbergasted. "You were bolder than I thought, Midori. Are all Japanese girls so free in their thinking?"

Midori became sober. "Freer with their thoughts than their actions, I think. There are reasons for that. I don't have family restraints for one thing. And I'm a single woman, alone in a big city. I was engaged to be married for a year. I learned all about sex and I enjoyed it."

"Straight sex," said Luke skeptically.

He had challenged her. "It was good enough for us," she said finally.

That led to some silence. Finally, Luke said, "Is it good enough for us?"

She held his gaze, thinking, finally "No, it's not good enough for us. We're different. I want us to be different. I gave it a lot of thought last week."

He rolled over and hugged her. "You're a natural girl."

"That's true. No hang-ups."

Luke realized that Midori was not quite the defenseless waif he had imagined on first meeting her. She controlled her emotions better than he did. In a moment of ecstasy he had been moved to say, "I love you." She placed a finger on his lips, silencing him. "It's too soon to speak of it," she said, and made love the more ardently.

Later, at rest, she said she could not give him her heart.

"It would hurt so much when you go away," she said.

Naked, side by side, their talk turned to politics. It was then that Luke discovered her nature, and the root of her radicalism. He had considered Kiah to be hard, the most independent woman he had ever known. Midori was just as tough, but with a soul and a purpose which enhanced her feminine character. There was a melancholy side also that he found disconcerting, something of a contradiction.

"I have considered suicide more than once," she said.

She saw the surprise on his face. "Many in Japan do."

"Americans always find that mystifying," he said, "Why is it so common? Why is it considered respectable here? There are other countries that have a high suicide rate, but only the Japanese approve, as though taking one's life is a legitimate alternative to living."

"That's because so much is demanded here. It is so easy to fail in Japan. Life is so difficult. The Eta cannot pass, even when they succeed."

"Shameful," said Luke, pitying her.

Midori seemed offended. "There is no shame in suicide, if it is for the correct reason. The shame is not to acknowledge failure. The shame is to impose one's failure on another."

Luke sighed. "So much emphasis on shame. I don't know if I will ever understand that outlook. The whole country is suicidal."

"That's extreme," she objected.

"In 1945 the entire nation was prepared to die rather than surrender."

"That was wartime madness. It could have happened to any people."

"You don't think the Japanese are fatalistic?"

"That's another question entirely."

"But are they? Are the Japanese people fatalistic?"

"Yes, I think so," she said quietly.

Luke was surprised at his own insight. "I think I see a connection between their fatalism and their acceptance of suicide as being a societal norm."

Midori was interested, turning over to give him a stare.

"Isn't sacrifice as old as Japanese culture?" he asked. "I mean Shinto, reverence for one's ancestors?"

Midori didn't answer.

"Karma is from the Buddhist religion, isn't it? It's fate."

She thought she knew what he was getting at, but quarreled with him anyway. "I don't believe in reincarnation."

"It doesn't matter. Do you have Karma? That's the question."

"Everyone has Karma. It's a moral absolute."

"Alright then. Karma, the moral absolute, is connected with the Shinto tradition of sacrifice, the veneration of ancestors. The individual, inclined to destroy himself on moral grounds, can be collectivized in times of crisis, to commit suicide on a mass scale. That is what gives the Japanese such tremendous drive as a people, their fanatical discipline. That's why for most of their history they have accepted an authoritarian figure to rule them, whether it's the local boss of an agricultural community, or the whole country, ruled by a divine emperor or a military dictator."

Midori thought about this. "That tradition has been broken," she said finally.

"How about the Samurai tradition?" he asked.

"Dead," she said flatly. "They were really gangsters of the Chicago variety."

Luke couldn't suppress a grin, wondering if Midori knew of the Italian godfather stereotype, since she had just evoked it. She saw his deprecating grin and it challenged her.

"Really, Samurais were victims of their own inferiority," she said. "They turned it against the common people, terrorizing them. Given life and death powers over any others than themselves, dependent upon the Daimyo in turn, they exhibited that double standard I mentioned before. Toward their superiors they were obedient, even supine in their acquiescence; but toward those inferior to themselves they were savage. On any pretext they might behead an innocent passerby. Is that a glorious tradition? Is that civilized?"

What could he say? thought Luke. Obviously not.

"Samurai who didn't war with each other became the administrators of the lord's fief. Their bureaucratic tyranny, their suicidal devotion to enforcement of the rule, was institutionalized until the Samurai mentality became an official attitude permeating government from top to bottom. It's that way to this day."

Luke had heard about Japanese left wing student rhetoric. Midori had learned her lessons well, combining what she knew of Japanese history and culture. It seemed plausible, and if true a condition which nothing could change. He thought she was suggesting that the Samurai outlook was more than tradition, perhaps a part of Japan's inherited character.

"So, if it's in their genes," he said, "why do you think the authoritarian tradition is broken?"

"Because we are finally eliminating poverty which bound us for ages to masters whose only purpose was to exploit us. There was a time not so long ago when poor farmers had to sell their daughters into a form of slavery, legal prostitution, just to keep the rest of the family intact. Those days are over and will not return."

"That sounds like a Marxist critique, human exploitation."

"I'm not a Marxist. It's a pragmatic assessment. You can't see it because you are an American. You Americans, in your great majority, have never known grinding, abject poverty. You have so much space, so many resources. You live in a huge country which reminds me of a great mansion full of fine things; while all of you, a little family, go idly from one rich room to another."

Luke raised his head to look around her tiny one room apartment, nearly devoid of furniture. For lack of it, they lay on the floor, a thin mattress between them and the bare boards. Plain, not unattractive, the apartment nonetheless reflected her material poverty. She earned just enough to pay the rent, buy food and the necessities of life. The natural inflation of a rampant economy kept her poor and needy.

"The struggle for survival is cruel," she said. "We have to work so hard. I think that is why we are a sentimental people. We love pathos. Kabuki fills that need. We need tragedy to entertain us, to remind us that even a tragic life is worth living, up to death. That is why we give ourselves to pleasure and religion so easily."

These were depths beyond Luke's comprehension. All that she had said seemed contradictory. She had told him already that she was a communist.

"Can one be a communist and be religious at the same time?"

"Yes, I am."

"Which religion do you accept? Shinto?"

"No."

"Buddhist?"

"Partly." She laughed, almost gaily; striking to him, how she went from melancholy to humor in a flash. "It's radical, as you might guess, both theological and political."

"A cult?"

"No. I wouldn't say that. More like a popular movement. It's called Soka Gakkai."

Luke puzzled over the word for a moment, "Creation, or value, or something like that. I read something about it."

"Correct. It means Creative Value. It is a secular movement, affiliated with a Buddhist sect, Nichiren Shoshu."

Her intelligence, her militancy, the boldness that first startled him in their sexual relations, left him a little intimidated. He could see how a poor girl from a rural segregated community might have been able, with sufficient financial aid, to surmount the notorious school examinations of the Japanese educational system for six years. But he wondered what unity or intellectual integrity could be found within the diverse radical movements she espoused.

"What are Buddhists doing with communists?" he asked teasingly, reaching over to ruffle her hair. "Does atheism and Nirvana become helpmates at some point on the socialist calendar?"

She resented his patronizing tone and pulled his hand away half angrily, trying to explain how Marxism could be adjusted to national peculiarities. Confucianist China had retained its familial tradition while adopting Marxist economic ideology. Japan, although Buddhist and Shinto in faith, was able to modernize without forsaking its traditions.

He wanted to know about Soka Gakkai.

"I gather it's political?"

"Yes. We have a party, Komeito, Clean Government. It is the political wing of Soka Gakkai, as Nichiren Shoshu is the religious wing.

Luke had to laugh. "Clean Government? Do they operate out of a bath house?"

Midori was offended by his cynicism. He had not been so sarcastic before. "I admit it; there is much party corruption, especially bribery, in Japanese politics."

"Graft is everywhere," Luke said gently. "Everybody's on the take."

He was suddenly embarrassed. An industrial spy, he could hardly assume a high moral stance. He was on the take, well paid to steal the secrets of his company's rivals. She had struck a nerve without realizing it.

"Not everyone is on the take," she said firmly.

He shifted the ground of their conversation. "Is Komeito Marxist?"

"No. I told you, it's Buddhist, secular, but spiritual, very moral. In the beginning Soka Gakki had been organized in cadres, like shock troops of the faithful."

More gangs, he thought cynically, religious gangs in this case. Through the women, tied to the house, Soka Gakki cadres attempted to reach the husband, tied to his place of employment, locked into another gang, the job affiliation that ruled him. Through the liberated woman, Soka Gakki would emancipate the enthralled man; deliver him from the domination of the gang bosses.

Luke recognized that the Japanese have a penchant for organization, an apparent need for regimentation. He had read of group activities which boggles the ordinary mind: groups of honeymooners, couples newly married beginning a conjugal life, join the aggregates of dozens, under a regime something like a tourist trip. All the facilities, as well as the felicities, are arranged with the precision and foresight that one would expect for an extended vacation. Where the newly married American couple seek privacy in a brief period reckoned one of the most precious in their existence, their Japanese counterparts give themselves to their fellows, seeking collective friendship in joint matrimony.

To organize the Japanese masses on the double bases of political action and religious certitude did not seem remarkable to Luke after all. The attempt had been made before. It had led to a military dictatorship, thereafter the conquest of Asia by dedicated Japanese soldiers. One necessarily thought of the Kamikaze pilots in World War II, suicidal in their faith. Soka Gakkai promised a moral revolution, the creation of a perfect society, without the need for foreign conquest without conventional suicide being a mandate. Was it possible? And he had to wonder which predominated, the political or the religious.

Midori anticipated his question. "They are equal. The values of one are suffused with the values of the other. That is Creative Value. Religion without politics is sterile. Politics without religion is amoral."

"What or who would unite religion and politics this way? Do you have a guru of some kind?"

"No," she said quickly, and then wanted to think about it. "What do you mean exactly?"

"Do you have a spiritual leader?"

"Not the kind you're implying. We're too democratic for that."

Luke scoffed. "All great religions have had a spiritual leader: Buddha, Christ, Mohammed, the Japanese Emperor, god-king of Shinto. Who is the founder of Soka Gakkai?"

"We're too modern for that," she retorted, slightly annoyed. Soka Gakkai just happened, fulfilling the people's needs."

That made him think. "Can you see the possibility of Soka Gakkai reuniting religious fervor and nationalism with the person of the Emperor a token?"

"No!" she said, almost angrily. "That's absurd."

Luke wasn't convinced. Soka Gakkai sounded like a theosophical doctrine. Strange, yes, but he could see why it was the impressive movement she described, the fastest growing cult in the country. National in its extent, with cells in every prefecture, its emotional base was a new nationalism;

not chauvinism of the old order, but national pride in touch with the past. Its political goal was social democracy. It seemed unique. But was it? Soka Gakkai sounded to Luke ominously like the totalitarian phenomenon of the 1930s: national socialism, a popular fanaticism; the Japanese masses again harnessed to the national will, mesmerized by the remote figure of the god-emperor, fascinated by the industrial and military elite's command to accept once more Japan's divine mandate to govern the universe. It seemed like fantasy, a script for Hollywood's film directors; in the eyes of pragmatic Westerners to be considered not so much a danger as a ridiculous posturing. But the thought was real, and Japanese ambition had been unveiled before, after long seclusion and introspection startling the world.

In Harry and Taki he had seen the belligerence and racial antipathies of the 1940s; he thought he saw the emotions and ideals of the same era being reborn. It seemed Midori had gone so far to the left she had arrived on the right. Totalitarian ideologies, left and right, always coincide on the same plane for action. She didn't seem to recognize the dilemma into which Soka Gakkai drifted.

He left her and went back to the hotel, regretting even a day away from the fascinating and demanding, radical, intellectual Midori. Mark was restless, however, and in his breezy way reminded Luke they were being paid princely salaries in the service of industrial piracy. They should earn their pay.

Chapter 15

Luke forgot to ask Midori about the editor of *Tradition*, a mental lapse not very different from a slip of the tongue. He didn't want to talk to her about Sakomizu, the Young Tiger, now an old tiger. His visit had been carnal, the need to penetrate her, body and soul. He had come away more satisfied, intellectually and emotionally; more determined than before to insulate the vulnerable woman from the world of force and deception in which perforce he moved.

"Can Midori help out?" Mark asked.

"No."

"Why not?"

Luke hesitated to say. "I decided not to ask her."

Mark wasn't sure whether he should pursue the matter. He asked anyway. "Why not?"

Luke couldn't tell him how much he had come to care for Midori, or the tangled motives that made him keep his occupation a secret. Industrial espionage is hard to defend. It can be rationalized, justified for the satisfaction of the one who engages in it. It is the way of the world, the way neighbors relate, the secret way in which they take from each other treasured thoughts. There is power in ideas, in symbols printed on paper; and, if the possessor will not relinquish them, they will be taken from him. Spying must be a form of social control, Luke thought, as surely as gossip that serves to discipline society by inhibiting its members. But neither espionage nor gossip can be justified in the eyes of those who see each for what they are: sins of some proportion, illicit invasions of privacy, hurtful, cunning, destructive of individuals. He wasn't going into all that with either Mark or Midori.

"I don't want her to get involved," he said simply.

That was enough for Mark. "You must have changed your mind."

"Yes and no. Midori's out of it. But we still ought to investigate Sakomizu."

Mark thought they were getting off the track again.

"What about Kiah? She's our only contact."

"What about her? She may be out of the country by this time. When did we see her last? I can't remember."

"About two weeks ago at least."

"We don't even know if she has the other half of the information."

"Do you realize," said Mark, "in terms of solid information, we're really no further along than the day we got here?"

Luke knew it. A little glum, they went to a bar, Mark's choice. One of the hostesses came up, slipped a familiar arm around Mark as he sat there. This was the girlfriend Luke thought, looking her over. Mark had good taste in superior tramps. She had adopted an American nickname, Jackie, a cute name like her personality. Her adopted American slang and clichés appealed without doubt to the humorous Mark. She was sharp, pretty, with bold eyes, an evident pleasure, and she knew how to please. Her English wasn't bad. Another Kiah, he thought, but without the special beauty of the Eurasian; not as firm and self-contained as Kiah; more like the geishas they had encountered at Akada's house, eager and adept in the social arts.

Mark made a date with her, and she went away with a show of reluctance to leave, that little regret which entices and makes the waiting seem more worthwhile.

"You know how to pick 'em," said Luke. He didn't mean it entirely.

Mark didn't know how to take that. "Listen, while you were spending time with your cousin I had to think of something."

Luke tried Mark's brand of sarcasm. "You mean the hotel's procurer let you down?"

Mark liked the banter. "I'm sorry, I need a permanent friend."

Luke pretended to be crestfallen. They moved into a booth, seeking a little more privacy.

"We can still work together," said Luke.

Mark pretended to be relieved. "What can we do?"

"We can find a way to get into that editor's house."

He caught Mark flatfooted. His mouth fell open a little. The jokes suddenly turned into something deadly serious.

"What the hell for?" he said finally.

"The Young Tiger, the old tiger now, isn't going to give us an interview, right? We can't arrange a charade like the one I used to talk to Professor Iwata."

Mark shrugged. "You're in charge of charades. I'll take your word for it."

"Believe me, there is no way we can go out to that old man's house and ask him about World War Two."

Mark was a little mystified. "Why do you want to talk to him anyway?"

"Because he was a Young Tiger, a rare animal by now, maybe the only one still alive. Let's suppose he was eighteen years old in 1945 when they tried to kidnap Hirohito. He would be eighty-seven now."

"Jesus!" Mark breathed hard. "You are obsessed with this. He would be among the walking dead."

"Maybe so, but that's all we've got going for us. Kiah is doubtful. We don't have any other contacts. Two of our people are dead. We're being threatened by someone we don't know. The Brass is pushing us for the information."

Mark wanted him to let up. "OK, OK, I see all this. What's your scheme?"

"I think we should slip in and search Sakomizu's house. Under no circumstances would he tell us what we want to know, even if we could arrange an interview on some pretext to get into his house. Our object would still be to make a search."

"So, we break in. Then we can go to jail for a long time."

"Only if we get caught, which we won't."

"Yeah, but an old guy like that must have a lot of security. You know what I mean? Dogs, bodyguards, electronic warning systems, the whole bit."

Luke was patient. "I have to believe you're right."

"What's your plan then?"

"We begin by scouting his place. We'll stake it out for a couple of days and try to see if there is a pattern to the old man's activities."

"Once a cop, always a cop," Mark said dryly. "How do we get his address?"

"We have it. The professor got it for me."

"Then it's cut and dried," said Mark, resigned.

They paid for the drinks and left the bar. "Cut and dried." Mark was a man with a thousand clichés, thought Luke. But he was loyal, and he had enough courage. What more could he ask for?

In five years on the Honolulu force Luke had probably encountered every trick and device which human intelligence can invent for getting into guarded places. It was as though his mind was a file, and from the appropriate drawer he must draw the blueprint that would best suit the present situation. For that some long hours of surveillance were required.

Mark had to be disguised: a wig of straight black hair, a phony mustache, the kind a Japanese dandy might sport. Luke diluted a bottle of iodine with alcohol and tinted Mark's face; a jaundiced complexion, eyeglasses with thick lenses. Sitting in the car with only his upper extremities showing, he could pass for a middle class Japanese gentleman in a neat business suit.

"Now there's a real Jap," Mark said, looking in the mirror.

"A walking caricature," agreed Luke.

They each changed cars at different rental agencies once a day, parking a different vehicle near Sakomizu's house every few hours. After two days, they could sum up their observations. Sakomizu lived alone and never left the house. Two men served him. In appearance they were domestic help. In another way the difference between the two men was remarkable. One was an Arab, easy to identify. He wore street clothes, a working man in appearance, but the visage was decidedly Middle Eastern. He was evidently hired for the night shift.

"That's the second Arab we've seen," said Mark. "The one we saw at Akada's house was wearing a long flowing gown and fancy headdress like a real sheik. This guy looks common as dirt."

Luke was mystified. "Arabs are rare in this part of the world. The big question is what are Arabs doing with a man like Sakomizu?"

"A hired hand, I'd bet."

"Yeah, but why would Sakomizu hire an Arab. The guy doesn't fit in."

"He looks like a bodyguard," said Mark.

"Probably armed," said Luke.

"And meaner than a junkyard dog," Mark added.

The other man was Japanese, evidently a domestic servant, working the day shift.

They decided the best time for their purposes was early morning, in that brief interval when the bodyguard was leaving and the day servant had not yet arrived.

"We still don't just walk in," said Mark.

"Sure we do," retorted Luke, "as though we had every right."

He had in mind one of the oldest of ploys used by confidence men. They spent a few hours driving around Tokyo's suburbs until they found what Luke was looking for.

"What are we after?" asked Mark.

Luke didn't answer directly. "A city this size, built on medieval foundations, has got to have a problem every day, somewhere."

After a few hours they came across a city crew, repairing a water main. Luke pulled up close and parked. He watched for a while, took some notes, made a few sketches then got out of the car. Mark watched while he talked to the man in charge. There were some gesticulations then Luke was escorted to a nearby curb and given a brief demonstration. After that, he came back to the car, and they drove away.

"What was that all about?"

"I told the foreman of the crew I was a reporter doing a story for *Nichi Nichi*, the Tokyo newspaper. He obligingly showed me how to shut off the water to each house on the street."

"How you lie," said Mark, his voice disapproving, a big grin on his face.

"You would have made one hell of a criminal. You know that, don't you?"

It sounded like a compliment, but it wasn't really. It touched a nerve for Luke. "They used to say at the Honolulu station, associate with criminals long enough and you begin to think like one. That really meant the only way you can track them and figure them out, is to become one of them. The line between the law and the underworld is always a hazy one," said Luke. "I think that's why I could adjust to security work so easily. In a way, I've been doing this for years."

"If the line is so blurred, what is the difference? Or is there any?"

"There is a difference."

"What is it?"

"Knowing what the line is and where the line is. The criminal has no integrity; he doesn't recognize any line between right and wrong."

That was a way of saying a criminal is what he is, a crook. But a spy is something less than that. It was all rationalization, Luke thought. He was straying close to the doctrine that a criminal is a pathological creature, incapable of knowing right and wrong. Courses in penology he had studied came back to him. How far over the line had he gone this time, in being loyal to the company, obedient to his superiors? He didn't want to think about it.

They drove back to the inner city and looked through a municipal phone book until they located a shop dealing in stage costumes. Mark remained in the car while Luke went in to tell the proprietor that he was preparing a neighborhood stage play. He needed uniforms that were as similar as possible to those worn by Tokyo maintenance men. After that, they found a rental store and picked up some tools.

It was evident to Mark what the scenario would be. Luke told him anyway. "We're going to shut off Sakomizu's water. He'll be glad to let us in. Once inside we'll look around, innocently you might say."

The next morning they rented a van, blue to match Tokyo's maintenance trucks.

"We ought to have a city emblem," said Mark.

Luke didn't think so. "You'd be surprised how little people notice official logos. They remember later, if at all. Con men count on human nature performing according to habit. In uniform, with tools, a van in the street, we will be accepted for what we appear to be: servants of the city of Tokyo. I'll keep Sakomizu preoccupied with my excellent Japanese while you look around without his realizing what we're up to."

Their timing was good, arriving about the time the Arab bodyguard was leaving. They watched him get in his car and drive off. Luke got some tools and went to shut off the water. They waited about ten minutes then Luke went to the gates and pushed the call button. Repeated efforts elicited no response from the house. A little puzzled, he came back and got in the van.

"What do you make of it?" asked Mark.

"Odd. We'll wait."

They waited without talking for about twenty minutes. Luke went back to the gate and tried again. Still no answer, he returned to the van.

"I don't like this. I wanted to be in and out of there in a hurry, like a thief, so to speak."

They waited another half hour. Luke tried once more. No response, he came back. "Let's go," he said.

Mark started the van and pulled away. "Do you want to scrub the operation?"

"No, first I want to get this van out of here. It can be traced to us."

"What about the water? It's still off."

"Shit, go back!"

Luke got out of the van and turned the water back on and they drove away.

"Let's return all this stuff," Luke said suddenly. The operation was over without a doubt.

"What do you think happened? Mark asked over a cup of coffee a few hours later. "That house seemed deserted this morning."

"I have a feeling something's gone wrong."

"Gut reaction," said Mark. "I think so too."

Another cliché, Luke thought, but it described his feeling exactly. "I told you, people generally don't pay close attention to what seems to be normal. They remember the peculiar circumstances later, when something exceptional makes them recall the details. Take that bodyguard coming out of the house this morning. We watched him for two mornings in a row and got used to it, right?"

"Right."

"Did you notice what kind of car he was driving this morning?"

"No. Wait a minute, it was a different car. I remember now."

He stared at Luke. "Why didn't we notice that this morning?"

Luke ducked his head, annoyed. "Because we're normal." We had things on our minds. I'm supposedly the pro. Now, that raises the question: Was that the same bodyguard we saw this morning, or was it another Arab?"

Mark couldn't resist a joke. "They all look alike, you know."

Luke was getting a little nervous. "We shouldn't have stayed there so long. It was taking too big a risk. If something has gone wrong in that house, people in the neighborhood will remember the blue van. It won't take the police long to trace it to us."

"What the hell have we stepped into?" asked Mark.

"I don't think we stepped in, so much as we've just sunk a little deeper."

He gave Mark a hard look. "We've got to find out what's going on in there. I think we should go back."

Mark shook his head stubbornly. "No way man, we're digging ourselves a grave."

"Listen," said Luke sternly. "If the police come knocking at my door, I want to know why."

Mark couldn't be convinced. "We're still clean. We haven't done anything illegal." He grinned weakly. "Except shutting off the water."

Luke had to laugh at that, mocking Mark. "A mere misdemeanor my good man. Look, here's what we'll do. I'll rent a car and go out there, posing as a pollster. You know the kind. They knock at the door, in this case ring at the gate, and bore somebody to death with a dozen questions on their survey sheet."

"What do you expect to gain from that?"

"Simple. If someone is there, he'll answer the buzzer. If there is no answer, we've got some difficult questions in front of us."

"Yeah. Like, do they have the Fifth Amendment in this country?"

Luke grinned. "I think MacArthur forgot to force the Bill of Rights on the Japs. Anyway, you can stay in the car this time."

"No disguise?"

"No."

"Thank you. I hate that iodine treatment."

It was afternoon by the time they got back to the house. Luke had purchased a clipboard and a tablet, ready to pose questions, as a pollster might. But there was no answer to repeated buzzing at the gate, and that gambit was dead. He came back to the car and threw the clipboard in with a show of disgust.

"Let's go," said Mark.

"No. I'm going in."

He said it firmly, a low tone almost savage. Mark had no doubt about his determination.

"I'll stay here."

That went without saying. Luke backed up to the wall and parked, got out and went onto the hood and from there to the roof of the car where he could look down on the other side. Nothing moved. He stepped onto the wall and dropped down into an enclosed garden.

A domestic Japanese house is about as resistant to intruders as a matchbox, a structure of light wood and oiled translucent paper. An impatient man might run through it without much resistance or injury to himself. Luke moved up to one of the sliding doors and tested it, prepared to force it open. It slid back at first try.

He went inside, stopped and listened to the kind of silence that rings in your ears. There was no one in the house. He knew it, he could feel it. He checked out a tiny room off the main one. It was a typical antiquated kitchen, not much more than a sink and a tap. A small refrigerator took up most of the space.

He went back across the main room to another set of doors and slid them back. He stopped abruptly, stunned by what he saw. A man, in black ceremonial gown, had fallen forward, face down. A pool of dried blood from the crumpled body was largely absorbed by the tatami mat.

"Hara-kiri," Luke said softly, almost disbelieving. He went forward, knelt down trying to see the face without the need to turn the body over. The twisted visage, only partly showing, fixed in rigor mortis, would have been almost unidentifiably in any case, contorted by pain and the death throws. The man had to be Sakomizu, he thought. Ceremonial immolation had gone out of style in Japan long ago. Only an old Young Tiger would still accept the excruciating pain involved in ripping open one's belly.

Luke straightened up. There were questions coming to mind. How long had Sakomizu been dead? Why had the bodyguard come and gone in different cars? Where was the day servant? Why suicide at this late date in the life of the Young Tiger, now a decrepit old man? Some crisis had risen without doubt, involving personal honor, to be atoned for by a painful death, the way of the Samurai.

He began a search that brought him here in the first place. There was nothing in the closets, only some clothing and bedding; no papers. He opened a small chest, went through its interior drawers, finding nothing. He rifled the garments, felt a solid object come between his fingers. He reached into a jacket pocket and brought out a small black box, something like a jewel case. Inside a medallion rested in a molded velvet setting, the rays of the rising sun glinting on one side. He turned it over and saw the replica of the mushroom cloud, and around the edge of the medallion the inscription: Kan Pai Nichi.

Luke's heart beat a little faster. He slipped the case into his jacket pocket and looked around a little longer. The absence of files, of papers of any kind in the house of a Japanese intellectual, was a puzzle. He started back across the central room toward the garden when he noticed that the heating table, which normally stands over the pit where the warming hibachi is kept, had been moved to one side. He knelt down and detected for the first time the distinct odor of charred paper. The hibachi was nearly full of fine black ashes. He poked a finger into the mass, felt slight warmth at the bottom and knew where the papers had gone. Some evidence of importance had been consumed by fire; thereafter the owner of the papers had consummated his life with steel. But why?

Luke looked at his watch. He'd spent enough time in the house. He went back to the garden, sprang to the top of the wall and stepped down onto the roof of the car. He was inside and had started the engine almost before Mark could recover from his surprise.

"What did you find?"

"You won't believe it," said Luke as he drove off quickly, not quite speeding. He didn't want their departure to attract interest in the neighborhood but he wanted to get away fast.

"Is Sakomizu in there?"

"Yep, he's there, spilled his guts, you might say."

He dropped the jewel case in Mark's lap. Mark opened it, staring at the medallion. The expression on his face told it all. For once he didn't have a wise crack for the occasion.

"We'll watch the newspapers," said Luke. "We'll wait."

Chapter 16

"Everything we touch turns to shit."

Mark's pessimism amused Luke. "Or suicide."

They were soaking in hot water, buoyed up, watching the women scrub at the faucets.

"I knew we shouldn't have gone back there."

"It was worth the risk," said Luke. "We've discovered another medallion."

"Big deal. We still don't know what it means."

"That's true. It doesn't have any intrinsic meaning so far, but finding another one means that if there are two, there are more. Medallions are generally cast to commemorate important events, or to serve as a bond for members of an organization."

"A keepsake," said Mark as he watched a good-looking female at the faucet.

"I think we've stumbled onto some sort of a brotherhood, Mark. Consider the connections, like links in a chain. First, there is Megen's medallion, converted to jewelry so she could wear it like a pendant. Let's suppose her boyfriend gave it to her. He was, or is, a Tushimi executive. Maybe he's a member of the brotherhood, or gang or whatever you want to call it."

Mark grunted enough to keep Luke going.

"So, Kiah puts us in touch with Megen, but she commits suicide. We suspect that it was really murder. Why? Because she was probably caught in the act of stealing and trying to sell Tushimi's secrets. The next medallion we find is stashed away in the home of a Young Tiger, an intellectual who had made himself a philosophical spokesman of Japanese conservatism. He commits *hari kiri* about the time we locate him."

"OK," admitted Mark. "All true. How do you size it up?"

"Tushimi, the multinational corporation, is in some way connected with a right wing military faction that was disgraced and driven underground over sixty years ago.

"Thought provoking," admitted Mark, "when you put it that way."

"The problem is," said Luke, "the Young Tigers did not commit ceremonial suicide to atone for their disgrace when their plot to depose the Emperor failed. Their candidate, a nobleman named Anami who intended to become a Shogun, a modern dictator, did disembowel himself; his followers did not. Why would a Young Tiger, one of the last of these old men, commit suicide at the end of his life, when he had a much greater reason to do so in 1945?"

"Beats the hell out of me." Mark said. "Why do you think?"

"Because I think they had something to live for, not to die for, in 1945. That's part of the answer, once you get inside the Japanese mindset, or better to say, the Samurai mentality."

"Doesn't make sense, Luke. Now you're saying Sakomizu had something to die for."

"It does make sense from the Japanese viewpoint. The custom Giri means everything to the Japs. Shame is something they can't live with. They prefer to die."

"What's giri?"

"Something like the honor involved in one's obligation to another, or to his peers. It's usually translated to mean saving face."

"Enough to commit suicide?" asked Mark.

"You bet. The Young Tigers were part of the tradition bound generation. Through allegiance to Kan Pai Nichi they have probably raised a second generation of Young Tigers, by now a third is probably on the way, dedicated to the destruction of the enemy they refused to surrender to in 1945, not then, not now. You see, it's a family thing"

"So the United States of America," Mark said softly, "is their eternal enemy. Have you stopped to think who our latest external enemy is?"

Luke had figured that out. "Al-Qaeda," he said, "and that explains the Arab presence, doesn't it?" The Arab we saw at Akada's mansion had a name that sounded like bin Laden, maybe a relative, maybe a son for that matter. They say bin Laden sired a huge family, maybe thirty children."

"You know," he said, "I'm beginning to think that Kan Pai Nichi is a brotherhood of believers. One of them must have made a mistake so big, they're liquidating everyone implicated. This much is certain, every paper in that house was either burned in Sakomizu's hibachi or carried off after he took his own life."

"I wonder why."

"Sakomizu sacrificed for something he considered larger than his own life. That's the Samurai way. It looks like we're going to keep stumbling into murders and suicides as long as we keep poking around in their business."

"Sure," said Mark somberly, "as long as we stay alive."

He absentmindedly flailed at the water, girl watching forgotten for the moment. "This isn't exactly what I had in mind when I signed up. The job was to make contacts, pick up information; Walt and Harry would confirm it and we would all be back in LA in about two weeks. What's happened instead? Everything has turned to puke."

"We've overlooked one thing in all of this," said Luke.

"I wouldn't doubt it. What?"

While we were watching Sakomizu's house, we were being observed. Have you thought of that?"

That sobered Mark a little. "No doubt. It's so easy to forget. They're watching us, whoever they are."

"We must have been closing in on something important, so important they destroyed the evidence and the owner as well."

"He destroyed himself," objected Mark.

"But he is one of them," Luke said. "Don't you get it? The brotherhood disciplines itself."

"Fantastic. But what I don't understand is why they don't confront us, or wipe us out? Why this cat and mouse game?"

"Beats me. We're being played out on a string, but we don't know why."

They went back to the hotel. The next morning Luke found a message waiting for him, a plain unmarked envelope, very familiar by now.

Kiah's renewed contact came as a surprise. He had just about decided she would not contact them again. He opened the envelope, with fingers a little impatient, finding another ticket. This time it was a masu ticket, to Sumo wrestling.

In the afternoon he went out to the Kokugi-Kan, a stadium designed for witnessing Japan's major sport, Sumo, a vast amphitheater so huge he couldn't quite believe it. Looking down on the sloping seats to the distant arena in the center, he estimated the number of spectators to be in the many thousands, all blocked off in individual cubicles, masu, a half dozen spectators hemmed into each little corral.

It seemed to him that even the venerable sport of Sumo had been reduced to group action. In each little enclosure bands of spectators sat or squatted, ate, drank and socialized, paying only periodic attention to the athletic pageant being conducted below them in the arena. It was the occasion, not the sport, that drew them; the fellowship that marks Japan's collective way of life in a thousand ways.

The usher took his ticket, led him to his masu, and relieved him of his shoes. At the usher's suggestion, Luke ordered beer and went in to sit down with the others.

Kiah was already there. If she was aware of his arrival, she didn't show it. Her attention was given by turn to the pageant below and several Eurasians sitting with her. Luke realized as he sat down they were konketsuji, "mixed blood," half-caste. Some were middle-aged men, about his age or a little older. They gave him an impassive stare, as though not surprised, expecting him. There were no introductions. He took his place next to Kiah as though he belonged there. In some sense, he thought he did.

Kiah gave him a glance that seemed devoid of recognition, and then turned her attention back to the arena where the champions had begun to come out of their dressing rooms.

The presence of several half-castes, and he one of them, sitting penned up in a single masu, seemed bizarre to him. One of the konketsuji sitting next to him was a Japanese Negro. The mongoloid and Negroid genes had combined to produce the distinct features. Kinky hair, saffron skin, the thick lips of a Negro, the oblique eyes of the oriental, reproduced in his person the salient features of two races.

Kiah never failed to arrange an exotic setting for their meetings. But what did this particular encounter signify? For once, Kiah was not entirely alone. These were evidently her boon companions. That was another mystery, he thought, another enigma, she the enigma within the larger enigma; a puzzle inside a riddle.

She turned to him about this time, and he spoke to her in English.

"Speak Japanese," she said, quickly turning her head toward the others. "They don't understand English."

Luke complied. "Who are they?"

"Friends," she said simply, and went back to watching the first match. The beer arrived and was distributed. For the next fifteen minutes they watched with interest as two immense fat men, naked except for the brief loincloth, contested each other's weight and sense of balance. Mountains of moving fatty flesh, hard smooth muscles and large bellies, the wrestlers engaged each other, beating their feet and bawling like bulls, insulting each other. It was a theatrical display not very different from professional wrestling in the States, Luke thought, the theatrical combined with the athletic; producing a show, partly serious and partly burlesque. A championship was at stake.

Sumo wasn't to his taste, Luke decided, massive pectoral plates of gigantic men on gnarled little legs, bulbous bellies, gargantuan appetites producing distortions and distention of the body. It was like meat accumulated to excess on stubby legs, a weight almost too great for the puny members to support, so that it seemed the wrestlers collided with each other in an obligatory crouch, always about to tip over. It was grotesque, excessive, like all things finally perfected in Japanese culture, overdone. He was glad when the preliminary matches had been completed. Now, the crowd awaited the appearance of the principal performers.

He turned to question Kiah and found himself silenced by a loud roar coming from the crowd. The wrestlers had begun to enter the arena, attended by their bodyguards and sword bearing escorts. The ceremony which followed was prolonged, a rigid etiquette. In precise movements each competitor made his obeisance to the Emperor's seat, which Luke noticed was empty.

Sumo is more than show business, he concluded. It is both an art form and a national ritual. Wrestling, a mundane thing, like arranging flowers or drinking tea, had been invested with traditions of symbolism and mannerism. The ceremony seemed to be as important as the outcome between two massive men who were roughly equal in size and ability.

They watched the remaining matches, until the final victory by the strongest man seemed certain. Then they all got up to leave, Kiah in their midst. Nothing had been said so far. Startled, Luke got up to go with them. They collected their shoes and went out on the street, somewhat in advance of the main crowd beginning to leave the stadium.

He came abreast of Kiah, a question on his face.

"We'll talk now," she said.

"Where are we going?"

"Sento," she replied simply, the universal word in Japan, public bath. There could not be a more private place in public for discussion, Luke thought.

The Sento was nearby, a five minute walk, accomplished in silence. It had been open only a few minutes when they arrived and was virtually deserted. He and the other konketsuji went into the men's dressing room and stripped without words or an exchange of glances. They seemed like aliens, from another world, as though they were strangers with nothing in common. None had volunteered a name. Luke considered it unwise to ask questions. Japan, he had come to learn, is a land of gangs, many gangs. That the konketsuji was a gang, or part of a gang, seemed apparent to him now. Elaborate tattoos on some of the naked bodies told him what he had learned at another time. They were likely affiliated with criminal gangs, Japan's underworld; and Kiah was obviously a part of that world.

They left the dressing room to scrub at the faucets, ladling the cool water over themselves with dippers from the buckets, still not speaking. Luke wondered whether his presence, a stranger, inhibited them. Silent in any case, they began to get into the pool, settling slowly, letting the hot water soak in a little at a time until at last submerged up to the chest.

Kiah took her time undressing. When she appeared, Luke was struck again by her physical beauty, her naturalness. She came out slowly from the women's dressing room, statuesque, erotic to him in her nakedness. Generally, Japanese women in the public baths hold in place modestly the tenugui, the washcloth or small towel, much like a fig leaf. She did not have one. Women bathe separately from the men, the sexes separated by a low wall, hiding little. Kiah chose to bathe with her companions. Luke kept to himself, his eyes on hers as she washed and rinsed. There was still something between them, something more compelling than desire. He wanted to know her. The possession of her body was not enough. She was more mysterious than before. He still thought to know her was to unlock, to explain, the essential questions for which he still did not have answers.

The medallion hung around his neck and he moved closer to show it to her once she had settled in the hot water. She seemed not to recognize it, disinterest on her face. He had a dozen questions for her. First the formula. Did she have Megen's half of the information? She said yes and his heart leapt up with anticipation, then his hopes were dashed. She was engaged in negotiations with another buyer.

"We had a deal," he said almost harshly.

Kiah seemed not to be intimidated. "Things have changed."

"How?"

"I told you before. Now that Megen is dead things are different."

Luke slapped the water in his frustration. "We've already bought one of the discs, Kiah. Either one is worthless without the other."

"I know that."

"Does your prospective buyer know that?"

She didn't answer at once. He wondered if there was in fact another buyer. Was she lying? Luke repeated the question. "Do you have another buyer?" He wanted a firm answer.

"Potentially, yes."

"Does he know what's going on?"

"I can't say. I don't care either way."

"You're going to sell him worthless merchandise?"

She laughed, dipping down, concealing for a moment her fine breasts. "Let the buyer beware. You bought, didn't you?"

He stared at her. Their eyes were hard, unrelenting. "You should give us first refusal," he said at last.

Another smile. "We might."

"Who is the other buyer?"

"An Arab. He speaks good English. We have an understanding."

A microchip knows no nationality, he thought. It is above commerce, a technology that touches upon military interests, space exploration, and the domination of the planet. Why wouldn't the Arabs or any other nationality have their own agents in Japan? They were all seeking the ultimate power in electronics, always getting closer to the acme of power, controlled power, invested in sub-atomic structures. The genius of some Tushimi mathematician had been replicated on a disc, and now had a street value. How much? He had to think. Probably the price was greater than money, greater than human lives, more than could be paid by any corporation or any state. How much did she want, he wondered.

"One million dollars," she said suddenly, as if his thought was hers.

He was surprised to think he was not surprised after all. Somehow he had known it. He had speculated with Mark that she would probably blackmail them, selling them one disc, then jack up the price for the second one. There might not even be another buyer. She could be bluffing but he wasn't going to bargain for long.

"I'll have to contact the home office," he said as though thinking out loud.

Kiah was confident. "We can wait a few days."

She kept saying "we", he noticed, where before it had been me and I. He wondered why the collective and the plural had entered her vocabulary.

"You must need a lot of money," he said, trying for a companionable tone.

"We need a lot of money," she replied.

She looked in the direction of the other kondetsuji, and he had a suddenly insight. These were the "we" of whom she spoke, street people, second generation, and perhaps third generation, produced by the illegitimate orphans American servicemen had sired in 1945 and left behind thereafter. Midori called them Ainoko, crossbreeds. He was one of them without thinking about it. Because his father had been smuggled into Hawaii he had been raised as an American boy. He had enjoyed a normal youth. But the many Ainoko had not been as fortunate as his father. The estimated number fluctuates tremendously, from as little as five thousand to as many as one hundred thousand of these unfortunate children. The progeny by now might be approaching a million. Why such large and imperfect statistics? Because the Eurasian children, technically Amerasian, were an embarrassment for both the Americans and the Japanese. They were unwanted bastards, fathered by one race, disowned by the other. Most were orphans, outcastes as surely as Midori's relatives were, the unwanted Eta. Growing up in the poverty-stricken back streets as cast off children, dying in such large numbers from disease and neglect that perhaps half had perished before reaching puberty. The survivors had made their way in gangs onto better streets, to receive their final education in Japan's underworld, learning how to survive; but more than that, to prosper frequently by their wits and cunning ways.

He suspected that Kiah was such an issue, sprung from Japan's urban seams, as Midori had sprung from Japan's rural spaces. The love and generosity of Christian missionaries had given Midori a lease on life, a chance. Kiah had received nothing but what she could take in her own way. He realized suddenly, buoyed up in the hot water, facing the delectable Kiah, that she, like himself, like Midori, was Eta, outcaste, unacceptable to Japanese society. Beautiful, she was unwanted, except for her carnal attraction.

Pearl Buck, a sensitive author, once pronounced Asia's love children "a new breed of people who can be the strongest, most beautiful, and most intelligent in history." Such a judgment surely applied to Kiah, Luke almost smiled at the thought; she, Cleopatra of the multinational world. Circumstances had driven her into an area of industrial crime where her sex and beauty could be used for survival. In knowing her a little by now, she had changed somewhat in his eyes. The carnal attraction was not less than before; but she seemed more than a mere object of his attention, more than a female magnet drawing him; rather, one who deserved his sympathy. She was a love child, Ainoko; but she was loveless, probably incapable of the feeling. For the moment, she was prepared to talk business, but no more. She was also evasive. Where would they meet next time he wondered. She couldn't say. When would they meet again? She did not know. She would send him another ticket.

Luke wondered if she would go to the Arab buyer after this and raise the ante. How many tickets was she sending out and to how many buyers? In their last meeting Luke had detected what he thought to be her insecurity, her fear of those she had betrayed, the omnipotent Tushimi people, still another gang. Now, she seemed quite at ease. He wondered if that had been an act. He suspected that she and her gang lived in Japan's underworld comfortably, enjoying a day-to-day opulence, a kind of security, unknown to most. It is protection gained by layers of influence, trading in favors; that kind of illegal immunity that insulates the successful criminal element from the harassment of the authorities, leaving them free to conduct their business. It is a condition of free enterprise that operates in every great city, from Tokyo to Chicago, Paris, Rome and around the world. Layers of influence connect Tokyo's underworld to the highest levels of international intercourse, carnal intercourse, most appropriate for Kiah's type. In her brief life she had learned to ascend and descend the escalator of crime and vice, from the streets of Tokyo to the bedrooms of the multinational corporations in Honolulu, and back again.

In some ways she was worldlier than he, more experienced. What she lacked was a soul and a philosophy. He could desire her, but he could not love her. He could care for her, pity her, but he could not give her his affection. She was human, but she was animal. She was just Kiah, a beautiful creature. They were both the product of the now almost forgotten American Occupation. Through her he thought the medallion might be traced to the violent Right wing in Japanese politics. But it was only apparent to him that she did not know the medallion. Her indifference to it was not feigned, he was sure, but a real ignorance and unconcern for its symbolism. Mundane crime and great ideological causes are rarely allies in any case.

Through Midori he had found that the medallion did not connect with the pacific Left, the anti-nuclear, anti-war community of believers. The Left, not being associated with the medallion, only the Right remained. But which Right? As there are two Lefts, pacific and violent, there were two Rights: the expansive, aggressive Right of the future, of progress and authoritarian social control; and the old Right, the Right of the past, of tradition, opposition to progress; withdrawn and enamored with a time when social control came about through familial ties and religious sanctions. Would it be the Right of the Young Tigers? Or the Right of the new technocrats? It occurred to him just now that the Old Right and the New Right might have combined. It didn't matter. It had nothing to do with Kiah or the information he sought.

She had moved away from him and joined the others. They talked little, almost out of range of his hearing. He realized she was the leader of these half-breeds. The confidence in her manner implied it; their deference toward her confirmed it.

It seemed strange to him, beyond calculation, that these strikingly attractive Eurasian street children, naked in a public bath, should discuss a business deal worth millions; while he, another Eurasian, stood by, an impotent witness. He heard them call her bosu. She had a title, "boss," traditionally limited to the male leader of a Japanese gang. She was their mistress, in terms of authority, but did she furnish them sexual favors as well? Was it sex that gave her power over them? Or her will and intelligence? Then, she was leaving the bath, without an adieu or a backward glance, with the rudeness she had always displayed; offering her finely molded back a final view that would remain in his memory: the slender figure, the tight butt and long legs, water running down the saffron flesh, as she walked to the dressing rooms.

The rest of the group was leaving the bath, as though her departure was the signal to follow. The gang, the authority of the group, the relapse of the individual into the collective action, was played out once more. At every level, he concluded, from street gang to bands to the clubs of corporate executives, it was a predictable behavior, whether in a noble man's mansion on Note or in a bath house in Asakusa.

He was alone in the pool, more informed, but also more unsettled. Half-Japanese, wanting to know a country to which he belonged by blood ties, he had to ask himself if he could relate to a society too much in unison, moving to concerted themes, regimented actions, as though orchestrated by a force larger and more inscrutable than life itself.

An astute critic of Japan has characterized this life form as a thermal drive, pristine energies arising out of the quaking earth, animating a whole population; a human anthill constructed on one of the world's most unstable geological faults; the frantic creatures are never at rest, always building, always working against the next inevitable disaster.

The metaphor seemed too grim, too zoological for Luke. Once upon a time divine power; the way of the gods, manifest in the Emperor, a living deity, had energized these people, giving them unity of action and purpose in life. But the way of the gods has lost favor with most of them by now. The Emperor remains, but only as a symbol. What now is that force which drives them to collective actions? As he would not want to be a lemming running to the sea, he would not want to be a Japanese running with the pack. But where were they going? What was their purpose? The hedonist would reply the pursuit of pleasures in this life. The pessimists would say for survival in a world of unrelenting competition and an unforgiving nature.

Chapter 17

Luke thought it was like being marooned in a ring of fire, a cauldron beneath one's feet, the ground in perpetual motion; the threat of fiery destruction, of being swallowed up by the unstable earth; the danger always present, conditioning all of one's waking hours. He could never be at ease in an environment that was at once precarious and threatening. There was something to be said for the idea that Japanese character, volatile and disciplined at the same time, is the result of ages of living in a land tempestuous and punishing, inscrutable in its silent loveliness, yet terrifying beyond comprehension when the earth quakes, cracks, groans; the land is shriven, and the molten lave comes boiling to the surface.

He had lost track, ceased to count, the number of times the ground had trembled perceptibly beneath him, each occasion a moment of transient fear, suspense forcing the adrenalin through his body. Lying in bed at night, in the most silent hours when most are inert in slumber, he could feel the slight continuous tremors of an unseen force, the earth beneath him in silent motion.

Japanese fatalism, an apparent religious and secular resignation, is perhaps a response to the stupendous forces of nature, always hostile, often consuming puny human lives. Small in stature, the Japanese can only feel further diminished in the presence of such sublime and destructive power.

On the other hand, ironically, cruel nature furnishes in abundance the pleasure and convenience of hot water, flowing from crevices at numberless points, an estimated thirteen thousand hot springs. On nearly every principal site where thermal water appears, there is constructed an inn, the Onsen, offering both rooms and hot baths. Life is easy it seems when attuned to what nature can provide.

Luke and Mark took Midori and Jackie on a weekend stay at one of these Onsen, a three-hour trip by train then another twenty minutes by taxi, into the foothills southeast of Mount Fuji. They chose accommodations complete with romansu-buro, two rooms and a private bath heated by nature, sparkling and pure.

After dinner they returned to their rooms, undressed, donned a light kimono and went to the bath. Midori and Jackie seemed comfortable with the arrangement. Mark and Luke betrayed the qualms of the Westerner, still not adjusted to intimate mixed bathing. In the recent weeks time they had frequented the Sento and were accustomed to bathing with naked strangers. In the presence of lovers, compounded by friendship and erotic relations, they were ill at ease.

For a time the women involved themselves with each other to the neglect of their men, two Japanese women who wanted to know each other. Midori had told Luke Japanese do not stare. They look past what they do not want to see. It is the condition of their little country. They see but they do not see. Midori looked past Mark and saw what she wanted to see of him. He was, like Luke, fairly big and heavy muscled. She liked men with big chests and flat bellies, narrow hips and a tight hard butt. He was well hung, like Luke, maybe a little smaller in that area. But, then, one never knows what that amazing organ will do under the stress of excitement.

She stared frankly at Jackie, thinking they were miles apart. She was a professional woman, salaried and independent. Jackie lived on small wages, she imagined, supplemented by tips. Presently, she was mooching off Mark and he was paying for the undoubted pleasure of her company. In the nude, Jackie showed what she had become, thoroughly westernized. Slight, almost invisible lines of past surgery gave evidence she had reshaped her bosom with silicone implants. Her breasts were large and full, and like most well endowed western women, they were heavy but uplifted to the maximum. Midori thought Jackie had what the western men call approvingly "nice boobs."

Unlike Midori, Jackie was not slant-eyed. Like many young Japanese women who aspire to western styles and physiognomy, she had paid a surgeon to snip crucial muscles, allowing the fold to slip up enough to eliminate the apparent slant of her eyes. Midori envied Jackie's boobs, thinking she was nonetheless content with large breasts that spread out too much. It didn't matter to her. Luke liked to fondle them, kiss them and in their love play suck them and that was enough. She was more than content with the "Mongolian fold," rather admiring her slant eyes, thinking her appearance was exotic, which she would emphasize whenever using cosmetics to enhance the attractive features of her face.

In the midst of her reveries Mark and Luke were getting out of the tub, announcing they wanted to go to their rooms. Obediently the women followed their men, one step behind, as custom requires.

Luke and Midori, still slightly damp, scrubbed fresh, tasted each other's flesh. They fused, as if one, and fell into a light sleep for a time. When they awoke, it was dusk, just light enough for them to see each other.

"What are you thinking," she asked dreamily, still half asleep, his head on her breast.

His brain was a whirl of thoughts and emotions. The weekend stay at the Onsen had been his idea. Sometime, somewhere, someday, he would reveal himself to her. This seemed to be the time and the place.

He wondered if he was being unduly theatrical, to think that he might not see her again. The forthcoming trip to Sapporo promised an unknown conflict, a danger he could not specify, yet sensed. He felt vulnerable, vaguely threatened. Perhaps even at this remote spa his unseen and unknown rivals watched. He who spied was being spied upon; of this he had no doubt. He had to consider in a way, not clear to him, that he brought his danger closer to Midori. Would they harm her? Should she know what she had gotten into?

"Let's talk," she said, stroking his back after he had been silent for some time.

"I was thinking that I love you."

"Don't say that."

"It's true."

"Think it, but don't say it. To say it once is enough for me to remember it always."

"Do you love me?"

She thought about it. "I think so."

"Say it then."

"It's not the right moment."

He raised himself to look down upon her in the dim light. "You want some fun this weekend, some pleasure." It was a question. She didn't respond.

He could just make out her form, all color gone in the gloom filling the room. He saw the outline of her breasts, rounded belly and crisp mound of black hair.

"I want to enjoy you," she said, legs parting, pulling him down, straining to drain him again, drawing him to a climax until a mutual orgasm relieved them both of their torment.

They rose late the next morning and joined Mark and Jackie in the dining room. Luke was surprised to find that Mark had been able to order an American style breakfast.

"What do we do today?" asked Mark.

The choices were few. A small tennis court was already occupied and the swimming pool was well populated by now. Luke looked in the direction of the women. Both were silent. He suggested a walk. They went to the desk and asked for a local map. Paths patterned the environs of the Onsen, most leading up into the hills. They chose a route that would take them to a noted teahouse, perhaps three miles away.

"We can have lunch there," said Luke, "then come back later in the afternoon."

He discovered on this excursion that Jackie, like Midori, was a rural girl having come to the city to escape the menial existence of the village. Unlike Midori, she was probably not Eta. But who could know for certain? That social curse is never acknowledged by the victim, the secret taint not openly searched for by strangers. It is the ingrained stain that only comes to the surface when Eta threatens Ippan the respectable ranks of Japanese society. It is not unlike the American doctrine, "Don't ask, don't tell." He concluded that Jackie had chosen to be a hostess for economic reasons only. Unlike Midori, she was poorly educated, shallow, but nonetheless a fun companion in the bath or on the trail.

Midori was enchanted, delighted to return to the countryside. They stopped often to admire a view, to examine a tree or a blossom. The remainder of the morning was required to cover a relatively short distance.

By early afternoon they emerged from a dense cryptomeria grove into a small clearing. The teahouse, an almost tiny structure shrouded by vines and small trees, was probably ancient and preserved both its sparse character and an elaborate tea ceremony.

The entry into the house, the preparation of the tea, the drink and lunch, lasted several hours. Eventually, refreshed and rested, they started back on a different path downhill to the Onsen.

After a light meal, they went to their rooms to undress, then went to the bath, lovers seeking pleasure in hot water. A day and a night together, and a previous exposure in the romansu-buro had changed their psychological relations fundamentally. The women seemed bolder and the men more at ease. This time the sight of the two women, nude before them there was an erotic tension that had been absent the previous day. There was less to say, and they remained in the bath a shorter time. They took the women to their respective rooms with greater haste than the day before, eager to satisfy the desire they saw in their eyes.

Contented, Midori said after a while, "Jackie has a better figure than mine."

Luke wondered if she said that with regret, or to test him. Women were an eternal mystery to him. Jackie had a voluptuous body, but he didn't intend to remark upon it.

"I wouldn't say so," he replied carefully.

Midori seemed to pout, so unlike her. Perhaps she was jealous.

"I saw the way you looked at her," she said.

"What look?"

She giggled.

He was growing hard again, her teasing arousing him.

"We were all strangers yesterday," she said. "Today we are companions, friends. We may stare if we like."

It was true, Luke thought. They had become close in a few hours, by shedding their clothes, sitting together in the hot water. It was the Japanese way, humanity reduced to its common denominator. He wondered what might happen if they should spend a week together in such a state of intimacy. Would they eventually change partners? He could easily lust after the shapely Jackie, and no doubt Mark would want Midori. The women could be equally promiscuous. He wondered if he would be jealous in that case. Could he share Midori with his friend? How could he say he loved Midori, yet share her? How could he entertain a desire for Jackie, yet treasure Midori at the same time? Mixed bathing had its pitfalls, he concluded. How did the Japanese handle it?

He heard Midori repeating her question. "Do you ever desire Jackie?"

He hesitated, lied a little. "No, she's Mark's girl. I have you."

"Can I really believe you?"

Luke was offended and turned her teasing back on her. "Do you desire Mark? He's a good looking guy."

He had caught her off guard and she looked him straight in the eye. "Of course not. It never occurred to me."

Now he had her. "Can I really believe you?"

"I want you Luke" she said, "only you."

She wanted proof, the best proof he could give her. Roughly he mounted her, fucking her hard, making her gasp.

"Tell me you love me," he said.

"I love you."

"How much?"

"As much as you love me."

He climaxed, feeling drained and exhausted. She seemed insatiable, wearing him out, as though she demanded his domination, and he must pay for it.

"Do you know why I love you?" he asked later.

She shook her head, curled up in his arms, contented.

"Because you have a superior mind to go with your nice body."

She wasn't impressed. "That's not much of a compliment."

"I think it is."

A small smile played about her mouth. "You should have said: you have a superior body to go with your beautiful mind."

"You do have a beautiful mind," he said soberly.

Dusk had enveloped the room by now. Midori rose and went to switch on a small lamp. She returned to stand over him, smiling down with a teasing expression.

"Curl up beside me again," he said.

They had come back to serious talk, the fact that most divided them when they were most united. "We're cousins, Luke," she said all at once. "We could never have a child together. That would be a mistake."

Luke attempted to make a joke of it. "The kid would have three eyes or something."

They were silent, musing. "Say, did you take a pill today?" he asked.

That angered her. "Of course I did. I'm not that careless."

Some more silence. She was thinking. Finally she said, "We have the life that was given us, for good or bad."

Luke just grunted. He was thinking the same, saying nothing.

"We're both still young," she said.

"The prime of our lives," Luke replied with a little sarcasm in his voice.

"We're both passionate Luke. We've found that out. We fit together perfectly. We should just live for each day and not think about tomorrow. You have your work, I have mine."

"Right, friendship. No marriage."

"No marriage," she replied at once. "But a full relationship, body and soul, heart and mind; a complete identity of two in one."

Luke grinned. "Just like cousins."

With that, she slapped him on the ass, hard enough to make him yelp.

They caught the midnight train back to Tokyo, willing to accept an uncomfortable night journey for the added time spent in the romansu-buro. They slept fitfully; Midori and Jackie slumped down in the arms of the two men. Luke half slept, the level of his consciousness allowing a stream of thoughts to flow, troublesome ones that kept returning. He still had not told the sweet woman what he was about, stealing a rival's secret.

The gulf between them was not biological after all. It was the moral divide that seemed insuperable. His life had become one of service to corporate greed, the war between combines that seek profits at any costs; and the gratification of his own lust for money, an urge as strong as the sexual drive. If he performed his job well he could expect to retire at fifty a wealthy man.

It was an offer not to be refused. His grandfather had performed well, a loyal policeman for over thirty years, retiring on a small pension but the ravages of inflation had made a modest income a kind of poverty for him within five years.

A creature of the materialistic west, Luke wondered how else he could respond, except in practical terms. He was well paid to do work, which, if not performed by himself, would be done by someone else.

Chapter 18

When they got back to the hotel Luke found a plain unmarked envelope waiting for him, inside a ticket.

"Kiah," he said, a little surprised how soon she was following up on their last meeting.

"What's on the agenda this time?" asked Mark. "Theater or sports."

"Neither one. It's a ticket to a June festival, a flower pageant."

"Well, ain't that just too sweet for words."

Luke ignored the acid humor. "Technically, it's a flower arranging show, Ikebana, by special invitation."

"That's exclusive. Maybe you and Kiah's Arab buyer will meet over a floral arrangement."

"I'm not convinced she has another buyer. I think she said that to get us to come up with a lot more money."

"I would never have believed the Brass would pay a million dollars to make this deal," said Mark.

Luke had thought the same. "The stakes must be tremendous."

"And the trust they put in us," said Mark. "Do you realize that we could split the money, take off, and live like kings for the rest of our lives?"

Luke grunted his objection. "You know better than that. If we double cross the Brass they will hound us for the rest of our days. There would be no place in the world we could hide. I'll tell you what keeps poor devils like us honest and loyal, the fear of reprisal."

Mark hadn't really thought about it before. "We're between two powers," he admitted, "the Tushimi people and our own employers."

"Multinationals are the third force in the world," said Luke, "the most deadly after organized crime and sovereign states. If I should be so unfortunate, I would rather be hunted down by a sovereign government before I would take my chances with a corporate business. They have no rules, no ethics, and no limits on the exercise of power or their ambitions. Some say that a world of sovereign states is like a jungle. Well, I can tell you after five years of experience, the multinational world *is* really a jungle, absolutely without law."

"They're ruthless," agreed Mark. "I'd say they *are* organized crime, on the ultimate scale."

Luke patted his shoulder holster. "This is a war, just as surely as if we were carrying weapons on the front lines."

"We are armed," said Mark gravely, "soldiers of fortune serving big business."

"That's a reminder for you as much as for me. If we want to survive, we better damn well come through with what they want."

"The formula, right?"

"Right, and so far Kiah is the key to our success."

"When will you see her?"

Luke checked the ticket. "Two o'clock tomorrow afternoon."

The flower show was being held in a western suburb. Mark kept the car, the better to entertain Jackie. Luke took the train, a twenty minute ride. He got off at the Sugashi stop. He realized it was not far from Midori's apartment. No necessary connection, he thought. For once a coincidence seemed reasonable and acceptable.

The crowd moving down the street from the station was large. He hadn't expected that, but then he had not considered also that flower shows are a passion for the Japanese that equals their taste for sex, a little short of the national obsession for immersing themselves in communal hot water.

He considered again that Kiah had a talent for arranging their meetings in the midst of many people, creating anonymity for both of them that seemed fool proof. He faded into the crowd, easily lost to sight, in case anyone had followed him. At the gates to the pavilion, he went beneath a replica of a Shinto Torii that embraced the entrance. He wondered if there was a religious implication in that, rejecting his own superstition.

He finally found a small house, something like a salon with the usual sliding doors of paper and lattice work. A smiling girl accepted his ticket and relieved him of his shoes. Inside, he encountered high culture, Ikebana, traditional flower arrangement. Outside the masses admired the blossoms of early summer: low culture, passing up and down the narrow lanes within the pavilion. Inside the salon there was high culture, a few aesthetes, perhaps two dozen people, sitting upright on a tatami mat. Luke waited for the performance, a demonstration of how to arrange beautiful flowers. It is an art form, almost as distinguished as the tea drinking ceremony. He looked around but Kiah was not in sight.

The demonstration began in an atmosphere of silent approval, continued for the better part of an hour with periodic restrained applause, and occasional "oohs" and "aahs." Still Kiah did not appear. Luke stirred, glanced about frequently. In another half hour the show was over.

He went outside with the others and claimed his shoes. Annoyed and a little worried, he had no choice but to wait. He stayed in the vicinity of the salon, pretended to admire the flowers. A girl came out in about an hour and closed the salon, pulling the lattice doors shut.

Time passed, darkness approached. Neon lights, the intricate, clever, multicolored lights that have become a substitute for the traditional lanterns, were turned on. Soft light, falling on myriad blooms, created a chromatic night time fairyland. Toward eleven o'clock the pavilion began to shut down. At midnight he followed the stragglers to the station and caught the last train back to Tokyo.

"So, she didn't show?" said Mark when Luke told him.

He was as disbelieving as Luke. "She's never failed us. Maybe you missed her."

Luke shook his head determinedly. "Not possible. I was there on time, and I stuck to the plan. For ten hours I drank tea and sniffed every flower there."

"She sold the disc to the Arab," Mark said flatly.

"No!" said Luke sharply. He didn't want to believe it.

"Didn't you say she was dickering with an Arab?"

"Yes, but I told you I had my doubts about that."

Mark was insistent. "There may be someone that outbid us."

Luke couldn't believe that either. "She would have come back to us, if that was her game, to raise both sides to the highest ante."

Mark's skepticism wouldn't go away. "She probably got such a good offer she took the money and split."

That thought was alarming, a disaster they couldn't overcome, a possibility Luke refused to consider.

"We'll wait a couple of days," he growled. "If she doesn't contact us in the next forty-eight hours, we're going to Sapporo.

They waited two days with no signal from Kiah. Luke was ready to go but Mark wanted to wait another twenty-four hours. He thought Luke was shifting the agenda too much anyway. "We're supposed to be looking for the Tushimi formula, not some old men who wanted to depose Hirohito seventy years ago."

"I haven't forgotten the primary goal," said Luke. "I have a hunch that those old guys, however many may be left, have something to do with that formula. In some way, they *are* Tushimi. I'm convinced of that. We need to find that castle."

Mark digested that. "You're staking everything on the idea that the military people and the industrial people in this country never separated after World War Two, in spite of American efforts to break them up. What should we call it? An unholy alliance?"

"In so many words, yes. But I think it's more complex. Laws can do no more than make legal prescriptions. They don't necessarily change the mores of a society. Look at the laws against segregation in the United States. Legally, it's not allowed, but day by day, segregation is practiced naturally, by both races. Consider Eta in this country. It was abolished by law in 1871 yet it's still alive and well today. After 1945 the US insisted on laws to abolish Japan's military industrial complex, called Zaibatsu. The Japanese complied. Then the old men just set back. They paid lip service to the new law, waiting for the Americans to leave. Today Zaibatsu has changed to Keiretsu. Different name, same old complex familial relations. Everyone who knows about this understands what it means, including the Americans."

Mark snickered. "A rose by any other name smells the same. It's just like Afghanistan. We show the Afghans the way to a happy life. They agree, and when we leave they'll go back to the old ways."

Luke agreed. "In the same way the old Right is alive in this country. There are probably half a dozen right wing groups operating openly in this country. They publish newspapers, promote political candidates, and beat up their left wing opponents from time to time. They are very public. What I'm thinking about is an ultra secret organization, a subterranean right, so to speak. We may have accidentally opened one of their hidden doors. I don't believe it's just a matter of industrial espionage we're into now. It may have been in the beginning, but something we don't know about happened along the way. There's no doubt, we're on somebody's hit list."

Mark couldn't resist that. "Somebody's shit list."

Luke accepted the jibe. "And they'll flush us down the proverbial toilet unless we find them first. I can't get what Kiah said out of my mind.

"What did she say?"

"She said they run this country."

"Wild. But who's they? And how good is her opinion?"

"She meant what she said, and it made me think. I remember my grandmother's Kenjin-Kai in Honolulu, the way it was organized and how it operated."

"What's a Kenjin-Kai?"

"It was an association of Iessi, the first generation Japanese immigrants, a custom for those arriving in Honolulu from the same prefecture in Japan to form a club, Kenjin-Kai. I recall how it was dominated by the elders, all men. In a way it was democratic. But in practice a few old men decided everything. Their powers were informal, but their opinions were decisive. The women participated, but actually they were submissive. I was just a kid, too naïve to see any significance in it."

"OK," said Mark, "call me naïve. What is the significance?"

"The way I see it is, if a society is organized along patrilineal lines, and the family is an extended one; the power of the old men is great, not diluted very much even if the society practices political democracy."

Mark was impressed with the thought. "Just like the Godfather situation in Italy."

"Sort of, but I have a better analogy. I believe the extended family and the gangs knit connections together in Japanese society, with the same rigidity that the institutions of caste in India hold an immense number of people together."

"So? Japan is by nature authoritarian and the people are submissive, is that it?"

"I think so, essentially. When Kiah said they run this country, I think she meant some old men, a few old men, crazy octogenarians."

Mark thought about it. "I'll go along with that. But the question is: what are we looking for, an imitation gothic castle or some octogenarians?"

"Maybe we're looking for both."

"Maybe we'll find them in the make-believe castle," Mark quipped.

"Maybe," agreed Luke soberly. "And maybe we'll find the other half of the formula at the same time."

"I still think Kiah's our best bet," said Mark.

Luke was of two minds on that. "She's our only contact. But I think we've waited as long as we can. She would have contacted us by now."

Mark sighed. "I guess we're off to Hokkaido land."

Luke returned the car to the rental agency early the next morning. After that, they took the bullet train to Sapporo. At mid-week, the lounge car was virtually deserted. They ordered beer and pretzels, watching the landscape streak by the windows.

Mark wanted to look at the photographs again. Luke spread them out once more. They looked them over, seeking that one clue that had perhaps escaped them all the other times.

"I've got these old guy's faces burned into my memory," said Mark.

"I always come back to the castle," said Luke at last. "To me, it's a clue, the only clue."

"A gothic castle in modern Japan," said Mark softly. "Right out of an American romance."

"And don't forget, a beautiful woman at the center of the picture."

They studied Megen's pictures again.

"She's a head taller than they are," observed Mark.

"I guess in bed it doesn't make any difference," said Luke.

"You really wonder if these old guys can still cut the mustard."

"They may not have kept her for sex."

"Come on!" said Mark.

"Seriously, Megen didn't have Kiah's looks, no woman could. You know what I mean?"

"Yeah, I know. Female machismo, the look of her. Her eyes say come on, try me. This blonde woman's eyes are gentle, and she has a sweet face."

"That's what the Japanese man likes. A submissive woman, something like a child."

"And white," said Mark.

"And blonde."

"Right," said Mark. "She really fooled them."

"Who?" asked Luke.

"Megen. I mean she stole their top secret, half of it at least."

Mark became serious. "Where is that half, I wonder."

"That's what we have to find out."

"I'll bet your first idea is the right one. Kiah's got it and she's had it all along."

"OK," agreed Luke. "She won't sell it to us, so where is it?"

Marked grinned. "In the castle."

"Where's the castle?"

They both laughed.

"God Almighty," said Mark. "This is like a mystery."

"A mystery without a plot," replied Luke. "I used to read a lot of mysteries when I was a kid, but there was always a plot, something to lead you on."

"Well, we're sure as hell being led on," said Mark. "Let's add it up. Megen and a middle aged Japanese man were photographed in front of a white limousine with Hokkaido license plates, a gothic castle in the background, probably less than a month ago."

"That's right," said Luke. "The date on the back of the photo was May of this year, just about the time we got here."

Luke pauses to reflect. "If it weren't for those license plate numbers, you might think they were vacationing in Switzerland."

"Second point: an article in a Japanese magazine called *Tradition* describes a castle exactly like this, a museum of some kind."

"Third point: two Americans, our company's employees, and two Japanese employees of the Tushimi Corporation, killed in a plane crash in the mountains of Hokkaido. Is this all coincidence?"

"Sure," said Mark. "Coincidence, like the deaths of five people, six counting the pilot, were all accidents."

"Add Sakomizu," said Luke. "That makes it seven. We've got to find that castle."

"That shouldn't be hard to do in a small mountain island. I wonder how big it is."

"I read somewhere that it's about the size of the state of Indiana," said Luke.

"Damn! That's a lot of territory. How can we cover it?"

Luke frowned. "I don't think we can until we get a plan established."

After awhile Luke went through the train and showed the photographs to several passengers. They didn't recognize the castle. He returned to his seat.

They arrived at Sapporo late in the evening. Carrying light luggage, they quickly left the station. A cab took them to the outskirts of the city. They checked into a modest hotel, showed the photograph to the proprietor. He didn't recognize it.

At dinner, Luke brought out the photo again. The serving girl looked at it with big wide eyes, gave a slight smile. She'd never seen it.

"We could go to the local police," said Mark. "They would probably know."

Luke rejected that. "We want to stay away from the police. We're not going to be so lucky as to run into another obliging guy like Masuro. I told you, some of the things he said make me think they suspect we're involved in a shady deal. We're treading on the edge of the law. The least that can be said is we're conspiring to buy stolen property. That's good for jail time if we get caught. You know the LA Brass would disown us and after that kiss Tushimi ass."

Mark relented. "I know. We're expendable."

They found a cab and went to a toruka to soak, get a rub down, and, as Mark put it, get relieved. When they got back to the hotel things were very quiet; seemed to be shut down, with little interior light. Dark shadows enveloped the lobby, a tiny neon lamp throwing out some feeble rays.

The antiquated elevator carried them up to the second floor, whining, slow, and finally hissed to an uncertain halt. The hallway was almost as dark as the lobby. They found the door to their room with difficulty. Luke struggled with the key, scarcely able to see the keyhole.

"I could pick this lock open quicker than I can get the key into it," he said disgusted.

Mark snickered. "Let's be legal for a change."

Luke got the key into the lock.

"Why did we choose this dump?" asked Mark.

Luke opened the door.

"Because we're trying to hide out."

He didn't quite finish his words when he flipped on the light switch. At the same time a body, coming out of the dark, emerging into the sudden light, slammed him into the wall. It was hard enough to stun him. Another body assaulted Mark at almost the same time, carrying him out into the hallway. A third man joined the one struggling with Luke, trying to wrestle him to the floor. Luke squirmed free, fell on the floor, and rolled, bringing his feet up in time to ward off one of them flying at him. He sprung to his feet, kicked the other one, a karate blow that doubled him up. Mark was being driven back into the room by a man as big as he, but harder, faster, hands slashing in deadly chops. Luke dived into him, butting his head into his midsection. Mark turned at the same time to catch another by the arm, twisting it. He heard a bone crack and a short sharp yelp from the injured man. Luke disabled one of them with a karate blow across the face. Stumbling, the injured man started for the door, another following him. The third one was ready to quit and went headlong out of the room.

They were in full flight down the hallway; Mark and Luke half-heartedly gave chase. A pounding of feet down the stairway in the darkness told them the assailants were leaving for good.

The fight seemed to Luke to have lasted a long time. He realized, as he bent over trying to catch his breath, that it had been a matter of seconds, probably less than a minute. Mark was equally winded.

"Are you hurt?" asked Luke.

"Just a little beat up," said Mark. He rubbed his nose, feeling some blood. "How about you, Luke?"

"I'm OK," he said. His ribs were sore. "It sounded like you broke somebody's arm."

"I nearly tore it out of the socket before it snapped."

They straightened up and stared at each other in the dim light.

"How the hell did they get in?" demanded Mark.

Luke walked back inside their room, Mark following, and he slammed the door in disgust.

"These doors are like cardboard. A twelve year old kid could pick this lock with a fingernail file. There's no security here."

"There's one thing about these Jap rooms," observed Mark. "There's hardly any furniture to break up in case you have a knock-down, drag-out fight."

Luke didn't feel humorous. He wondered what the intruders were after.

"It just occurred to me," said Mark.

"What?"

"They can kill us anytime. They can shoot us on sight. We don't know who's following us. They can drop on us at will. We're really helpless. As far as that goes, they could have stuck a knife in either of us just now."

"They don't want us dead, that's for sure, at least not just yet. But I don't get it. It's like stalking terror. First, they try to run us down with a car, then they work us over."

"Who are they? We don't know who we're after. At the same time, we don't know who's after us."

Mark had a sudden thought. "Does Japan have something like the American CIA?"

"No," said Luke. "I don't think so. Actually, they don't have a foreign policy worth talking about, so little power in the world. I can't imagine the need for covert action."

"How about the equivalent of our FBI?"

"No. Criminal gangs are more or less institutionalized in Japan. The FBI tried to root the criminal gangs out of American society beginning in the 1930s, without success, which explains the American FBI's origins and its continued existence as a national police agency. But the Japs have never taken on organized crime that way."

"So, with no FBI, how do they deal with organized crime?"

"They live with it, work with it, and use it. Criminal gangs are a way of life that has earned a measure of toleration. Midori told me that Eta continually fills the ranks of the criminal gangs."

"Then we can say it's not a Japanese FBI or CIA that's after us?"

"I think that's safe to say."

"Maybe Japanese crooks are after us; or maybe Kiah's half-breed gang."

Luke doubted that too, but he couldn't say why exactly. "I think they would rather do business with us."

"Let's pack up and move to another hotel," said Mark.

Luke raised his hand, a futile gesture. "Where? Which hotel? They'll just follow us. We would be under their eye there just as much as we are here."

"So, what do you propose?"

Luke took out his pistol. "We'll have to play soldier for the rest of the night, take turns standing watch."

"Makes sense," said Mark.

"What are you're best hours?"

"My sleep clock shuts down about two in the morning. Death staring me in the face wouldn't keep me awake after that hour."

"OK. I'll try to sleep until two, and then relieve you."

Mark stationed himself at one end of the room, sitting against the wall, watching the door.

"I really don't think they'll come back," said Luke, dropping onto a futon he'd spread out on the floor.

Chapter 19

The next morning they rented a late model car, stick shift, small and fuel efficient, perfect for exploring the mountains and uplands of Hokkaido. It is a country of tall hills and dales with deep valleys, overall a mountainous terrain. They drove east and by noon they began to encounter some of the more formidable country, the mountains not tall, being submerged by the sea, but precipitous. They drove up the Surai River Valley for about an hour, and then turned off into some rough country. Switchbacks soon appeared, the usual necessary method for primitive roads forced over steep ranges. Mark became discouraged by their slow progress and Luke shared his gloom.

They intended to show the enlarged photo of the castle to people they might encounter along the way. The wish had not been realized since they encountered a region seemingly devoid of human life; rugged, primitive beauty, but of no use for their purpose.

"We could be up here for the rest of the summer," said Mark.

Luke said nothing, shifted down a gear then started climbing another long grade. They attained the summit, descended into a narrow valley and soon commenced another challenging series of switchbacks.

"I'd like to know where the hell we're going," said Mark, disgruntled.

Luke merely grunted. Miles of poorly maintained roadway ate up more time.

"I had an idea coming up on the train yesterday," he said at last. "It might be a little crazy."

"What's that?"

"I think we should go into the Ainu Country."

"Ainu, what's that?"

"They're some of the most primitive people in the world, a remnant of the Caucasian race lost in Asia thousands of years ago. How and when they got on these islands no one can really say. They're definitely white people.

You know, tall stature, heavy muscles, and fair skin. The men are hairy with long beards. What's left of them now live in villages on a system that's sort of like a government handout, welfare in the western manner. I understand a few still live in the backcountry, the way their ancestors did, on a mixed economy of hunting and primitive farming."

"What's to hunt up here?"

"The usual critters, mainly brown bears. There used to be a lot of bears up here. That's one reason the Japanese don't like the Ainu. The Ainu are meat eaters and the Japanese are rice eaters. It's the old story of agricultural people competing with a hunting people. It's been going on for thousands of years."

"And the Japs are winning, as always," said Mark.

"If you mean against the Ainu, that's for sure. But that's the history of the world anyway. The people who can make the most food make the most babies. They win."

"That's simplifying history alright."

"You'd better believe it. There are about a hundred and twenty-eight million Japanese today, and the best guess is about six thousand Ainu, most of them half-breeds. There was a time not so long ago when they were roughly equal in number to the Japanese."

Luke pulled the car over to the side of the road and shut off the engine.

"Let's see the map."

"Where does it say Ainu Country?" asked Mark.

"It doesn't."

"Some map."

"Ainu Country is a regional expression, not an exact territory. They're scattered through here."

Luke ran a finger over the map, tracing out a large area. "I think this might be it."

Mark was impressed. "How do you know?"

Luke started the car and pulled onto the road again. "I was raised on Japanese culture. It was my grandmother's passion you might say, and my grandfather's hobby. I remember old Japanese geography books, old history books. Many things were taught me from the time I was a kid: the Japanese language, Jiu Jitsu, Kendo. Mind and body, Gramps would say, the two must be conditioned to be as one. He had a tremendous admiration for the Japanese capacity to correlate the aesthetic and the athletic, the highest of culture and the martial arts. He thought it was a unique society in that way."

Luke's face had become fascinated by latent memories, invoking things he had learned when he was a child. Tucked away, they were returning with a clarity that surprised him.

"This is one of the most remote regions in the world, next to Siberia. Who would have any occasion, or desire, except us, to go into Ainu Country?"

Mark snickered. "An Ainu maybe?" He became serious. "The Japanese might."

"Very few."

The remark seemed to galvanize Luke. He pulled over to the side of the road, sitting there, letting the engine idle while he stared ahead. "We've got to go back to Sapporo," he said finally.

Mark was mystified. "What are you getting at?"

It was as though Luke did not speak, but murmured in a dream alone. He turned the car around without answering, and started back down the mountainside.

"It's all coming together." he said. "It's been on the top of my brain. So close. *So* close!"

He pounded the wheel, pulled the medallion out from around his neck, extending it for Mark to see. "Look at it!"

"I've looked at it a dozen times by now," said Mark wearily. "The rising sun on one side, the mushroom cloud on the other. The inscription: Kan Pai Nichi. To The Day."

Luke drove in silence, thinking, and then said, "Suddenly I know what it means! Incredible!"

"So, tell me," said Mark. He was getting worked up himself.

"I'll tell you this. Japan today is a planned society. True?"

"If you say so."

"Everybody says so. You know why the Japanese compete so well in the world of business. They plan years ahead."

"Sure. They beg, borrow or steal technology from everybody."

"That's part of the answer. Like sovereign states, all the multinationals steal each other's secrets. But there's honor among these pirates. They don't kill each other's agents over lost secrets. If they did, we wouldn't be for hire."

"So? What's your point?'

"Why this series of killings? Why are we being harassed?"

"We don't know," said Mark.

"We know it has nothing to do with the formula we've been trying to get for the company."

"You may know that, I don't."

"Believe me, I'm right on this."

"OK. So what has a planned society to do with it?"

"Akada told us, in so many words, during the drive to his family estate. Don't you remember? Without resources of its own, Japan must gain control of resources abroad. In the 1930s they did it through the conquest of their neighbors. Today, they do it through peaceful trade relations; the multinational corporation is their chosen instrument. State and industry in this country are joined, like fingers inside a glove. There isn't anything going on in big business that the big shots in government don't know about."

"And logically," observed Mark, "vice a versa."

"Absolutely," replied Luke.

"So?"

"So, when we started pirating Tushimi's technology, we accidentally opened a door to a state secret. I believe it now. Still, it seems unbelievable."

"God damn it Luke, you're driving me crazy. What is it?"

"They're making an atomic bomb."

"Jesus! But wait a minute, that couldn't be a secret, it's too big."

They drove in silence. "You don't believe it," said Luke flatly.

Mark frowned. "No! To The Day! What does that mean? Have you figured that out?"

Luke shot him a quick glance. "I think they're waiting for the day when they can blow us up."

"Blow who up? The United States?"

"Sure. It means pay back for Hiroshima and Nagasaki."

"That's sick," said Mark.

"Sure," replied Luke. "But I'm beginning to think that's what we're onto."

"You can't believe that."

"OK, then you tell me what *the Day* is."

"I've got to think some more about it."

"We've been thinking," said Luke, irritated, "for almost a month by now. I'll tell you this, once they get this medallion back, you and I are going to have an accident. Do you have any doubts about that?"

"Let's get back to Tokyo," said Mark. "We can tell the American Ambassador."

"I don't think we'd make it alive. Anyway, what kind of cock and bull story would it sound like? You don't believe it yourself. Beyond that, are we going to tell the United States government we're in the process of stealing Tushimi's technology? The big shots in LA would deny it anyway."

There was more silence. "Well, what do you think?" Luke finally asked.

"Let's say you're right. Why do you pinpoint the castle as being in Ainu Country?"

"For a couple of reasons. It's isolated. The country is under populated. The Ainu are ignorant and subservient to the Japanese government. Secrecy is assured to any project up here. Also, I understand the production of fissionable materials requires heavy water, and a tremendous amount of electricity. These mountains are full of swift streams for producing hydroelectric power."

Mark said nothing.

"It all fits!" argued Luke.

"It sounds like a fantasy," said Mark. He seemed to hesitate. "It's almost paranoid."

That annoyed Luke. "I'm not paranoid. Think about it. The manufacture of an atomic bomb requires an immense capital outlay. If the bomb was internationally financed, it couldn't be a secret. The Japs have the second or third largest economy in the world today. Their economy was all but destroyed in World War Two. Cyber technology has allowed them to rebuild. They have the wealth they need to finance the bomb. They have an isolated place to do the work."

"Right here on this island," said Mark.

"Exactly."

"What you're saying then," observed Mark carefully, "is a country has meditated on vengeance for two generations, over a lost war. I don't think any society is capable of that."

"Not a country, Mark, not a people, but a few old men, and their children and their grandchildren. They keep the hatred alive."

"That's scary," said Mark.

"Actually, I'm exaggerating. Hatred and vengeance are not the right words. The right word is one a Japanese intellectual would approve of."

Mark scoffed. "Intellectual! Here we go again. What's the right word?"

"Nihonjinron."

"That's a mouthful."

"It sure is. It means something like tradition, but in another way it means honor, pride, dignity and self-respect. The humiliation experienced in 1945 can never be forgotten, never to be forgiven."

"That's a lot to swallow." said Mark.

"This isn't a free society, Mark, not in the sense Americans understand individual freedom. I believe the oldest social cement is still in place here. Extended families operate at every level of Japanese society, innumerable associations, many gangs, all run by bosses, intimately affiliated with the families; they call it IE, the chain, which translates into vertical lines of authority. Tradition rules and means everything to the average individual. All are acquiescent, even if they do not blindly obey. The bond of obedience between the common man and the classes above cannot be described, much less defined."

"Huh," said Mark. "That's pretty deep stuff Luke."

Luke pulled over and parked, shutting off the engine. He wanted to clear his mind and let Mark be his sounding board.

"The Japanese are probably the most cerebral people on earth, and maybe the most religious. It couldn't be otherwise. They live in a part of the world where everything around them is at any moment about to destroy them. They cannot be other than fatalistic."

"Here today, gone tomorrow," Mark mused. "That's believable."

"There's a huge literature on the subject. I've read a couple of books about it. As a belief system, it is as old as these islands and the people who live here. Like the Jews, they believe they are God's chosen people. Their origins are found in their religion, Shinto. The story sounds like the one in the Bible, but more sexy in the Japanese manner. One day the Sun Goddess encountered the Sun God, I don't remember their names. She looked him over and realized there was a difference between them that fascinated her, that thing hanging down from his belly. "Come," she says, "let us join that which is superfluous in you with that which is lacking in me and we shall be as one."

Mark chuckled. "So, they had great sex and a baby afterward."

"Naturally, a little "godlette." As the story developed over time the Japanese emperor was recognized as the descendent of that happy fornication."

"That's a terrific story," said Mark.

"Yeah, like the story in the Bible. It explains the uniqueness of the Japanese people. Eventually the common run of Japanese humanity was connected with a divine creation. The only difference was social status and authority, the emperor at the top and the rest arranged below in ranks and degrees of importance."

"So," said Mark, "the Japanese are the real chosen people, not the Jews."

"It looks that way. But the plot thickens in my mind."

"How so?"

"The Jews, God's children, lost their way after Abraham was promised Canaan, or the Holy Land, or Palestine, or whatever you want to call that territory. Arabs took over the Jewish myth and established their own religion. Since the Jews had strayed too far from the straight and narrow path, or Sunna as the Moslems call it, the prophet Mohammed chose to worship Allah and urged his followers to take up a mission called Jihad. The aim was to establish one religion in the world and one religious law, Sharia. The Jihadists are here. We've seen a couple of them ourselves."

Mark scoffed. "Man, that's stretching it, Luke."

"So, why are those guys here Mark?"

"I don't know, you don't know."

Luke let out a little sigh of exasperation.

"Granted, we both don't know. But we can speculate. During the nineteen thirties the Japs got into the contest for world supremacy. They were obeying an ancient Japanese tradition in a modern way. They called their program for expansion The Greater East Asia Co-prosperity Sphere, which entailed military occupation and dictatorial control of their neighbors. Once they had possession of Asia they intended to extend their conquests worldwide."

"But it didn't turn out that way," interjected Mark, tiring a little of Luke's long story.

"Right," said Luke. "Now, it seems to me Japan's East Asia program is back, if I understand Baron Akada's ideas. Domination in trade, not military conquests, is the new Japanese mantra. Suddenly rich, they're buying up the world's resources."

Luke started the engine and got back on the road. "We'll go back to Sapporo, get some camping equipment, then come back up here."

Chapter 20

Once they had another car and picked up the equipment they needed Luke changed his mind. "I think we should take a different route this time," he said as he looked up.

"What do you see up there?"

Mark shaded his eyes with one hand. "I see an electric line."

"Not just an electric line. It's a high voltage line that probably comes from a hydroelectric station somewhere inland. If I'm right about all of this, atomic work of some kind is going on up there and that requires large amounts of high voltage electricity."

"I know, you said that yesterday."

"So, what do you think?"

"Right now I'm for anything that's plausible."

They got in the car and started out, soon on a country road, lightly graveled and festooned with innumerable potholes. The road paralleled the high line for about thirty miles, and then diverged from the great towers marching up a steep incline. Several miles more and the line appeared again. They were back in the same rough country as the day before. A steeply inclined terrain required switchbacks to reach what seemed endless summits and endless valleys.

"I think we're back in the land of the Aniu," said Mark after awhile.

"We're further north too," said Luke.

"Why do you think that?"

"More evergreens. Most of the deciduous trees have disappeared."

Luke felt his hands grip the steering wheel involuntarily as he looked down on a switchback below them. "Hey Mark, does that limousine look familiar."

They could see a white limousine coming up the mountainside.

"It looks like the one in the photograph," said Mark.

Luke chuckled. "A limousine in these mountains. Can you believe it?"

They met the limousine at the curve, both vehicles slowing as they passed, the occupants in each looking into the eyes of the other.

"Taki!" Mark shouted in amazement as they went by.

"I saw him," said Luke grimly.

Disbelief was on Mark's face. "And we thought he was killed in that plane crash."

"Obviously not, Taki must have engineered the crash and put a substitute for himself on that plane."

"I think I saw Taki's bodyguard in the limo as they passed," said Mark.

"I wouldn't doubt it."

"They're above the law," said Mark softly.

"Or else they're with the law, if you know what I mean. That would be even worse."

"Let's move out of here fast, Luke."

"We can't go down this mountain any faster."

Luke looked in the mirror and saw the limousine on the switchback above them. It had turned around and was in pursuit.

Mark looked back, judging the distance between them. "We've got a half mile lead I'd say. But they'll overtake us when we get to the flat land."

"That heavy limo takes the curves better than our car," said Luke. "They'll catch up before we're out of these mountains."

"Do you want to stop? You know, ambush them? Shoot it out?"

"Hell no! All we've got are two pistols and a box of shells. That limo is probably a rolling arsenal."

"How about forcing them over the edge of the road? It's a long way down from here. They wouldn't make good scrap by the time they got to the bottom."

"Forget it. This little car can't stand up against that big tank."

The drove for a few minutes in silence, taking the curves wildly, gravel spitting out as they careened down the mountainside.

"We can't outrun them," said Luke. "but maybe we can outsmart them. Watch for a side road."

He saw one almost as soon as he said it. He pulled up in a sliding halt, the little car skidding down the steep incline. Turning around, he drove back at high speed and went into the side road without slowing. Hardly were they out of sight when the limousine came streaking down the slope. It went by and they were safe for the moment.

Luke drove slowly down a long winding road, more a woodland trail than anything else. It was overgrown, washed out; somewhat like a green corridor. Finally they came out onto an open space, a small plateau on the mountainside. Ahead of them they saw a hut and emerging from it, an old man, stooped, distinctive because of his heavy white beard.

"An Ainu, I bet," said Mark.

"Probably not, a half-breed I would guess. Old Japanese men never live alone. They stay with their children until they die. That's the nature of the extended family. This one is half-caste, Japanese-Ainu, a forest hermit shunned by both races. He's no doubt living off the land."

They stopped and Luke got out of the car to have some words with the old man. He came back in a few minutes. "He says it's OK with him if we camp here for the night. We'll ignore him and I'm sure he'll return the favor."

Chapter 21

Early the next morning they left the primitive road after hiding the car, starting up a track through thick undergrowth. The backpacks, heavily loaded, dragged them down. The new boots chafed their feet. By noon, they needed more than lunch. They had run out of steam and they had blisters to deal with.

Mark dropped his pack to the ground. "I thought I was in pretty good shape until this morning." He still had bruises around the face and his ribs were tender from the beating he had taken two days ago.

He sat down and took off his boots and socks, then gingerly picked his way over a rocky shoreline until he reached a fast moving stream. Luke joined him and they cooled their feet in the chilly water.

"How far do you think we walked this morning?" asked Mark after a while.

"I don't know. What would you say?"

"Maybe fifteen, twenty miles."

"No way. Probably about half that."

Mark looked at the ridgeline above them. "I can see why primitive people might have felt small and insignificant, swallowed up in the world around them."

Luke had to admit it. "Nature cuts you down to size."

Mark hobbled back up the slope to get his boots. "I'll take my chances with nature. They, whoever they are, will jump us if we go back to Sapporo."

The realization had come to them. They couldn't go back. They were quarry, hiding from hunters, driven into the woods because they were in peril on the roads or in the cities. They started to set up the tent, deciding that they had hiked far enough for one day.

"This is crazy," said Mark when they started to cook a meal. "Who is his right mind would construct a European style castle in empty country like this?"

"Obviously, it wasn't built to be a fortress. This was always a primitive region, a refuge for aboriginal people until at least the nineteenth century. The construction of a medieval castle in these parts had to be the whim of some rich man, or some group who had a special purpose for it."

"Like making an atomic bomb?"

"It does sound farfetched," Luke admitted. "For every mystery there is an answer. Maybe we'll find this one."

They had had the foresight to buy fishing equipment and tried their luck. Without a bite in two hours, they heated some canned food, rigged up the mosquito netting and got inside the tent, removing themselves as far from nature as they could. Luke, the bookworm, had brought some paperbacks. That killed the hours for him until dark. Mark had brought his iPod and settled for Japanese music to entertain himself.

They slept late the next morning. By the time they had cooked breakfast and packed their gear, it was getting on toward noon. The long rest had allowed them to recover from the beating they had taken. Their feet felt a little tougher, and they made better time. In an hour they passed over the ridge, descended the other side and came down into a narrow valley. They crossed over and started another steep climb.

Mark couldn't get over it. "I thought Japan was wall to wall with people. This country is more deserted than the western United States."

Luke had come to a halt on the steep trail, a little above Mark. "The Japanese economy and life style forces them into a congested existence. The surplus rice farmers are pushed off the land and crowd into cities. Hokkaido isn't rice country. And the Japanese don't like it for another reason. It gets cold up here in the wintertime, and the snow is deep. The Japanese survive each winter in the south with just a minimal amount of fuel. The average family huddles together around a charcoal burner in one room and wait for spring. Aside from a few livestock and dairy farmers who have adapted to Hokkaido's cold, the great majority of the Japanese people prefer to live in the southern islands. That's probably what has saved the Ainu from extinction up to now. A hunting people can survive only so long as a wild environment remains intact."

"I want to see some of these museum people," said Mark.

"I think we will. I've read they live scattered, all throughout this country."

They started up the trail again, crossed another ridge, came to the top and stopped to look over a tumbled country that seemed to be without people. Their resolution wilted at the sight. The game trails were narrow, overgrown and impeded their progress.

They started down the slope, soon came to a rushing stream, and running alongside it a wide, well worn trail. Human beings, without a doubt, used it. Their hopes picked up and they followed its gently sloping turns, always downstream. After a mile or so they reached a point where they could get a view of the valley below. The sight heartened them. A small cluster of wooden buildings, standing alongside the brawling stream, suggested a village in the forest.

"Ainu," said Mark.

"Has to be," said Luke. "Japanese wouldn't live this far up the valley."

He took off the pack and got out a map.

"There's a town about five miles downstream from here."

"Japanese?"

"No doubt. I bet it's a farming community, probably dairy operations."

It took another fifteen minutes to descend to the valley floor. They came into a dirt square, like a little compound and were met almost at once by curious children. Half naked they followed at their heels, playing and giggling.

"That sounds like Japanese they're jabbering," said Mark.

"It is. I understand that the Ainu language died out sometime during the 1920's or 30's. They're like American Indians. Losing their language over time, they took up the language of those who defeated them."

Beyond the half dozen huts they could see a gravel road running off down the valley alongside the stream.

"These Ainu probably hold this land as a grant from the Japanese government," said Luke. "They go to town for what they need, that includes schooling for their children."

"Sounds like the American Indians."

"Sort of," agreed Luke. "But the American Indians, technically, are captive people. They became wards of the state through losing wars and treaties. Superintended by Federal agents they were restricted to reservations. They were and are, second-class citizens. Most of them are satisfied to stay on the reservation. They live hand to mouth, on welfare checks and free clinics. The same is probably true for the Ainus, but they are full-fledged Japanese citizens. They're really Eta, outcasts in fact, but equal with the Japanese by law.

"Sounds just like Midori and her relatives," said Mark, as they walked toward the largest of the several buildings.

A young Ainu came out to meet them. Mark waited while Luke talked to him.

"He says we can talk to the headman," said Luke.

"When?"

"Pretty soon. I told him we're tourists hiking through the country, and we want to pay our respects. The Ainu like attention. They've been conditioned to think they're special."

"Which they are," said Mark. "What's the delay?"

"He says the headman is old. I'll bet he's taking an afternoon nap."

They had to wait about fifteen minutes, the children drifting away in the meantime. The young Ainu appeared again, beckoning them to enter the hut.

Their first impression was a fetid dank smell, somewhat gamey, as if they had stepped into an animal's den. The darkness of the single room, illuminated by a small window, seemed complete after the bright sunshine outside. When their eyes adjusted, they saw an old man lying stretched out on a raised platform on one side of the room. He was naked to the waist, a heavy beard covering his chest. At the end of the room there were two women, one old, the other young, who sat staring at them.

Rough sawn planks, laid out side by side on the earth served as a floor. A low table, some well-worn cushions and a large chest were the only items in the room.

Luke approached and made a deep ceremonial bow. The old man acknowledged this with a slight nod. He motioned for them to sit. They complied, dropping down on their haunches. The young Ainu squatted beside them.

"For fifty yen the chief will tell you of his exploits," he said.

Luke took some money from his wallet. The young man got up and handed the bills to the old woman, then returned and took his place beside Luke. The young woman left the room and returned shortly with a jug of saki and cups. She served the chief, then the visitors.

The sockets of the headman's eyes were unusually deep, Luke thought, almost like sunken fossae, from which the sharp old eyes gleamed. He reached for a carved stick, about eighteen inches long and elaborately carved. Luke wondered if it was a homemade scepter. He raised his heavy mustache with the end of the stick and put the saki cup to his lips. After a sip, he adjusted himself more comfortably on his side and commenced his story.

Luke interrupted him when he got a chance, asking the young Ainu, who seemed to be the intermediary, if he could translate the chief's story to Mark.

Mark was puzzled by this time.

"We've got to humor him," said Luke.

"OK." said Mark, "but why the fee?"

"I understand that Japanese tourists come through here occasionally and will pay to hear about the myths of the Ainu. If we cooperate, the old man may help us."

They listened to a long story, interrupted sometimes by Luke when he thought he could sum it up for Mark.

"The spirit of the gods is in all things," the old man said, "in the heavens, the wind, the water and the earth. The great brown bear is the messenger of the gods. In killing and eating the bear, we propitiate the gods and the spirit of the gods is returned to them. This cycle will endure through all time."

"Or until they kill off the bears," said Mark with a grin when he was told this.

The chief related how he had served in the Japanese army during World War II as a soldier and scout. From his father he had learned how to track and kill the great brown bear with poison tipped arrows.

The description of how he, a lone hunter, and a half dozen trained dogs, could entice the bears from their caves in the early winter before full hibernation had set in, then kill them one at a time by a technique of harassment and poisoning, fascinated Luke.

The last of the chief's tales was not so pleasant. He related the bloody episodes over centuries that had seen the Ainu driven little by little into the vastness of Hokkaido Island. He was among the last of his people to speak their language as a child; but the proximity of the Japanese schools and the death of his father caused him to take on Japanese ways.

"Then, why are you here?" asked Luke.

"I have returned to my village. It is my hope in old age to restore our customs, our way of life."

Luke looked around. The old woman, sitting silently at the end of the room, was perhaps aged enough to be the old man's wife. The young woman could not be a daughter, he thought. Perhaps they were relatives nonetheless.

"Do you speak Ainu still?" asked Luke.

"I have a good recollection," said the chief. "Japanese scholars come to visit me in the summer time. From me they learn the tales of our people. I am but one of a very few who still remember. They also wish to see the Ainu people survive, as a people."

"Damn," said Mark, "that would be great. But I bet the Japanese government doesn't really want that."

They rose, bowed, and the young Ainu escorted them outside. Luke had forgotten the purpose of his visit. He took out the photograph and showed it to him. He didn't recognize the castle.

"Ask your chief," said Luke.

The young Ainu returned in a few minutes.

"He knows about it," he said simply.

"What is the castle?"

The Ainu looked puzzled.

"What is it used for?"

"The chief says it's used for hunting. The owner brings his friends to hunt bear in the autumn."

Now that made sense, thought Luke. He might have guessed it. It was a rich man's hunting lodge, a rich man with western tastes in architecture and a devotee of the hunt. In earlier times, the Japanese nobility were avid hunters of the wild boar in the southern islands. But they had always left the brown bear to the Ainu. Why the change, he wondered. Was it because of contacts with the West?

"Can your chief give us directions?" asked Luke.

"He will see that guides are furnished for you."

After that they camped down by the stream, interfered with somewhat by the children who came gawking, then skylarking as they became bolder. Luke tried again to catch a fish, finally at dusk reeling in a large trout. It made a small meal for the two of them, supplemented with some canned food.

They were up shortly after dawn. Going outside the tent they found two Ainu men, squatting nearby, stolid and silent, as though they might have been waiting for some time.

Luke guessed what they were doing there.

"Did the chief send you?"

They knew Japanese. One of them nodded and Luke sent them away for a while. After a quick breakfast they broke camp and were on their way out of the valley, their two guides somewhat ahead of them.

This time the Ainu guides led them on a graveled road. It went up into the hills for a few miles, and then petered out in brushy woodlands. They ascended higher slopes and encountered virgin timber, a mixture of hardwoods and tall evergreens. A game trail became their path once more. By noon they were as worn down as the first day when they started.

Mark called a halt. They started their small butane heater and made some tea, the Ainu squatting with them and sharing the green brew.

"How much further?" asked Luke.

One of the guides raised three fingers.

"Three days?" said Mark, much discouraged.

Luke talked to the guides. "Three hours," he told Mark. "Also it will be easier going. We will hit a better trail that leads to another Ainu village. From there it's about an hour's walk."

When they reached the village they had to wait while the guides passed a sociable hour with friends. Then they started out again, going back up into the highlands. In about an hour, they came out onto a ridge, heavily wooded. Through a break in the trees they could see below them another narrow valley. Tucked in a wooded recess, only partially visible, sat the castle.

"Pretty as a postcard," said Mark softly.

Luke was more inspired, more literary. "End of a quest." He turned to the two Ainu and nodded his satisfaction. They started to turn away.

"Wait," said Luke. He took out his wallet, handing them each a five hundred note. They were pleased, grinning with the unexpected windfall.

"Tell your chief I am more grateful than I can say."

The Ainu faded into the woods, almost at once. Luke turned to Mark and saw that he was studying the castle through his binoculars. He got out the photograph and made a comparison.

"That's it all right."

Mark was looking at a chain link fence, about ten feet high, that ran down the slopes below them and then out of sight through the trees.

"I'll bet they've got the place fenced in entirely."

"It's electrified too," said Luke.

He took the binoculars from Mark and studied the distant gates in front of the castle. A small sentry house stood to one side of the gates. A uniformed guard came out occasionally, paced with apparent boredom, and then went back inside. Luke watched for a few minutes before setting down the binoculars.

"Let's camp here tonight. Tomorrow we'll move down closer, stay under cover and see what's going on."

Chapter 22

About mid-morning they came down the ridge, keeping beneath the trees for cover, establishing themselves in a grove about a hundred yards from the gates. After setting up camp they worked their way to the edge of the clearing where they could remain concealed, yet have a view of the gates.

The guard came out of the sentry house after a while, yawned, scratched himself, took a leak, looked down the gravel road, then went back inside.

"A single sentry," said Luke, watching through the binoculars.

"He doesn't look very military," said Mark.

"I think you're right but he's armed like a security guard."

"Electrified fences and armed guards," said Mark. "If they need this much security there must be something important going on in there."

In about an hour the sentry was relieved by another. Luke checked his watch. They maintained surveillance for the remainder of the day. They concluded the sentries changed shifts every six hours, around the clock. At dusk, lights came on, illuminating the gates. Lights began to appear at three levels in the huge stone building, suggesting activity, perhaps a large number of people.

Soon there were sounds of an approaching vehicle, driving at high speed, the tires spitting out loose gravel, pinging off the chassis as it came to a halt before the gates. It was the white limousine. Taki's unmistakable profile could be seen in the back seat, and next to him the burly bodyguard.

"The intelligence man," said Mark softly.

"Another connection," replied Luke. "Something tells me Akada's in there."

Once the limousine was inside the gates they scouted the fence for several hundred yards, learning what they had suspected. Dogs, set loose at night were beginning to patrol the fence lines. Vicious looking they came up to the fence. They backed away before setting them off in an uproar.

Back in the tent they prepared a cold meal, not taking a chance the small flame from the butane stove might reveal their presence. The next morning they resumed their vigil at the edge of the woods, keeping well out of sight.

"I think this is Tushimi's headquarters." said Mark, as he leaned against a tree.

Luke thought it might be even more than that. "The Ainu told us this castle is a hunting lodge, belonging to some Japanese who come up here to hunt in the fall of the year. Right?"

"So?"

"The Japanese people don't hunt wild game. It's not in their culture. Some of the aristocrats do, or at least they used to."

Luke paused, letting that sink in.

"Who do we know likes hunting? Who likes to kill bears for the sport of it?

Mark whistled softly. "And who likes to hunt bears with a bow and arrow? Damn! Akada!"

"It's my turn to say fantastic," said Luke.

"So this is Akada's hunting lodge? Man, what a lodge!"

"It figures, doesn't it?" He took us to see his family's medieval fortress so he could impress us. It turned out to be phony, built by his great grandfather who was addicted to western fashions, even down to the nineteenth century habit of the European *nouveau riche* to construct imitation castles. Who else would be rich enough and eccentric enough to build a fake gothic castle in a wild place like this?"

Mark's cynicism evaporated. "Akada's grandfather. Listen, I'm on your wavelength. I had to wonder when he started bragging about his family's success. The way they were able to revive after becoming destitute Samurai. Their aping of western ways and all that. The incredible trophy room with all those stuffed animals, as though they had to outdo every great white hunter who ever lived. It really fits together."

Luke was convinced. "And his real weakness is pride; he had to show it off. This is his lodge. I'd bet my life on it."

"His lair," said Mark. "I wonder if he's in there right now."

"I think I know how we can find out."

"How?"

"We'll take over the sentry house for a few hours."

"That's risky."

"True, but the traffic is light. Yesterday we saw only one vehicle all day and the guards don't change shifts for six hours at a stretch."

Mark sat up straight to face Luke. "You've got a charade in mind. I know it."

"I'll distract the sentry. While I'm talking to him, you slip up behind him and we'll take him down."

"How?"

"I'll pretend like I'm a hiker who has lost his way."

Luke went to get his backpack. When he was ready, he took a long detour through the woods and slipped onto the road, then started back toward the gates.

Mark remained in hiding, watching with interest. As Luke approached the sentry house, the guard came out, a little surprised, one hand on his belt near his holster. Luke came up to him with a grave innocence and engaged him in conversation. The guard seemed to relax. Luke took off his pack, setting it on the road. That was Mark's signal. He began to worm his way over the open space, elbows digging in, a hundred yards to the sentry house.

Luke took a map out of his pack, spreading it on the road, squatting as he searched for the place he was seeking. The sentry bent down, the better to follow Luke's aimless finger as he traced a course on the map. Engrossed, the guard did not hear Mark stealing up. A karate chop to the back of his neck stunned him. He dropped inert and Luke caught him by the arms as he fell. They picked him up and dragged him off to the woods in a few seconds.

"Like clockwork," said Mark, exalted.

Luke got out of his clothes as Mark began stripping the guard. While Luke put on the uniform, Mark tied the sentry to a tree.

"Gag him good," said Luke. "He's going to be there for awhile."

Mark went to sit in the sentry house while Luke opened the gates to go inside. He strode up to the castle with as much casual authority as he could muster. Passing the main doors, he went along one wing of the building until he encountered a side door. Testing it, he found it open and went inside.

A long corridor led back to the front of the building. When he arrived at the end, he came into a large formal hall. A wide staircase led to the second floor, letting out onto a railed mezzanine.

As he approached the stairs, he saw a Japanese man, dressed in a western business suit, beginning to descend the steps. He returned the man's stare as they passed each other. There was no surprise on the man's face and Luke suspected that he had been seen for what he seemed to be: a security guard going about his duties.

At the top of the stairs he turned back just in time to see the man go into a room off the hall. Reassured, he started down the hallway. He passed several rooms, some with doors closed, some open. All that he saw were furnished in the western style elaborate expensive furnishings. He wondered where the art pieces were he had read about in the magazine *Tradition*.

His thoughts were interrupted by the sound of voices. Double doors, slightly ajar at the end of the hall, allowed a buzz of conversation to escape. He came up slowly, placing himself where he could hear what was being said. The view through the slightly separated doors allowed him to view a narrow section of the room's interior. Men were seated around a long conference table. At one end, the chairman without a doubt, sat Akada. Next to him sat the Arab sheik he had seen at Akada's mansion.

The sudden sight of Akada made Luke draw in his breath inadvertently. Mark called this Akada's lair and they had found him in his den. Luke listened for a few minutes, and then moved away. He estimated that there were perhaps a half dozen men in the room.

Back downstairs, he looked in several rooms on the first floor. They were filled with artifacts, treasures from Japan's Middle Ages. Satisfied, he started down another wing. Here he came upon a broad flight of stone steps leading to the basement. At the bottom he found a central corridor. A string of pale light bulbs furnished a weak illumination.

A door opened at the far end, men's voices filtering out at the same moment. Luke pressed himself into a nearby door niche, rigid while he watched. A man came out, naked except for the *fundoshi*, the traditional loincloth, and a towel over his shoulder. He watched him go into another room, waited a few minutes then stole up to look inside. The man had gone into a tub, sitting in water up to his chest. If he knew the Japanese, Luke thought, he would sit there for a considerable time.

He moved carefully to the partly open door the man had just left. Inside he could hear the voices of other men. A short period of eavesdropping and he knew they were sentries off duty.

Coming back to the first floor, Luke started to explore still another hallway. About halfway down a door opened and a Caucasian woman emerged. Startled by this sudden apparition, Luke broke stride for a moment, then resumed his normal gait and went past her. She was tall, a strawberry blonde with pale skin and good looking. He had no doubt about her function in this place.

When she was out of sight, he went back to the door she had just closed and stepped inside. A suite of rooms, elegantly furnished, evidently the sumptuous quarters for a woman of pleasure. He scouted the several rooms quickly. Finding no one, he went back to the main room to wait for her return.

More than half an hour passed. Trained in patience, Luke's nerves were nonetheless taut. Mark could not sit in the sentry house very long before being challenged. The big risk was an unexpected visitor who might approach the gates expecting entrance. A Caucasian unable to speak Japanese would never be able to handle that. He was about to leave when he heard the door open. He slipped into an adjoining room. As it turned out, the precaution was unnecessary. The girl had returned alone.

She came in, evidently morose, bored, dropping listlessly onto a sofa. Luke came out to confront her. Her astonishment on seeing him was as great as his had been when he first saw her in the hallway. She drew back, alarmed, eyes wide.

"What do you want?"

Luke smiled slightly. "I'm a friend, I hope."

"You don't sound Japanese."

"I'm not. I'm an American."

"So am I."

She was suspicious, trying to size him up. "You look Japanese."

"Part-Japanese," he said, hoping to reassure her.

The suspicion and the fear having passed, she became sullen.

"What are you doing here?"

Luke sat down in a chair, facing her. "I'm looking for information."

"About what?"

He took the photographs from his pocket, searched until he found the right one and handed it to her.

"Do you know this woman?"

"It's Megan."

"Who's the man?"

"What's it to you? Why all the questions?"

"I'll tell you if you'll help me."

She was puzzled by that. "Help you do what?"

"Help me with information."

"Are you one of the sentries?"

Luke grinned, looking down at the uniform. He realized that it was too small, the trousers too high up on his legs, the arms of the jacket riding well above his wrists. He half-laughed. "This is a sort of disguise."

That earned a stare from her, a stony silence.

"Who's the man?" Luke repeated, more firmly this time.

"Soyoka."

"Is that his real name?"

"It's his nickname. I don't know his real name."

"Is he a big shot?"

The girl nodded. "He's important, I know that."

"What's his relationship to Megen?"

"Megen's his pootch."

"Pootch? What's that?"

"It's like a code word. Girlfriend. You know, sort of like a mistress."

Luke couldn't suppress a smile. "A kept woman, huh?" He paused, holding her eyes. "Are you a pootch?"

She gave him a hard stare. "We all are."

"All? How many?"

"Two, besides me and Megen."

Luke handed her the other photographs. "Do you know any of these men?"

She looked them over then pointed wordlessly to one.

"What do they call him?"

"Mura."

"You don't know his real name?"

She didn't. He thought it was time to ask her name. She said it was Sandra. He wondered if that was an alias. Everybody seemed to operate under code names or nicknames.

"Is your boyfriend here?"

That annoyed her. "He's not my boyfriend."

"You're with a man. Is he here?"

"Yes."

Luke thought he would test her. "Where's Megen?"

Sandra answered, steady as a rock. "She went to Tokyo last month."

"Alone?"

"No, with Soyoka."

It seemed like the right moment to tell her. He said it flatly, wanting to see her reaction. "Megen is dead."

Sandra was obviously shocked, no doubt about it. "What?" she said in a small voice. It wasn't disbelief, but rather as though she had expected it, rather like resignation on her face. It seemed to Luke like the same kind of pain and bewilderment he had experienced when he learned of the death of Harry and Walt.

He still kept up a harsh exterior, wanting to get all he could out of her. "Don't you keep up with the news?"

"They don't let us watch TV; only old black and white movies here, some videos, you know, American stuff we can watch."

"Megen's death was in the newspapers."

"I can't read Japanese. Anyway, they don't let us know anything."

Sandra's voice seemed to tremble slightly. "What happened to Megen?"

"According to the news reports she took an overdose of sleeping pills."

She seemed unconvinced. "I don't believe that, Megen didn't use drugs."

Luke couldn't help letting a little sympathy creep into his voice. "How did you get into this anyway?"

She didn't seem to understand him. He became blunter. "How did they pick you up?"

"At a trade fair in New York last year."

"Do you know how Megen became Soyoka's pootch?"

"She met him at the Tushimi firm in Kyoto."

"Did she work there?" He knew from Masuro that she did.

Sandra nodded. "She had a job as a computer analyst."

That explained things for Luke, the reason and the way that Megen had probably been able to get into Tushimi's computer system.

"What if I told you they killed Megen because she stole some of their secured data?"

Sandra hesitated. "I'm not surprised. Megen told me she had found a way to get out."

"Get out? Was she a captive here?"

"We all are."

That brought a long silence. Luke wondered what he was getting into. "Do you want to leave?" he asked all at once.

"Not if it means getting killed, like Megen."

"But do you want to get out? Tell me."

Sandra shook her head, wouldn't speak. But it was affirmative, some fright with it he thought.

"What about the other girls?"

"They're fed up too."

"How come?"

"How would you like to be locked up this way?"

"Why don't you walk out?"

She shook her head, showing some spirit. "Are you kidding?"

"Do you know what's going on here Sandra?"

"I don't know what you're getting at."

That was too quick, too easy for him to believe. "Aren't you curious about this setup? Don't you girls at least talk about it?"

She shook her head stubbornly. It was Luke's turn to get up, pace around a bit. He was trying to think of a plan. Scouting the castle was one thing. Finding three women who described a condition just this side of white slavery was something else.

"What's going on upstairs?" he asked.

"I don't know what you mean."

He wondered if she was playing dumb again. Maybe she was just that, dumb. Good looking, sexy, but dumb. "There seems to be a meeting on the second floor," he said patiently.

They have a meeting almost every morning."

"How long does it last?"

She looked at her watch. "Most of the morning, a couple of hours usually."

Luke checked the time. It was about ten A.M. "Do you know what they talk about?"

"No."

She was too positive again. He doubted her. "Do you ever eavesdrop?"

Her eyes widened with that. "I wouldn't dare. You don't know what they're like."

That sounded like Kiah talking, he thought. They, who run the country.

"How many guards on the premises?"

"Three or four, I think."

"Where do they stay?"

"They live in the basement."

"Where are the other girls?"

"Upstairs."

"Can you talk to them?"

"Of course."

"All right. Tell them to be prepared to leave any time."

He'd made up his mind. They would leave together. He didn't know how, but that would have to be the plan.

"What are you going to do?" she asked.

"Just tell them to be ready. I'll let you know."

Luke went over to the window where he could look down on the gates. He could see Mark's head inside the sentry house. All was quiet, but that could change at any time. He went out of the room in a hurry, Sandra still sitting there, watching him, somewhat dazed, with an uncomprehending look on her face.

Luke knew what he was going to do, what he had to do. He went directly to the basement, started back along the corridor toward the guardroom, his pistol out, stalking and listening. He checked the bath first, the tub was empty. He crossed the hall, pushed the door open slowly, and then moved in fast.

There were three of them, two at the table playing cards, the third one getting dressed. They saw the pistol in his hand, astonishment on their faces. He gave them a sharp command, and they dropped to the floor, face down. They knew he meant business. He pulled the partly dressed one back to his feet and told him to take off his uniform and boots, then ordered him back on the floor.

Near the door was an old-fashioned wall phone and a modern intercom panel. He pulled the wires from the phone and disabled the panel, smashing it with the butt of his pistol. He quickly rifled the drawers and cabinets, finding a number of weapons, handcuffs, several rolls of surgical tape, and a knife. He manacled the men and found some old rags, stuffing them in their mouths and running tape around securely. They could grunt but they couldn't speak. He used some of the tape to bind their feet together. The rest was used to lash their arms to the legs of the table. A ring of keys was hanging near the door. He clipped them to his belt and went out, locking the door behind him.

Chapter 23

It had taken less than half an hour to truss up the guards like so much beef. He went back outside and crossed the courtyard to the sentry house. Mark saw him coming. Luke threw the guard's uniform and boots to him.

"Make like a sentry."

"That was quick," said Mark, beginning to get out of his clothes.

"The place is ours," Luke said.

"What do you mean?"

"I tied up the sentries and locked them in the guard room."

Mark stopped undressing for a second. "This is a little crazy. What do you mean tied them up?"

"I locked them up and tied them up. What choice did I have? We can't let them loose. They're hired guns. As far as I'm concerned this is war."

"Christ! This is more dangerous than spy work. We can be jailed for kidnapping, breaking and entering; I don't know what the hell else. We could spend the rest of our lives in some Jap prison."

Luke had considered the same possibility. "We're between a rock and a hard place, buddy. If we show ourselves anywhere near civilization, the Tushimi people will jump us. On the other hand, we can't sit out here by these gates forever."

Mark saw the futility of it, the necessity of it. He resigned himself, buttoned his jacket, set the guard's cap on his head and came out of the sentry house.

"What's the layout in there?"

"I'm guessing there are four or five important people in there." He let the words hang, watching Mark's face. "And one big fish."

Mark knew immediately. "Akada," he said.

"Right. To use your words, he's in his lair. And (he let the words hang again enjoying Mark's curiosity), three very good looking females."

"Really? Three broads? What's the story?"

"They're Megen's friends. Pootches."

"Pootches?"

"I'll explain it to you later. They're the mistresses of these old guys, American women, and they're mighty unhappy."

"We should make them happy," said Mark. His bravado had come back.

Confident in their uniforms they went back to the castle. Once in the central hallway they started up the staircase to the second floor, drawing their pistols. They slowed up when they came near the double doors of the boardroom. Luke pushed in, slowly at first, then quickly. Mark came in beside him at the same time.

Startled, the men around the table turned, disbelief etched on their faces. Akada was at the head of the table, Taki next to him; their faces were like a study in bronze. For just a second Akada stared, and then stabbed with a finger at a button on the nearby wall.

"It will do you no good," said Luke. "I cut the lines. You have no communication. Your men are under lock and key."

He could see Akada wilt slightly, just the smallest sag of the big shoulders. He said nothing. There was an immense silence in the room. Luke didn't quite know what to do next. He and Mark looked around, taking in whatever seemed significant. Their eyes came to rest on two large medallions hanging on the wall. One depicted the rising sun, Japan's national logo. The other a replica of the mushroom cloud. Over the two medallions there were large characters attached to the wall. Mark had seen then often enough.

"Kan Pai Nichi," he said aloud, softly, with something like awe in his voice.

"To The Day," said Luke.

Akada finally found his voice. "What is the meaning of this?" he said in a hard, dull voice.

Luke felt almost like laughing. So banal, like trivial theater, as though Akada had memorized the appropriate English lines. He holstered his pistol, Mark training his on the frightened men. Luke quickly swept up the dossiers as he went along the length of the table. The pile was considerable when he arrived at the head of the table. Akada looked down at what had been assembled before him. Luke scooped them up and carried them to a table near the window, looking back at Akada, whose head was turned, following Luke with his eyes.

"The meaning you asked for," said Luke, "is in these folders, no doubt."

He waited for Akada to respond. The Baron said nothing, turning his head back, stubbornly staring straight ahead. Luke went through some of the documents, a great silence again coming over the room, only the rustle of papers to be heard as Luke scanned the contents. In a few minutes he let out a low whistle, turning to Mark.

"I wouldn't have believed this."

"What is it?" asked Mark.

Luke looked back at the men around the table. "Just about what we guessed."

He and Mark exchanged looks, reading each other's minds.

"Let's lock up these guys," said Luke.

"Where?"

"The basement."

Mark waved his pistol, a motion they understood. They got up uncertainly. Another threatening gesture and they started out of the room, stumbling on each others' heels. The Arab continued to sit in his chair, as if transfixed. Luke grabbed his gown at the shoulder and pulled him to his feet, then shoved him into the moving line of men. Mark got in front of them, Luke coming up from behind. Akada stopped suddenly, as if he might resist.

"Move," Luke said savagely, "or I'll blow your head off right now."

Akada started walking again and the others followed him. In a group, they started down the staircase to the main floor. When they came to the central hall, they saw Sandra standing there with two blonde women.

About the time they had arrived at the bottom of the stairs the thump and rumble of their feet alerted a man in a nearby office. He came out, curious at first, and then startled with what he saw. He started to retreat. Luke stopped him with a sharp command. Another order and he came forward hesitantly to join the others.

They were marched into the basement, a little band of anxious captives, shifting their weight from one foot to the other, waiting while Luke fumbled with the keys until he found one that unlocked the door. It was a large windowless room without furniture, just a few storage boxes and a lot of litter. They went in without protesting. The Arab hung back until Luke pushed him in.

"Maybe we should tie them up," said Mark.

Luke examined the door and tested the heavy bolt on the outside. "They're secure here. We should look at those papers first. We'll deal with these folks later."

They locked the door and went back upstairs. This time the three women fell in behind them, curious and apprehensive at the same time. When they got to the boardroom Luke took the dossiers back to the conference table and spread them out. It was an imposing array of materials, charts, maps, formulae and correspondence.

The women wandered around, soon bored. Sandra sat on the edge of the table, swinging a slim leg carelessly. When Luke came upon a large map of the United States and spread it out, they all crowded around.

It was an unusual map, physical relief without state boundaries, showing only the principle cities. A grid work had been established, concentric rings radiating from the centers.

"What do you make of that?" asked Mark.

Luke tried to interpret the symbols at the bottom of the map. "Each center seems to be a site for detonation."

"Does that mean they're operating in the states?"

"They either are, or they intend to. I would have to read some of these documents to know."

Luke glanced around the room. "I wonder if there is a safe in here, maybe a vault."

"Nothing in sight," said Mark.

Luke went back to the papers before him. "Check the room, will you?"

Mark commenced a systematic search of the room, running his fingers along the paneling, probing for something that might trigger a mechanism and reveal a safe. Luke interrupted him with a sharp exclamation.

Mark went back to the table. "What is it?"

"Here's a mind expander for you. They're trying to produce, or maybe they have by now, a miniature bomb, just as we thought."

Mark snorted. "Just as you thought."

"It sounds like science fiction, but I've heard that some countries, including ours, are trying to construct a miniature dirty bomb."

Mark stared at the diagrams. "What do you mean by miniature? How small?"

Luke laid out some more papers to look at. "Small is small but this is tiny."

They examined the sketches, amazement growing on their faces.

"A bomb that could fit inside a small satchel," said Luke.

"Now that's science fiction," said Mark.

"I think I see their general plan," said Luke. "They intend to plant one of these miniature bombs in each center they have pinpointed on the U.S. map, and then detonate them electronically in sequence."

"Ok," said Mark. "Who would do the planting? That's the big question."

"Easy to answer my friend." Luke opened another file. "The answer is in here. The Jihadists will do the essential work. Islamic extremists have been infiltrating mosques nationwide since 9/11, waiting for orders. When the day comes they will start planting these devices wherever they are, all across the United States. With the work done, they will go back to where they came from."

The two men were silent, reflecting on the implications.

"The idea behind this is unbelievably diabolical," said Luke. "Instantaneous radiation released across the continental U.S., maybe as far as Canada and Mexico. It would sicken whole populations in hours, with no means to recover under those circumstances. After that the Japs would move in without encountering any resistance."

They thought about it. Finally Mark said, "This castle would be their base of operations for this, no doubt."

"Yes and no," said Luke. "This would be the nerve center, so to speak, the brains behind it. The actual electronic transmission would come from a space satellite."

"Is that really possible?"

"I'm no scientist but I believe sophisticated technology can make almost anything happen. What's needed for results is willpower and intelligence. Men with money and a compulsion to compete and to dominate are capable of anything."

"We're talking about Akada."

"And others like him."

"Ex-Samurais," said Mark grimly.

"Worse than that, born again Samurai. That's what we've been dealing with; men who not so long ago wanted to rule the world."

"Yeah, I know, you called it Toa Dobunkai or something like that."

Luke had to grin. "Exactly, Toa Dobunkai, East Asian Common Culture Society. The westerners translated it as Greater Asia Co-prosperity Sphere, but it meant the same thing. The Japanese economic system would be spread across Asia by means of the heavenly sword. Eventually, every country would come under Japanese domination."

"A universal economic dictatorship," said Mark.

"Right, economic hegemony over the world, the Japs called it bakko ichiu, meaning the Eight Corners of the World, all under one roof, maintained by earth's superior race, the Japanese.

Mark grunted. "Fantastic. The Chosen People."

They were both silent for a moment. "You know, they might have pulled it off," said Luke, "if they hadn't lost most of their fleet in the naval battles in the Coral Sea and Midway."

Mark laughed slightly. "Seems like history turns on a small hinge of fate."

They went back to the papers dealing with satellite communications. The three women, bored again, began moving about restlessly.

Sandra went toward the door. "Come on," she said to the girls, "let's go back to our rooms."

Luke brought her up short with a sharp command. "No. Stay here."

Sandra came back to the table, a little belligerent by now. The other two followed her.

"Let's get out of here," she said.

"In a few minutes," Luke promised her.

They went to some chairs and sat down, obviously annoyed. Mark and Luke found more maps, more elaborate sketches showing missile launchers and launching pads.

"These guys were living in a fantasyland," said Mark. "You don't need to know the Japanese language to understand these diagrams. They're going from computers, to miniature atomic bombs, to killer satellites. This fills out the theory you've been talking about for two weeks. The question is, though, can this be part of the Japanese government's policy or just the wild ideas of a few crazy people?"

Luke gave that some thought. "It could be a combination of the two, in what proportions, I don't think anyone could say. The military Right Wing before World War Two was never an integral part of the political Right that ran the country. The military men were auxiliary, close to the seat of power but always ready to usurp that power; and when their chance came, they took it in 1945. The attempted coup by the Young Tigers is proof of it. They intended to replace the emperor with a Shogun, a military dictatorship."

Mark gave that some thought. "In other words, the alliance of politicians and industrialists who now make Japan's policy and their prosperity possible, are potential victims of these maniacs."

"Right, potential victims of second generation Young Tigers."

Luke opened a pamphlet lying on the table, finding a passage underlined in dark ink. "Listen to this, Mark."

"The Japanese could majestically command the world in every direction, and by virtue of the awesome presence of this Imperial Land they could readily subjugate the puny barbarians and unify the world under their control."

Luke stared at Mark. "What does that sound like?"

"Lunacy," said Mark.

"Have you ever heard of any other country making a boast like that?"

"No," admitted Mark. "It sounds like the rhetoric of the Japanese before World War Two."

"You probably think that quotation I just read came from the 1930s, right?"

"Well sure," said Mark, "sounds like a classic statement of Japanese militarism in World War Two."

"It's a classic statement of Japanese megalomania. What I just read is from a Japanese writer who lived during the first part of the nineteenth century, well before Admiral Perry opened this country up to western trade."

Mark was astounded. "No kidding."

"Yeah. It was a kind of patriotic writing called Nihonjnron, very popular with the intelligentsia. For three hundred years Japanese intellectuals have been celebrating Japanese racial purity, its potential for racial supremacy. Racial purity is still all-important to the Japanese, as much to the common man as to the intellectual class. That probably explains why it is hard for Eta, and mixed breeds in general, to be accepted by the Japanese. Even now the Koreans, if they can get Japanese citizenship, are politely ostracized. They segregate themselves voluntarily, out of defense, just the way Eta does."

"You could say it's a natural prejudice," said Mark.

"It has deep roots. Westerners used to think that Japan's military and industrial ambitions began after World War One, provoked by their compound sense of military inferiority and belief in racial superiority. The fact is the alliance of industrial and military power, men dreaming of world conquest, goes back to a time when Japan was a hermit country, without modern industry."

"I thought that dream became a nightmare for them," said Mark. "We beat the hell out of them, occupied them, reformed them, and financed a new beginning for them."

Luke had a grin on his face. "You mean they should be grateful to us."

"No," said Mark. "I mean they should have learned their lesson, once and for all."

"Mark, what we've found here is proof to the contrary. This castle is a big think tank, and I know now just about when it started, 1964 or 1965."

"How do you know that?"

"I told you, when I went through the past issues of *Tradition* I found a short article published in 1964, describing the medieval treasures stored in this place. It was a private museum then, the owner not named in the magazine. In 1965, *Tradition* obtained a new patron, also anonymous, and the magazine's masthead was changed. After that, the characters, Kan Pai Nichi were printed discreetly in each issue on the first page."

"That man would have been Akada," said Mark softly. "He was the patron."

"And he couldn't help bragging. We noticed his real character when he showed us around his family estate. That probably accounts for his compulsion to advertise the motto, Kan Pai Nichi, and why he had those medallions minted and distributed to the faithful."

"A symbol they could be proud of," said Mark.

"A boast they intended to keep. That article in *Tradition* made me do some more research in Japan's *Who's Who* and some old newspapers. Akada's father died in 1964. Akada, the present baron, became the head of the family. He also became one of the chief executives of Tushimi that same year."

Mark was impressed. "Man, you've done a lot of research. Talk about pieces of a puzzle falling into place!"

Luke took some photos out of his pocket and picked out one. "Do you see any resemblance in this face and that of the present Baron Akada?"

Mark looked at it briefly. He couldn't suppress a smile. "They all look alike," he cracked.

Luke was insistent. "Look again. Tell me what you think."

Mark tried again. "OK. I'll say yes. It's possible. Are you suggesting that Akada is related to the man in that photo?"

"I am. In an obituary column in 1964 there was a photo of Akada's father, the former Baron Akada. That newspaper picture resembled this photo."

"You lost me there."

"The similarities are enough to make me think this is a photograph of a Young Tiger in 1945, Akada's father."

"I'll be damned! Then Akada is a second generation Young Tiger."

"And he's converted his father's hunting lodge and private museum into a scientific laboratory."

Mark let out a little whistle. "And now they're making an atomic bomb, a very tiny one!"

"That's what I've been thinking for awhile. But we've been off track a bit. They're trying to make a neutron bomb."

Mark knew about that vaguely. It didn't mean much to him. "A sort of super bomb, right?"

"Yeah. Sometime in the nineteen seventies the hydrogen bomb was modified. The blast when detonated was minimal, but a massive radiation was released. It was intended to be an anti-personnel nuclear weapon for military operations in the Cold War."

"Hm," said Mark, "very interesting."

"I was just a kid then, like you, when talk about the neutron bomb started. My grandfather was a news junkie and a policy wonk. Sometimes he would lecture me like I was a student. But, you know, a small boy is like a sponge. His words seeped into my mind like the air I was breathing. He was dead set against the weapon. It reminded him too much of what the atomic bomb had done to two cities in Japan. My grandmother was a victim of the bombing. I remember when President Carter decided not to deploy the weapon."

"Something doesn't jibe here," said Mark, looking toward the large medallion fixed to the wall. "To me it represents an atomic bomb."

"That can be explained," said Luke. "Kan Pai Nichi was formed right after the war by the Young Tigers. They were young and filled with the spirit of revenge. They wanted to get even for Nagasaki and Hiroshima. But time passed and new technology came along, first the hydrogen bomb, then the neutron bomb; then what amounted to a revolution in technology, mainly satellite communications and cyberspace inventions."

"Sure," said Mark. "The old medallion didn't square with the new technology."

"Absolutely. The Young Tigers were becoming what you might call old tigers, but they were keeping up with the changes around them. They were also keeping alive their spirit of revenge even as they were getting old."

"Their children and grandchildren likewise," said Mark

The three women were beginning to move around again. Luke turned to Sandra, half embarrassed. "Mark and I have a habit of getting into long winded conversations."

"It's fascinating," she said. "How do the Arabs fit into all this?"

Luke turned to Mark. "You tell her."

Mark hesitated. "I can't put it in a few words. All I can say is the Arabs want to get even with America, for reasons no one can really explain, mainly religious I guess."

Silence filled the room. Finally Luke said, "I have a theory."

That amused Mark. "Another theory. Let's hear it."

"Well," said Luke, "you have to admit most of my theories have panned out so far."

Mark nodded.

"Here's my theory. The Cold War didn't end just because the news services around the world proclaimed its end. It goes on, but in a new way."

"I know," said Mark, "The War on Terror."

"Yeah, which really means the Jihadists don't make war on the United States in particular, but western civilization in general. That motive makes them the logical partners of Kan Pai Nichi. Both Japanese extremists and Islamic extremists have two things in common. They want to destroy the United States, one way or another. They both have a universal agenda. Kan Pai Nichi is a program for making a pure Japanese race become lords of the world, the same fantasy that dominated them in World War Two. The Jihadists want Islam to be the universal religion, its believers obedient to the sacred law, Sharia. That's their fantasy."

"They haven't figured it out all the way to the end," said Mark.

"How so?"

"After the Japs and Arabs wipe out the United States and are on top of the world, they'll turn on each other. There can be only one winner; that's how the Japs think, and the Moslems too."

Luke liked the idea. "Shinto vs. Islam, Gotterdammerung, twilight of the gods, or the End Days, as some Christians see it. Meantime, there is no doubt they have an immediate agenda. We are the potential victims in their wild scenarios. Both want to bring an end to western civilization as we know it. They hate everything that is modern. To them the U.S. is the symbol of everything evil."

Sandra had gotten into the conversation by now. "It's ironic when you think about it. They want the old days to come back but at the same time they want the best that modern times can give them."

"I grant the contradiction," said Luke, "but part of my theory is this: we're dealing with a religious fanaticism in both the Japanese and the Arab mentality. They are willing to use the sophisticated means of the present in order to bring back, shall we say, the good old days of their imagination."

Mark slammed his hand down lightly on the table, "Well spoken, Mr. Sullivan. I accept your theory."

Luke as usual played out their little game of banter. "Thank you sir, for your most cordial acceptance of my modest theory."

He turned back to the table and reached for a pointer, tracing out a pattern before them on a map. "Here is the practical matter that has nothing to do with theory. The two partners, Jihad and Kan Pai Nichi, have a mutual need of each other. The one has access to satellite communications, the other has an endless reservoir of inspired terrorists, trained to follow orders and prepared to die for what they believe in."

"Like Kamikaze pilots in World War Two," said Sandra.

That got Luke's attention. He turned toward her with a quizzical look. Here was a well-informed concubine.

"How do you know about that?" he asked.

Sandra slapped him on the arm playfully, "I like to watch old movies."

Luke went back to his lecture. "The Jihadists have been infiltrating the United States, ever since 9/11. Their agents are established everywhere. The numerous mosques, from the Atlantic to the Pacific, give them all the security they need. They blend into Moslem communities across the country, innocent in appearance yet deadly in their purpose.

"They serve Allah," said Mark, "You know, like Kan Pai Nichi, To the Day. They're waiting for the day, just like the Young Tigers."

Their eyes followed the pattern Luke was beginning to trace on a large map. "On a given day, with a signal from outer space, hundreds of Jihadists would start planting these devices, in briefcases, satchels or whatever. Another electronic impulse, and presto, ignition. The rest is left to your imagination."

Mark drew in a breath. "Apocalypse. Jesus! But where do the Young Tigers get the neutron bomb?"

"You mean where do they get a lot of little neutron bombs?"

"Yeah, where?"

Luke pulled up a chair and sat down, staring at the pile of papers on the table.

"My atomic bomb idea was wrong."

Mark sat down and gave Luke a grin. "So, now what do you think?"

"I think I didn't get the whole thing right in the first place. Japan isn't in the nuclear arms race. They signed the nuclear non-proliferation treaty years ago."

"Whatever that means," said Mark.

"It means there's no fissionable material in this country."

"Akada could have smuggled it in."

"I thought that too," said Luke. "That's where we went wrong."

There was silence. Luke finally shifted his weight a little.

"I've been thinking about the Korean guy we saw at Sakomizu's place last week."

"I didn't know we saw one. What's a Korean got to do with this?"

Luke turned around and stared at Mark. "There are a lot of Koreans in this country; they're one of the largest ethnic groups in Japan. It didn't seem significant until now. These people here are North Koreans. I'm sure of it. The guards are Japanese but the people we locked up in the basement are North Koreans."

"You mean Akada is a Korean?"

"No way. He's one hundred percent Samurai and proud of it. But the others are Koreans."

"How do you know that? Personally, I can't tell a Jap from a Korean."

"That's because you were raised in a white world Mark. I bet you can't really tell one black person from another, or one Hispanic from another. That's just the way it is. You don't see the details."

Mark chuckled. "Yeah, that's right. I'm colorblind. They all look alike to me."

"Not to me. I grew up in a Japanese community. I see what you don't see. I can always tell a Jap from a Korean or a Chinese; maybe it's instinct."

"If you're right about all this Luke, what are the Koreans here for?"

"Well, I might ask why are the two Arabs here."

"Sure, it's the same thing. Revenge! The North Koreans hate the Americans because in 1950 we kept them from taking over South Korea. The Arabs hate the Americans because they won't let them force the Jews out of the Middle East."

"Like you said Mark, it's revenge; and we know where the Young Tigers come into this story. The scenario probably goes like this: the North Koreans furnish the neutron bombs, the Arab agents plant the bombs, and the Young

199

Tigers detonate them with cyberspace technology. Presto, three hundred million Americans; along with some Canadians and Mexicans, are wiped out. The Jews are driven out of Palestine and the North Koreans take over South Korea."

"That's crazy, really unbelievable."

"But it is believable Mark, if you're a fanatic like these people."

"But where do the neutron bombs come from? That's the question."

"That's easy to answer. The North Koreans have a longtime friendly relationship with Pakistan, a country that hates the United States. The CIA reported last year that the North Koreans are constructing a cavern along the DMZ, estimated to be around one hundred miles long, for the purpose of training its spies. It is deep enough underground that atomic research cannot be detected. The fissionable material comes from Pakistan, then smuggled into North Korea and processed underground."

Mark stood up. "I think we should talk to those guys, maybe shoot them in the head after that."

Luke laughed. "Let me do the translating first."

Chapter 24

They were headed for the basement when Luke suddenly stopped.

"I think we have to reason with these people, Mark. We still don't have a plan."

"I just said, Luke, the plan should be to kill every last one of the bastards."

"That's not reasonable," said Luke, "cold blooded murder? Anyway, we need a lot more information than we have now."

"There must be some other way," said Sandra mildly.

That made both Mark and Luke laugh a little, agreeing with her. "We'd better go down and tie them up," said Luke, "temporarily, at least, until we can figure out what to do."

He turned to the other women. "Stay here. We're going to the basement."

Sandra insisted they all go together.

"Ok, we'll stick together," said Luke.

"Did you check out the other rooms down here?" asked Mark when they got to the basement.

"I didn't have time," said Luke.

He took the ring of keys from his belt and opened the first door they came to. It was pitch dark inside. Mark walked in slowly, flailing with his hands above him, trying to find a cord or chain. He finally made contact and flooded the room with light. They were confronted by a large store of weapons, ammunition, flares, explosives; a few unpacked but most were still in crates.

"I'd say they're ready to start a small war," said Mark.

Luke looked around a little. "There are enough explosives here to blow this place off its foundation."

They turned off the light and went down the corridor to the next door. They entered a room slightly illuminated by a tiny neon lamp. They could see a figure on a makeshift cot at the far end of the room. As they approached Luke suddenly stopped, riveted in place.

"Kiah!" he exclaimed.

"What the hell!" said Mark at the same time.

The three women came crowding forward, silent and curious.

Kiah was bound hand and foot, staring up at them. Her eyes implored them, too proud to speak. They untied her and she sat up, attempting to rise. Luke helped her, supporting her when she was on her feet.

He had a lot of questions. "How long have you been here? Who did this?"

Weak and a little disoriented, she said, "I don't know, a few days I think."

They led her toward the door, her spirit recovering with each step. "How did you find me?"

"I'll tell you later," Luke said as they headed toward the stairs.

"Wait a minute," said Mark, "we've forgotten why we came down here."

Luke turned and went back to the room where they had left Akaka and the others. He unlocked the door and pushed it in with difficulty. A sense of alarm came over him. At the same instant the door gave way enough for him to see inside. He stood there, looking in, stupefied. Bodies lay on the floor in a grotesque heap.

Mark came up behind Luke. "My God!"

Luke motioned to the women to stay where they were. He and Mark went into the room, stepping around the dead bodies.

"Can you believe this?" Luke said, "They do everything in groups in this country, even suicide by group."

He knelt down to smell the partly open mouth of one of them.

"I bet its ritual suicide," said Mark.

Luke stood up. "They swallowed cyanide, you can smell it. Once a Samurai, always a Samurai. We should have searched them."

"They used to cut their bellies open," Mark said, "now they've gone modern, they poison themselves. We should have searched them."

"I'm sure as hell not going to feel guilty about this," objected Luke. "How could we know they had suicide tablets?"

They went back into the corridor. The three women huddled nearby, signs of panic on their faces. Luke was not surprised to see Kiah standing somewhat apart. Composed, silent, her face was like a mask, the disciplined features of the survivor.

They started back to the boardroom, the women tagging along behind. Kiah kept pace with Luke. He put his arm around her, pulling her along with him.

"Who brought you here?"

"I don't know. They chloroformed me I think. When I woke up, I was tied up in that room."

"What did they want?" he asked even thought he knew what she would say.

"Megen's half of the formula."

"Do you still have it?"

"I know where it is, it's in a safe place. I wouldn't tell them. They would have killed me once they had it back."

"Where is it?"

"It's in Tokyo."

They went into the boardroom. The women were staring at Kiah. They didn't know her. He could tell, but he asked anyway.

"Do you know each other?"

"No," said Kiah.

Mark had gone out into the hall again, coming back in a few minutes, concern on his face.

"We forgot something else."

"What?"

"That big bodyguard. He usually sticks to Taki like wallpaper."

Luke swore softly, "Damn! He's got to be around here somewhere."

He turned to Sandra. "What's the name of Taki's bodyguard?"

The name Taki didn't register with her. Luke remembered that the nickname they had employed was only a part of his name. He described Taki and she said she knew the bodyguard.

"They call him Yamoto."

"Have you seen him today?"

Sandra looked at the other girls. There was a little chorus of no's.

"Where does he usually stay?"

"In the servant's quarters," said Sandra, "on the third floor."

Mark and Luke went out in the hall. A narrow stairway led to the third floor. Pistols in hand, they came out on a broad corridor, a tall window lighting it at one end. They began entering the rooms carefully, each working a side of the hallway. Mark opened a door and saw an Ainu maid at work. She looked up to see him at the same moment. He closed the door gently and went on to another room, tried the door and found it locked.

Luke went into a couple of bedrooms, quickly checking them then went back into the hallway. By this time Mark had gotten to the end of the hall. Luke opened the next door slowly and started in. He saw the bodyguard lying on a western style bed in his shirtsleeves with his shoes off. Yamoto's eyes were on his as he opened the door.

They stared at each other, that second or so when reaction time and the mind are out of tune. A moment seemed like a long time, as hard eyes bored into each other. Yamoto moved a fraction of a second quicker than Luke, rolling off the side of the bed and out of sight.

As he hit the floor, Yamoto reached for his holster, lying on a chair next to the bed. Luke slammed the door open the rest of the way and charged into the room. He rolled headlong toward the floor and came up on the far side of the room, lying in a prone position. They both lay there. They couldn't see each other and neither one was ready to stick his head up.

Mark heard the commotion and came running through the door. Yamoto fired on him, driving him back against the wall, the bullet going deep into his shoulder. He slowly collapsed, sliding down the doorframe. Yamoto rose, prepared to shoot again. Luke had a clear line of sight now. He fired, the shot spinning Yamoto around. He screamed, lurched, and then remained on his feet, running toward the door. Luke got up and fired again. He either missed Yamoto or just grazed him as he went out of the room.

He ran to the door in time to see Yamoto starting down the stairs. Taking aim with two hands, he got off a shot but it was too late. He could hear Yamoto's bare feet pounding down the steps.

Luke pulled Mark to his feet then quickly started after Yamoto. Mark was holding his arm, his face white from pain as he struggled to follow them.

At the second floor, as he came off the stairway, Luke collided with the women who had come running out of the boardroom. He knocked one of them down, almost losing his balance. He could hear Yamoto racing down the main staircase and he started after him again.

At the head of the stairs he could see Yamoto rounding the corner, headed for the hall that led to the basement. Going down the steps two at a time, Luke came out to the main hall leading to the basement. He was just coming to the first steps when he felt the blast from below. It picked him up with its force, throwing him backwards, stunning him. Black billowing smoke began to pour out of the basement, flames licking their way up the walls of the hallway. It was the last thing he remembered before passing out, thinking dimly Yamoto must have set off a prearranged charge. The arsenal they had discovered was blowing the basement apart.

Chapter 25

Mark hobbled down the stairs in considerable distress. Each step sent sharp spasms of pain through his injured shoulder. The panic-stricken women quickly passed him on the stairs. Explosions from the basement were beginning to tear up the floor at the foot of the stairs; flames licked their way up from below in a dozen places. The whole building seemed to be shaking with each new explosion.

Through the smoke and flames they could see Luke near the entrance to the basement. He was coming to, moving a little but still out. There wasn't much Mark could do with one arm. Futilely he tried to pull him up by the shoulder. The women had already started outside. At the threshold, Sandra hesitated, and then started back inside. Kiah followed her. Together they grabbed Luke's feet and began pulling him toward the door through a confusion of smoke and flames as the floor rippled under them.

The walls were engulfed in flames by the time they reached the door. A shower of glass came down on them, the intense heat causing the windows to explode. Mark never imagined such a huge building could become engulfed so quickly. He concluded every floor of the mansion had been set with mines ready to blow.

They drug Luke's nearly inert body down the long flight of steps onto the lawn, trying not to injure his head at each step as they descended to the ground. Struggling, they stopped temporarily, exhausted. The sparks and falling debris from the building pelted them.

Regaining consciousness, Luke sat up, then slowly got to his feet feeling weary and disoriented. They gathered around him, waiting for some word. Across the way, half dozen servants had gathered, having fled the building in a matter of minutes.

"Do you know where they keep the cars?" Luke asked Sandra.

"In the garage."

"Where?"

She pointed. "On that side. It's separate from the main house."

"Let's get out of here," he said, moving in that direction.

They followed him, running around the castle that had now become an inferno. The intense heat forced them to make a wide arc as they rounded the building. They found the chauffeur standing in the open doorway of the garage, the white limousine behind him. His face was a picture of fascination, an intense preoccupation with the burning building, so great he did not see them until they were nearly on him. Luke barked orders, a flood of Japanese that turned the man on his heel almost instantly. He brought the limo out in a hurry and they all piled in.

"Go!" shouted Luke.

The limo sped off, passing through a hail of sparks and flying debris. Explosions continued to destroy the structure as it burned.

They didn't look back until the driver had made the first sharp ascent onto the ridge overlooking the valley. Luke ordered him to pull over and stop. Silently, they looked down on the fiery devastation. The small group of Ainu who stood momentarily watching the early progress of the fire was gone. Luke figured they had taken to the woods, scattering to their villages.

Mark was visibly moved. "Those guard in there, the poor devils were roasted alive."

Luke tried to shut that horror out of his mind. He knew it sounded callous when he said it. "They were expendable."

"Like us," responded Mark soberly. "Say, what about the one we tied to the tree?"

Luke shrugged. "I'd say he's lucky to be alive. Somebody will find him."

The walls of the castle were beginning to fall in, sending a tower of flames and smoke up into the sky. Luke turned to see Kiah's face. It was sharp, hard as always, riveted on the destruction below them. The heat of the fire seemed to have taken the heat out of Luke. He was cold to her now. She had the other half of the Tushimi formula. They could do business, but he wanted nothing more to do with her. He felt liberated. He wanted Midori. He needed to go to her, get into her mind again through her body. She was his contact with the past, perhaps the future. He heard Mark say something.

"What?"

"I said that's the end of Kan Pai Nichi."

"This is not the end of it, I'm sure," said Luke as he tried to remember what Winston Churchill supposedly said one time. How did it go? "This is not the beginning of the end. It is the end of the beginning."

Mark couldn't suppress a chuckle. "Luke, you're a damned poet. But you're right. There are more people like Akada out there. We just got lucky and found some of them."

"Akada-Al-Qaeda," said Luke. "Now that's sort of like a rhyme, something to think about."

"How's your shoulder, Mark?"

"You know the old line, Luke. It only hurts when I laugh."

"We've got to find a doctor."

"If we do he'll probably turn us in."

"We'll pay him off. And if he can't be bought, believe me, it'll be sayonara for that doctor. We're desperate."

He clapped his hand on the driver's shoulder. "Let's go to Sapporo."

"Hold on," said Mark. "what about the car we stashed two days ago?"

"We'll leave it. We're getting the hell off this island as fast as we can."

Chapter 26

The driver knew the location of a doctor on the outskirts of Sapporo. He dropped them off and Luke paid him generously, sending him on his way.

Dr. Hatachi, a middle-aged man, and his assistant stared at the large number of foreigners arriving suddenly in his waiting room. The problem was apparent to him. He led Luke and Mark to an inner office to remove the bullet.

"My friend stumbled and fell, accidentally shooting himself," said Luke, as the doctor probed for the slug.

"A deep wound," said the doctor, "no damage to the bone, I think."

A local anesthetic did not eliminate the pain very much and Mark began to sweat profusely. Finally, forceps brought the bullet to the surface.

"It must have been a big gun," said Dr. Hatachi quietly.

"Very big," Luke agreed.

The doctor strapped Mark's arm to his side with surgical tape. "Your friend's shoulder should remain immobilized for the next two days," he told Luke.

Luke began slowly counting out bills, his eyes on those of the doctor. "You won't need to report this, I suppose?"

"No," said Dr Hatachi as he watched the yen piling up on his surgical table. "Obviously an accident. The authorities wouldn't be interested."

They took a taxi downtown and found a first class hotel, booking four rooms. After the women had settled in Luke and Mark went to their room. Gingerly, Mark slipped onto the bed, lying on his good side while keeping his weight off the injured shoulder. His good humor had come back. "You know, these women probably look on us sort of like heroes since we rescued them from their slave chambers."

Luke sat down in a chair. "Yeah, they're grateful, no doubt."

"We should take advantage, don't you think?"

"Meaning?"

"Under the circumstances, if you think about it, they're ours for the taking. I think they would be happy to reward us."

Luke sighed. "I'm not in the mood, Mark."

"I'm in the mood but that doctor made a cripple out of me with all this tape and stuff."

"So what? Considering how they make their living anyone of them would be glad to blow you off."

"But not Kiah, right?"

"That's for sure. She's a proud woman and she always calls the shots."

Mark struggled to sit up. "Given my situation I'd love to have a blow job from one of those babes."

"Here's an idea for you, Mark. Tell them to take pity on you. You're helpless. They can help you get your clothes off and clean you up. After that my friend it will depend on your winning personality."

"Good idea Luke, I'll take the three babes and you take Kiah."

"I don't want her."

"Why not?"

"I've got a girlfriend."

"Oh sure, Midori, your cute little cousin."

"That's right."

"I call that loyalty, my man. But I thought you had a thing for Kiah."

"I did, but not anymore."

"True love for you and Midori, is that it?"

"Something like that."

Luke had only unfinished business to do with Kiah. With Midori, he wanted a future.

After arriving in Tokyo late the next day, they found a good hotel for themselves and the women. For the first time they finally felt secure. The president of Tushimi had been reduced to ashes along with his elaborate think tank. His demise, like the destruction of the castle, could not be connected to them.

The next day Kiah provided them with Megen's half of the formula, accepting her ill-gotten reward with evident pleasure then quickly disappearing. Luke made an appointment to meet the newly appointed head of Tushimi. They planned to leave for the States the next day, certain the purloined formula was safely in the hands of the Big Brass in Los Angeles.

"What about Midori?" Mark asked as they settled in their seats for the long flight home.

"She'll join me in Honolulu at the end of July when her summer classes are over."

Looking out the window as the plane commenced its ascent, Mt. Fuji's perfect cone was coming into view. The scene seemed symbolic of something. Mt. Fuji was the last sight when leaving Japan, as the white-capped mountain had been his first sight of the country when arriving. He relaxed, leaning back in his seat, breathing a sigh of relief that this assignment was over. His thoughts quickly turned to Midori and their future together.

Edwards Brothers Malloy
Oxnard, CA USA
December 9, 2014